He stimate

"I want you here, exactly as you are now."

Anne gasped. "But—you are to sail! You told me you must meet your ship! Your home is in France!"

All the time she spoke, Edouard kept shaking his head slowly side to side. "My home is here, my love. Here with you and our sons. I meet the ship to collect all that my factor has sent from my estates. How could you believe that I would wed and then leave you?"

Anne gave no answer, for she was speechless. Speechless and terrified.

Even the concern evident in his words did nothing to reassure her. "It is small wonder you are surprised," he said, "but I never realized you had so misunderstood me. Are you not happy that I am returning soon, my sweet?"

Returning? Oh, mercy. What now?

Dear Reader,

This month we're giving you plenty of excuses to put your feet up and "get away from it all" with these four, fantasy-filled historical romances.

Let's start with a spine-tingling arranged marriage in *Bride of Trouville* by rising talent Lyn Stone. It's a spin-off of her terrific Medieval, *The Knight's Bride,* but you needn't have read that one to enjoy this breathtaking romance. Here, the Comte de Trouville flees France to marry a young Scottish widow. Lady Anne MacBain has no wish to wed again—especially since she must hide her son's deafness. But she never counted on her husband falling in love with her—or she with him—which makes her secret harder and harder to contain....

USA Today bestselling author Ruth Langan is back with *Conor,* the second book in her miniseries, THE O'NEIL SAGA. The roguish rebel Conor is charmed by an Irish noblewoman who helps unravel a plot to murder Queen Elizabeth. And if you enjoy soul-searching Western romances with half-Apache heroes, don't miss *The Merry Widows—Sarah* by the gifted Theresa Michaels. Here, a single father finds love—and a mother for his sons—with the self-reliant Sarah.

Finally, we have a pretend marriage between an abandoned wife and her widower neighbor when she moves in to help care for his daughter in *The Rancher's Wife* by Lynda Trent.

Whatever your tastes in reading, you'll be sure to find a romantic journey back to the past between the covers of a Harlequin Historical®.

Sincerely,

Tracy Farrell
Senior Editor

Please address questions and book requests to:
Harlequin Reader Service
U.S.: 3010 Walden Ave., P.O. Box 1325, Buffalo, NY 14269
Canadian: P.O. Box 609, Fort Erie, Ont. L2A 5X3

LYN STONE

BRIDE OF TROUVILLE

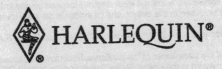

HARLEQUIN®

TORONTO • NEW YORK • LONDON
AMSTERDAM • PARIS • SYDNEY • HAMBURG
STOCKHOLM • ATHENS • TOKYO • MILAN • MADRID
PRAGUE • WARSAW • BUDAPEST • AUCKLAND

ISBN 0-373-29067-5

BRIDE OF TROUVILLE

Books by Lyn Stone

Harlequin Historicals

The Wicked Truth #358
The Arrangement #389
The Wilder Wedding #413
The Knight's Bride #445
Bride of Trouville #467

LYN STONE

A painter of historical events, Lyn decided to write about them. A canvas, however detailed, limits characters to only one moment in time. "If a picture's worth a thousand words, the other ninety thousand have to show up somewhere!"

An avid reader, she admits, "At thirteen, I fell in love with Brontë's Heathcliff and became Catherine. Next year, I fell for Rhett and became Scarlett. Then I fell for the hero I'd known most of my life and finally became myself."

After living four years in Europe, Lyn and her husband, Allen, settled into a north Alabama log house that is crammed to the rafters with antiques, artifacts and the stuff of future tales.

This book is dedicated to my son, Eric Stone, and
all the others who have conquered the silence
and made their way in the hearing world.
You are my heroes, every one.

Chapter One

France, Summer, 1318

"Another wife is what you need. And I have the perfect woman for you this time!"

Edouard Gillet, comte de Trouville, shot the impertinent baron a weary look of forbearance. Here was all he needed to make a disastrous day complete. "I do believe we indulged in this conversation four years ago, Hume. To no good end, I might add."

He spurred Bayard gently and rode on ahead. The killing heat had abated somewhat as they pushed farther north, but he itched from the collected sweat beneath his padded gambeson and chain mail. Thank God, he'd dispensed with the heavy helm. His troubling thoughts gave him headache enough. And now he must tolerate Hume's noxious presence. *A wife, indeed.* The man must be mad to suggest it.

Dairmid Hume maneuvered his mount so that it drew abreast again, and continued, blithely undeterred by Edouard's contempt. "Your fine lad there could use a mother to impart the ways of courtesy, could he not?" He nodded toward young Henri who traveled several lengths ahead of them. "And if I recall correctly from our former dealings, my lord, you are well past thirty now. Not getting any younger!''

Edouard grunted, a near laugh. ''You are the soul of tact, Hume. I do wonder how you have kept your head attached.''

He could not abide this man. Wed to a French noblewoman, the Scots baron had long served as a go-between for the kings of France and Robert the Bruce of Scotland. Hume used any royal association he could foster to elevate his stature at court.

Just as he had four years earlier, the baron obviously had in mind Edouard's kinship to King Philip and how it might prove useful to him. What would be the man's reaction if he knew his current prey had just been banished from court by his royal cousin, Edouard wondered?

Philip's order was not official, but when this particular king grew red in the face and shouted, ''Get you from our sight!'' he left little room for debate. Not that Edouard would have argued the matter. Though he had spent almost all his years in royal company, he welcomed the change if not the circumstances that caused it.

As comte de Trouville, he counseled the king and planned strategy. He fought and would die for France, but insinuating himself into the English court and gathering intelligence in the indecent manner suggested definitely was not his way. Philip was wrong to demand it of him, and Edouard had told him so.

The king would deal out some kind of punishment for Edouard's rebellion, no doubt of that, and it would not be long in coming. A wise man prepared for the worst. He would not only leave court, he would leave France altogether.

Thus it was that Edouard, his son, and two knights found themselves upon the road headed north. That they had happened on Hume and his retainers along the way had done nothing to brighten Edouard's mood. Even so, combining their small parties and riding seven together provided a safety from brigands that Edouard, in his haste to leave court, had found no time to arrange.

He was bound for the low countries. From there he would await word of the king's plans for him. Possibly that would entail nothing more than forfeiting his role as counselor. Or he could lose his estates, certainly a more dire consequence. In the worst case, he might face a charge of treason.

Wouldn't Hume fly into retreat on this offer if he knew that! Edouard was almost tempted to tell him, just to see his reaction. But, thus far, he had told no one, not even his son or the two knights who accompanied him. Their duty was to follow where he led and to do so without question.

Hume pushed on. ''I've only your best interests in mind, my lord.'' He held up a hand to halt Edouard's objection. ''You remain unwed, disgusted by my daughter's foolery, no doubt. But all that's over and done, and needs be forgotten, eh?''

''Believe me, I have no great desire to recall it,'' Edouard said with a wry twist of his lips. ''Nor should you if you are wise.''

The baron sighed. He clicked his tongue and shook his head as if sorely dismayed. ''You know I would have preferred you as a son-by-marriage to that highland mercenary she chose. I truly do regret my daughter's actions and her declination of your suit.''

Declination of his suit? Edouard almost laughed aloud at how prettily Hume phrased it. She had run for her life four years ago, or so she thought. The poor woman had been terrified at the very idea of wedding him, the dreaded comte de Trouville, a man who had buried two wives and held a reputation worthy of the devil's own get. Even when Edouard had traveled to Scotland to reclaim her, the little spitfire had defied them all. *Declination of his suit,* indeed. Small wonder Hume bore the title of diplomat.

Edouard had only himself to blame for his black reputation. He might have changed Lady Honor's opinion of him, if he had bothered to explain away the rumors that made him so feared.

Since he had not, the woman took it upon herself to arrange her own destiny and fled to Scotland, altered her marriage documents and wed another. He secretly admired her spirit and courage even more than her incredible beauty. In an uncharacteristic fit of sentimentality, he had even fancied himself in love with her for a time.

He had gone after her to slay the Scot she'd wed, intending to make Lady Honor a widow. Perhaps he should have killed them both when he had the chance. Instead, he had given the Scot a sword and offered to fight for the woman.

Edouard's sudden sneeze in the midst of that encounter had decided the matter. Lying flat with a blade at the throat tended to cool a man's ardor considerably.

Now here he was, riding along the road beside the woman's wretched father, with the idiot eager to propose yet another match. Risking an attack by brigands might have been preferable, after all.

He paused in his mental diatribe as a sudden idea occurred. Hume might be of some use yet. Edouard needed lands outside of France now. Living in the low countries, even though most of his shipping enterprises were based there, did not appeal to him in the least. But Scotland might. What he had seen of the wild, free country had impressed him.

Edouard turned in his saddle to speak directly. "How does that daughter of yours these days?"

Hume's chest puffed out. "Ah! She gave me a grandson

this year. That is where I am going now. Business and pleasure."

"A portion of Lady Honor's dower lands lie in Scotland, do they not?" Edouard asked the baron.

"Aye, a small keep to the north." Hume assumed a penitent expression. "I still say you should have taken at least a part of her dowry as settlement for her treachery. Honor even suggested that as reparation, if you recall."

"No. The lands are hers." Edouard paused only a moment before adding, "However, I might be willing to purchase that particular property if she and that husband of hers are like to part with it. And if it suits my needs, of course."

"I have a much better idea, my lord, if you would only consider. You may gain an estate, free and clear! And the income from another!" Hume straightened in his saddle, his calculating smile warning of the aforementioned proposal.

"I do hesitate to ask how," Edouard muttered.

Hume ignored the sarcasm. "You see, I have a niece, my sister's only get, who was recently widowed. A comely lass, Anne was when last I saw her, and now she is mother to a fatherless lad of ten. Both of you, as well as your sons, would benefit by an alliance. And it would soothe my conscience with regard to my daughter's treachery," Hume said. "I shall have to match my niece with someone while I am in Scotland, and who better than yourself? You see how fate has intervened here?"

Fate. As much as he disliked the man, Edouard wondered if Hume might not be right. Strange that providence had thrown the two of them together at such a time. A time when Edouard really did need a new home, a wife and a mother for his son.

If this niece of Hume's was anything at all like the Lady

Honor... Well, it would not hurt to listen to what the old devil had to say.

"You have disposition of her? What of her parents?"

"Dead for some years, my lord. Her son inherits the Baincroft holdings, but Anne owns those adjoining it. You should gain an adequate income from both. Also, you will have at least eight years to enhance her property while administering her young son's estate for him. War never touched either place and profits from both are excellent. Trust me, these lands are better located than those you offer to purchase from my Honor and Alan of Strode."

Edouard did not reject the notion out of hand. No woman since the Lady Honor had appealed to him as a candidate for wife. So unsuitable were those available, he had not even considered marriage for some time now. The French court tended to attract women like his mother, jaded, promiscuous and power hungry. Hume's suggestion bore looking into.

"One lad of ten, you say, and none since? She must be past bearing," Edouard said. No man wished a barren wife.

Hume appeared worried as he fingered his beard. "Anne's twenty-seven, I believe. Aye, that would be right, for she wed at sixteen." He brightened. "'Twas her husband's fault she quickened no more. I'm certain of it. He was near sixty, after all."

"Could be," Edouard replied noncommittally, but Hume's supposition made sense. She had already borne one child successfully, and would very likely have more with a younger husband. Being a father again appealed to Edouard.

Owning an estate outside of France appealed even more at the moment. Hume's offer had merit if the woman did prove suitable.

And the baron was right about a mother for Henri. Living between their bachelor keep and the debauchery of the court had rendered the boy something of a hellion. Learning a few social graces from a feminine hand might soften his rough edges.

The more he thought on it, the greater Edouard's interest grew. He disliked Hume personally, but the man *had* fathered that wondrous creature Edouard once despaired of losing. Might his sister have produced one as well?

"Describe her to me, warts and all," he ordered.

Hume laughed. "No warts, my lord. Anne's very like my Honor in appearance. Skin smooth as new cream. Her hair, a bounteous length of fine, dark waves. Eyes like the deep, mysterious waters of a highland loch."

So Hume would wax poetic, Edouard mused. He listened tongue in cheek as the proud uncle continued, "I recall that shining mane rippling to her waist the day she wed. Exquisite eyes with a wee tilt to them. Both lasses carry the look of my mother, who remained lovely well past her prime. In temperament, Anne has proved far more tractable than my Honor, however. She did her duty as she was bidden, and will again."

Edouard wondered what kind of persuasion had been required to compel a sixteen-year-old girl to wed a man more than thrice her age. But Hume seemed confident of the woman's acceptance should Edouard choose to offer for her.

On the off chance that he might do so, Edouard decided to send Sir Armand with a letter to his factor in Paris. He would order the man to collect and forward all the portable goods from the French properties to Scotland.

The bulk of his ready coin and jewels, Edouard carried with him now, in the event his royal cousin leaned toward confiscation of the estates. The profits of his investments in the low countries could easily be directed to Scotland, as well.

Even if nothing came of the meeting with Hume's niece,

Edouard could build or purchase a place and live quite comfortably near Edinburgh.

The more he thought on it, the more he welcomed this necessary change from his former life. Yes, why not begin anew in Scotland, free of the intrigue and machinations necessary to retain his niche in the royal circles of France? That would suit him admirably, whether he wed this Scots-woman or not.

Until now, he had never seriously considered how weary he was of it all, or how detrimental life at court might be proving to Henri's character.

Fate might very well be at work here.

Hume shifted impatiently in his saddle. "Well, what say you, my lord?"

"Very well. I will meet this niece of yours. Then we shall see. But I warn you now, I would have no unwilling woman to wife. Should I decide to offer for the Lady Anne, there will be no coercion on your part as there was with your daughter, Hume. Is that clear?" He pinned the man with a warning glare. "None at all."

The baron answered with a beatific smile. "Oh, none will be necessary, my lord. My niece will delight in you, I am certain."

Two weeks later, Lady Anne stood in the hall of Bain-croft's Keep, aghast at her uncle's dreadful suggestion. *Another marriage?* She could not accept this, *would* not.

She cursed the wretch who notified him that her husband had died. Though she realized that news from Scotland must reach the French court with some regularity, Anne had hoped that the death of a minor Scots nobleman would prove too mundane to report. Apparently, it had not.

"The comte de Trouville delayed to inspect your dower lands and will be arriving directly. I came ahead to prepare you and to assure you that he is perfect! Just think, my dear, his title equals that of earl, and you shall be a *comtesse,* a countess!''

He reached for her hands, but she jerked them away. Then, mindful of his absolute control over her, she softened the hasty act with a forced smile. Nothing would be achieved by rebellion.

True, she had met her uncle only twice before in her life including this visit, but clearly, he took their kinship quite seriously.

''I know what his title equates to, Uncle. But I swear to you, Robert and I can manage Baincroft quite well on our own. He gained the age of reason three years ago. His people love him and are eager to serve him as lord, despite his youth. I truly have no wish to wed again. Kindly humor me in this, I beseech you.''

She saw at once how his choler rose, and that she could not reason with him, no matter how sweetly she spoke.

''Humor you?'' He spat angrily into the rushes and then leveled her with a furious look. He shook a finger in her face. ''You heed me, Anne, for I have no time to bring you round nicely or whip you into submission. Trouville is cousin to the French king. I need this connection and I'll brook no reluctance on your part. You utter one word, offer a single look of denial to this man's proposal, and that son of yours will be on his way to France with me on the next ship.''

Anne could not stifle her cry of protest.

He nodded and smiled evilly when he heard it. ''Aye, you did strike me as a mother hen when you spoke of your one and only chick. You will not see your precious Robert again if you refuse me this. I have the right to his fostering, you know! Eight long years, Anne. Think on that.''

Anne closed her eyes and fought the fury exploding inside her. First, her father had forced her to marry MacBain, a man much older, wealthier, and more hateful than her sire had been. Eleven years, she had spent in hell here. Eleven years of enduring constant calumny, sometimes outright cruelty. And nearly nine years of hiding from his sight the son MacBain grew to hate.

Now her uncle would throw her right back into the pit of despair she had just escaped by the grace of MacBain's death.

Though it galled her to submit to yet another marriage, keeping Robert by her must be her first concern. Even had he the ability to survive fostering with another, she could never allow him into her uncle's keeping. He would not last the day.

She could tell her uncle the truth, of course, and he would not wish to foster Rob. But if Dairmid Hume ever discovered Robert's one weakness, he would never allow her son to keep Baincroft. Her uncle would apply to the king to give the lands to him as next male kin to Rob.

He would demand to know how a lad who could not hear or properly speak could ever hope to rule or hold what he had inherited. All would be lost. No one in authority would uphold Rob's rights or stand for him in the matter. The courts would agree with Lord Hume.

This she knew, because not one year past, Gile Mac-Guinn's castle and his title had passed to his younger son when the elder, not yet eighteen years of age, had been blinded in an accident. The former heir now lived upon his brother's charity. The precedent seemed all too clear to Anne.

She alone could save her son's birthright.

Thank God, Robert's problem proved invisible. Even so, deafness was not an easy thing to conceal. She had counted upon MacBain's reluctance to admit publicly that he had fathered such a child, and on his hope for another son not so afflicted. Now that the old man was dead, she depended upon the love of those who served Rob to assist her in hiding his disability.

As it was, if their secret remained secret, she could hold Baincroft in her son's name until he came of age. By that time, she would have surrounded him with so much support, no one could oust from him his rightful heritage. And she would have proved to his liege, Robert Bruce, that her son's demesne had run smoothly and profitably for years under Rob's care, despite his deafness.

Her marriage would remove the immediate threat of her uncle, right enough, but would only supplant it with another. This comte he had brought to wed her could just as well usurp Rob's lands and, using his influence with the French king, attain King Robert Bruce's blessing on the theft.

The best she could hope for was that this French noble only wanted her adjoining property and the income from it. She needed to find out how things stood now. "You mentioned his royal affiliation. Will the comte be returning to France soon, then?"

Hume spoke more calmly, obviously assured of her obedience. "Oh, definitely he will. Trouville's a very important man and King Philip will have need of him. Aside from his role as advisor, Trouville always participates in the tournaments as the king's champion. Aye, I'm certain he must return there soon."

She nodded. "I see. I suppose he merely wishes to establish an estate here for the added income it will bring him. Is that not right?"

"Of course. What other reason would he have? It is not as though he desires your person!" He smiled at her then, as if he had not just resorted to threats to gain his way. "Though he *will* want you once he sees you, my dear. If you serve him well as wife, he might even ask you to ac-

company him to court. Every woman's dearest dream, of
course. You will love it there.''

Well, she would see to it he left her *here*. Here, so that
she and her son might go on as they had since MacBain's
death. She would keep Rob's secret from both of these
men, at all costs, even though she would have to concede
in the matter of this marriage.

This comte could hardly be worse than MacBain had
been, and she could bear anything for the duration of his
time here. Anything, to regain a measure of the peace and
freedom she had found, and safety for her son. If she refused this man, her uncle would only find her another, one
who might remain at Baincroft forever. And, in the meantime, he would take Rob away. God forbid that should happen.

Anne nodded once. ''Very well, if you vow to leave my
Robert to me, I will do this for you.''

''Gladly promised.'' He nodded, all affability. ''I knew
you would see the wisdom of it.''

She quickly ordered one of the maids to go above and
clear the master chamber for guests, and have an additional
room readied for her uncle. There was no time to do more.

The door to the hall swung open. A stalwart young lad
wearing rather costly-looking raiment marched through it
as though he owned the keep.

Two knights entered behind him, their spurs scraping the
floor beneath the thin layer of rushes. Shining basinet
helms, jingling mail aventails still attached, rested in the
crooks of their left arms. Massive swords hung in scabbards
at their waists. A formidable sight, these two. Anne resisted
the urge to step back.

The boy halted a short distance in front of them, bowed
formally to her and her uncle and announced, ''The comte
de Trouville, my lady, Lord Hume.''

Anne had no trouble discerning which knight bore the

title. He would be the dark one. If his air of absolute supremacy had not proclaimed it, then his exemplary attire would have done. He wore a knee-length *surcote* of deep madder lake—near the color of ripened plums—emblazoned with a black-and-silver device. His sword bore several magnificent jewels in the hilt, and Anne marked not a dot of rust marring the links of his mail. Travel dust would never have dared settle on such a one.

His companion paled rather literally by comparison. Fair-haired, garbed in sky blue trimmed with white, the other stood a hand width shorter and not so broad. Even were he as richly turned out, Anne would never have mistaken him for his lord. He lacked the commanding presence and assuredness of the other.

Still, they both appeared so grandly dressed to impress, she felt like asking where the tournament was.

Her uncle gave her a little shove from behind. "My lord comte, may I present my niece, the Lady Anne."

The comte extended his right gauntlet to the boy who promptly tugged it off. Then, gracefully, he bowed and Anne automatically extended her hand. He raised it to his lips and barely brushed the back of her knuckles. He would have missed the contact altogether had she not shuddered at his touch.

"Welcome to Baincroft, my lord," she said, trying not to sound as breathless as she felt. Many men had visited her father and her husband, but never in all her days had she laid gaze upon one such as this.

Dark as sin, he was. Midnight hair hung to the edge of the curved steel gorget that protected his neck. Long-lashed eyes the color of polished walnut regarded her with frank curiosity and not a little admiration.

Anne felt her face redden under his scrutiny. She wore one of her older gowns, a russet linen, and no headrail at all. MacBain had required her to don those old-fashioned wimples, since discarded, and she owned no other head coverings. No matter. So much the better if Trouville thought her unfashionable. He would leave her in Scotland where she belonged.

For a man coming off a tedious journey, he arrived remarkably groomed, clean-shaven, combed and exuding no unpleasant odors. Did he never sweat?

His features, while refined, held none of the soft comeliness she would have expected on a courtier. Nor did his form. He appeared battle hardened and muscled by frequent exercise, judging by his carriage, the width of his shoulders and narrowness of his waist and hips. Devastatingly handsome and self-confident described him well. Frightening described him better. Dealing with this one would take some doing.

He straightened and finally released her hand. "My lady, may I make known to you Sir Guillaume Perrer, knight in service to me." He waited until the man made his bow. "And our herald this day, my son and heir, Henri Charles Gillet, Esquire."

Anne regarded the serious young face that mirrored the father's. Young for a squire, she thought. He looked hardly more than thirteen. His manners seemed as impeccable as his sire's.

"Henri? See that fellow there beside the stair? He will show you to the chamber where you and your father will bide."

As an afterthought, knowing well the constant hunger of growing lads, she added with a smile, "We sup in one hour. I trust you like sweets?" He rewarded her with a sudden grin that changed his whole appearance.

When she returned her gaze to the father, she noted an expression of relief, almost as transforming as the grin on his son. "Will you sit and take wine, my lord? You and

Sir Guillaume must be weary.'' She gestured toward the dais.

"My thanks, but I would go above with my son and disarm.'' He turned to his knight. "Find the barracks, Gui, and join us here for the evening meal.''

Anne hurriedly took herself to the kitchens to give orders for extra food. Then she sent Simm, her steward, to locate her son quickly and send him to her chambers.

During supper, the comte held the seat of honor, her uncle on his left and she, at his right. Young Henri served his father and stood behind his chair. His man and her uncle's attendants sat at the lower tables with her priest, just above the steward, and others of the household.

Never once did the noble lord comment on the meager fare dished out to her unexpected guests. Neither did he remark upon the state of the keep itself. While scrupulously clean, Baincroft boasted none of the frivolous amenities he must be accustomed to in his own. Surely he would have no wish to remain here for long, she thought with satisfaction.

Best of all, he made no mention of her missing son. Robert, by all rights, should have joined them at table, or in lieu of that, served as page.

Anne noted that, unlike Sir Guillaume, Trouville did not cast disparaging looks toward either the hall itself or her people. If he thought himself consigned to a large hovel full of backward peasants, his lordship hid it well and appeared quite content to be exactly where he was. Quite polite of him, she decided.

She accepted the offerings the comte held out from their shared trencher. He spoke of the weather during the crossing and the vicissitudes of their travel overland with a touch of wry and unexpected humor. Anne made certain that her soft laugh greeted his words in all the correct places.

Everything considered—and despite his fearsome appearance—the comte seemed a pleasant enough man. But Anne dared not deceive herself. His wittiness surprised her, but deception she would expect. He did, after all, want her hand and her property. Why would he not act charming at the outset? MacBain had done the same at their first acquaintance. It had not lasted long.

After the meal concluded, the comte asked to speak with her privately. Girding herself for the imminent and unavoidable proposal, she calmly invited him to share a cup of wine in her private solar just off the hall.

"All will be quite proper, my lord, for it is not my bedchamber," she assured him as they entered. "I find it convenient to conduct business in the solar during the day, due to the better lighting. We also sew and spin there, for it is warmer and better lighted than the hall itself. I have rooms on the floor above this for my private use."

He offered his arm. "I would never question the seemliness of it, Lady Anne, for I see that you are a model of propriety."

Her face warmed at his ready compliment. "You are very gallant, my lord, seeing as how you hardly know me."

His free hand covered hers which rested on his sleeve. "A condition I hope to remedy in short order."

The moment they settled in the high-backed chairs beside her fire, he said, "I know that your uncle spoke of me before I arrived. Are you agreeable to a match between us, my lady?"

Welladay, this one obviously did not believe in dallying about once he made his decision.

"Aye," she said after only a moment's hesitation. She met his gaze directly and, she hoped, without expression of any kind. "I am agreed." Damned if she would thank him for the honor, however.

He downed the contents of his simple chalice and set it

on the floor. Then he reached for her hands, set her own cup aside, and drew her up to stand before him.

Without warning, he leaned down and pressed his lips to hers, putting a seal to their understanding.

Anne remained motionless, shocked by the warmth of his mouth on her own and the tingling pleasure it evoked. He released her and stepped away. They touched no part of each other now, but she could feel him still.

His compelling gaze held a measure of such satisfaction, he must know how easily, and how deeply, he had stirred her feelings with what should have been a formal gesture.

This would not do. She blinked her eyes to break the trance and shook her head to clear it. If the man could disable her thoughts with but a clasp of hands and a kiss of peace, what mischief *might* he wreak when it came time for real intimacy?

Nay, this would not do at all. Now she must beware herself, as well as him.

Thank goodness he would not remain here long.

Chapter Two

"Your uncle has the contracts already prepared, I do not doubt," Trouville said. He inclined his head and quirked his mouth to one side in a conspiratorial grin. "I've watched him scribbling away like a maddened clerk every night for the past week."

"He does seem most anxious to promote this union," Anne returned, wondering whether the comte knew why. If so, did he object to being used to advance her uncle's ambitions? Trouville did not strike her as a man to be used unless he thought he would gain more than he gave. Well, he certainly would do that in the event of her marriage to him.

"Need we wait for banns?" the comte asked. "Have you a priest who will accept our word there is no impediment? Hume could vouch for us on that."

Anne wished they could have done with it immediately, but she knew better. "My uncle will likely want as many to witness this as he can gather."

The comte's dark brows drew together in a frown. "I must return to the coast in three days to meet a ship, and I would have it done ere I leave. There is no need to make a May Day of this. It is, after all, your second marriage and my third.''

Then he seemed to think better of the abrupt announcement. "Unless, of course, you wish to make some great event of it."

Anne quickly shook her head as she struggled to hide her relief that he would go so soon. "Oh, nay, I prefer not to do so."

Her ready concession earned her a smile that made her heart skip. "Do you feel need of a longer time to prepare your son? I failed to consider that. Did he avoid our presence apurpose this evening?"

"Oh, nay, my lord. He knows nothing of this as yet. How could he, when nothing was settled between us until now? Robert will give you no problem. That I promise."

"Fine. We need not wait longer, then," he said firmly.

"As you wish," she agreed. "I shall speak to Father Michael tomorrow morn. He can perform the ceremony the day after, if that suits you."

He raised a brow and crossed his arms over his chest, leaning his weight on one foot. Anne thought the pose a practiced one, but she did not mind his preening. He was extremely good to look upon and seemed to know it. "You have no reservations, my lady, to wedding a stranger of unknown means? Would you not care to know what I bring to the bargain?"

Anne knew well the power of flattery, though she had found precious little chance to employ it these past years. With a shy duck of her head, she employed it now. Staying in his good graces could only benefit her cause. "You are extremely well-favored, my lord, and courteous. Obviously, you are not destitute, and you have traveled far to honor me with your suit. I married a stranger before for no cause other than to alter my single state and because my father arranged it. How could I do less now when I have more good reason than I ever dreamed?''

''How sweetly said!'' he remarked as he raked her full-length with a warm and suggestive appraisal. ''I begin to think this troth of ours heaven-sent.''

Or hell-bound, Anne thought. ''Indeed,'' she replied with a small tilt of her head.

Anne could swear the man's chest expanded as she flattered him. Most likely his head did, as well, she thought wryly.

''Ah, lady, how you humble me,'' he remarked. He sounded incredibly sincere, but Anne doubted anyone had ever humbled this fellow. He wore his arrogance well, however.

Even as he reveled in her compliments, he gave as good as he got. ''I do pray your son proves as agreeable to the match as does his winsome dam. If so, I envision this event as a high point in my life with not a thing to detract from it.''

Anne cast about for a reason why Robert had not joined them at board. The comte must wonder at it since he mentioned him again. ''Robert meant no disrespect to you this eve, my lord. 'Tis only that he is very shy of strangers. And not feeling well. I shall speak to him upon returning to my rooms.''

''He sleeps by you and your women, my lady? A lad of ten?''

Anne shook her head as though she shared his amusement. ''Of course not! He did reside in the lord's chamber, as was his right. But now that you have come, I ordered his things removed to my anteroom.'' She lowered her voice as though to share a secret. ''Robert believes he is to sleep there as guard to me while we house our unfamiliar guests.'' She laughed lightly to insure that he appreciated the small jest and did not take offense.

"How thoughtful you are of a young man's pride," he said. His face softened and Anne had to stifle a sigh. The very looks of the man made a woman weak at the knees. And the cause of it had little to do with fear. She truly must be wary of her own reactions to him. This was her first dealing with a man who attracted her. She had never before met one.

Once they were wed, Anne knew she dared not refuse him his rights. At the back of her mind, she even wondered if it might not be quite tolerable. Tolerable or not, she must please him, of course, and send him away contented. The thought of that necessity did not trouble her nearly as much as it should.

She must see that no occasion arose while he was here to prick his temper. A joint of meat underdone, a cup of wine leaning to vinegar, a kitchen drab who screamed at his rough sporting. The comte would react no differently in those circumstances than had her father or MacBain. But the fact that she only had to keep this one happy for less than three days, comforted her immeasurably. She could do that.

Anne cleared her throat and raised her chin. "Day after tomorrow, then, and we shall marry so that you may be off to the coast the next morn. But I would you told my uncle yourself, my lord. He may think I am behind this rushing to wed."

The comte laughed aloud and Anne blushed. She realized he must think she had just admitted to eagerness.

"I shall assure him it is I who would put paid to the deal! And I do thank you for considering my need to leave you so suddenly after our wedding, Anne. I may use your familiar name, may I not?"

He smiled that charming smile of his again, and reached out to touch her face with one long finger. Anne stiffened at the impertinence, and then made herself relax. He was her betrothed now, after all. She must allow touching. And indeed, it did feel rather nice.

"You may call me as you wish, my lord."

"A saint's name seems appropriate for so kind a lady. My Christian name is Edouard, should you care to use it. I wish that you would." He spoke very tenderly as he said the words. Oh, a practiced charmer, this one, but the sweetest fruit could hide the most rotten of cores. There was a known fact.

"Edouard." She allowed a subtle promise of pleasure to enter her voice. "Yours is a strong name. It means *protector,* does it not?"

He nodded once. Then he crossed his arms over his wide chest and regarded her as though considering something further. "I have decided ours will be a love match," he said in that determined way of his.

"Oh, have you now?" Anne replied, laughing merrily in spite of herself. This unexpected tease of his delighted her. The man seemed perpetually amused at life in general and she liked that. Though he wore a serious look at times, as he did now, Anne thought he used it only to enhance his dry witticisms.

"Yes, that would be best, I believe."

She sobered a little, determined to match his worldly nonchalance. "Ah. Well, that would explain our day-long betrothal and hasty marriage, should anyone care to question it."

He nodded and shook a forefinger at her. "That, too! Good thinking. But no, I mean that you should love me. Sincerely."

Anne bit her lips together, trying to stifle any further laughter. She cleared her throat and took a deep breath before speaking. "Love you. I see. An unusual idea. Why on earth would you want me to do that, I wonder?"

The comte shrugged and held out his hands palms up.

"I think it would bode well for our happiness. Would you rather hate me?"

She swept past him to pace the room, uncertain what to say next. This sort of exchange was new to her. "Well, of course I would not *hate* you! But be reasonable, my lord—Edouard—I hardly know you yet! Are you so imminently lovable, that you assume I will—"

"Oh, I shall be quite lovable," he interrupted with a sensuous half smile. "Though some might argue the fact, I *do* know how to be."

She did laugh then. "I daresay you do! What of me, then? Shall you love me as well? How do you know that I haven't the blackest heart in Christendom, hmm?"

He grinned full out and raised his brows. "Because I know the owner of that particular heart, my dearest, and she is not you! And to answer your question, yes, I shall love you."

Anne shook her head and rolled her eyes. "Well, love or nay, we'll not lack for laughter, will we! What a notion, to wed for love. You do not strike me as particularly sentimental. Tell me, when did you make this decision, to love and be loved? And by a wife, of all people?"

He walked to the solar window and looked out, his back to her. "I suppose I should say it was the moment I beheld your sweet person. But, in truth, I have thought on it for years. Would it not be unique?"

That it would, Anne admitted. But it would hardly matter one way or the other, if the two people concerned were living apart in different countries. Then again, that might be the only way such a love would survive. That must be his reasoning as well.

It did occur to her that he might have put forth this offer of love to keep her faithful to him while he lived away from her. On that count, he need not worry in the least.

She had no intention of engaging the attentions of any other man.

"You are one who truly believes in love, then?" Though she asked the question playfully, Anne really wanted to know his thoughts on it, for she did not think the emotion existed between men and women, other than in songs and poems. It certainly had not existed within the realm of her experience.

"Absolutely, and without question," he answered readily, as he turned from the window. "I do know that many caution against combining love with marriage, but I have endured two marriages without it, and—"

"And I have, one," she added, interrupting him. "But if you never knew love, when did you decide yourself capable of loving?"

"When I looked upon the face of my son after his birth. Did you not love yours?"

"Aye, of course, above everything! But that is not the same thing, surely! Loving a child is not the same."

"Not at all the same," he agreed. "But it does prove that a deeper feeling, that a caring for someone else more than oneself is entirely possible. I would like to feel that for a woman. For you. If you could return the favor and love me, likewise." He brushed a hand over her cheek and she could not resist leaning into the caress.

Then she looked up at him. "I think love is not given upon conditions such as that, my lord. One either loves, or one does not."

He tapped her nose with one finger. "We will make our own rules, you and I. No unrequited love for *us*. You will love me, and I shall love you, all unreserved. I have decided."

The man was a little mad, or else he engaged in all of this foolery to make her laugh and lighten this cursory proposal of his.

That sparkle of amusement in his eyes at the moment told her which it was. He was showing her the way of things within his exalted circle of acquaintances, no doubt. Country-bred she might be, but she had heard tales aplenty of how the more worldly nobles behaved. Bantering about love and such was considered a right wondrous pastime at court, so the traveling bards proclaimed. It had been so since the time of Queen Eleanor.

What did it matter? He could prate on about it all he wanted. 'Twas pleasant enough debate, after all, and highly entertaining. Once he returned to France, he could regale all his friends at the court with tales of how smoothly he had wooed and won his Scottish wife, and then left her longing for him. What did she care, so long as he departed soon and let her be?

If he wanted games for the two days he abided here, she would play. "Love, it is, then!" she said with her most elegant curtsy.

"Shall we go and share our happy news with the others?" he asked.

"With all haste," Anne agreed.

He placed her palm on his arm as they returned to the hall. And she smiled for all she was worth. Not for a sure place in paradise would she allow her Uncle Dairmid to think she had bowed to his threats out of fear, even though she had. Men pounced on fear, she knew that. "This is *my* choice," her look told her uncle as clearly as words could have done.

The trouble was, that in Dairmid Hume's sublime fit of joy and copious felicitations, he did not seem to care one way or the other whose choice it was.

Anne consoled herself that she had gained much more by this arrangement than her uncle. She would have a husband in absentia, no further dealings with Dairmid Hume as a guardian, and her son would remain with her. Aye, everything about the situation suited her at the moment. She could not have hoped for more.

Now all she had to do was to keep Rob away from her uncle and the comte until they quit Baincroft and returned to France. Assuming that Robert would cooperate.

That worry alone threatened her hard-won, and well-practiced composure. Her lad had a mind of his own and more pride than was practical.

The next morning, Edouard woke in a happier mood than his usual. Sun streamed in through the arched window, its warmth mellowing the breeze that accompanied it. Even the weather welcomed him to this place. If he were superstitious, he might consider it a good omen. But his cynical nature warned him that Scotland's weather was notoriously fickle, and so might be the lady. For now, he would give her the benefit of the doubt. Once wed, he would give her good cause to remain sunny, Edouard thought with a wry smile.

Anne of Baincroft did not strike him as a guilt-riddled girl obsessed with the myth of original sin as Henri's mother had been. Nor did she exhibit the hesitancy about marriage that his second wife had shown. If Anne loved another man as Helvise had done, she certainly concealed the fact well. Her words, expressions, and attitude indicated that she was exactly what she appeared to be, a bright and beautiful widow who welcomed a very advantageous match.

Such natural beauty and grace proved more than he had hoped for at the outset. Her laughter was like sweet music. And her enthusiasm for a short betrothal was definitely an added boon.

He had teased her to set her at ease last evening, and she had responded in kind. Though she could be coy, he had seen immediately that she possessed none of the traits of the sophisticated jades he was used to. He had found himself going half-serious with his talk of mutual love. Would it not be astounding if she really—

"The keep is a ruin, but this lady is not, eh?" Henri interrupted his thought with a sly grin. "She is right handsome for one so old."

"Impertinent whelp," Edouard admonished as he splashed his face with water from the basin. "Shake out my blue cote-hardie and find the belt, will you? No, the silver one."

Baincroft must seem rather impoverished by Henri's standards, Edouard thought. His son had never lived in so modest a place as this. Not that it was in ruin as the boy described, but it did lack the well-appointed comforts and rich trappings of their various estates in France.

And after many occasions of sharing palatial accommodations with the kings they had attended, Henri must believe he had fallen on mean times indeed. But Edouard knew this sound old castle, small though it was, possessed great possibilities.

Lady Anne kept a spartan household, though there were woolen blankets aplenty for warmth, and victuals plentiful enough so that no one suffered hunger. She prepared plain food, missing the customary spices save for salt, and served it up on humble trenchers and unembroidered linens. Economy was good in a wife, though it would no longer be necessary for Anne to employ it.

The old-fashioned square keep boasted only three stories above ground level, all its rooms accessed by a spiral stairway. Some wise ancestor had thrown up a high wall to add protection, creating the spacious ward where stood several outbuildings. All the stone, inside and out, remained undressed and not even whitewashed.

His wealth could change all of that. He would meet the ship this week and receive all the items his factor could gather and transport from the holdings in France. His belongings could make Baincroft a right habitable abode for the next few years, a place suitably grand for a lady such as Anne. By the time her son claimed it for his own, Edouard planned to have built her a home fit for royalty on her land adjacent to this.

Would she welcome grandeur, or would she remain the unpretentious, dignified soul that she seemed in spite of it? He secretly hoped that she would stay as she was. She wore a glow of serenity, a mantle more dear than any he had acquired thus far. Though even now, Edouard could feel a calmness seeping into his soul to replace the constant watchfulness and suspicion.

He straightened the hose points he had just tied to his belt and stood waiting for Henri to assemble the rest of his clothing. "You approve of the lady, then?" he asked his son.

"Dare I not?" the boy returned, holding the velvet garment out to be donned. "Would it matter? It did not the last time."

"No," Edouard admitted. He should have cuffed Henri for his sarcasm, but the lad did come by it honestly. Instead, he softened the truth with a smile of affection. "However, I would appreciate your support in this."

Edouard sighed and laid his hands on Henri's slender shoulders. "Son, you are nearly a man now. I have done you ill by remaining unattached so long. Who is to teach you manners and the way with proper ladies if I do not take a wife? True, I could foster you with another lord, one with a wife who would take on the task, but I trust no other to train you up as I will do."

Henri nodded. "I would learn from the best there is, Father."

"Not above boosting the old man's pride, eh?" Edouard did feel immensely proud that Henri felt this way. He brushed nonexistent lint from the shoulders of his son's finely stitched jack. "So! Shall we go below, break our fast, and charm my bride-to-be?"

"Why not?" Henri replied. "At least she does not serve up sheep guts as I have been told they do here. One must like her for that, I suppose."

Edouard did cuff him then as they laughed together.

As they descended the stairs, he wondered whether Lady Anne had her own son convinced this marriage would be a good thing. A half-grown lad could harbor jealousy of a mother, hatred for a man who would replace his dead father, and resentment for anyone who had charge of his lands these next few years.

She greeted them, all gracious and soft-spoken, as they entered the hall. "My lord. Henri. Do come and eat. My uncle left Baincroft some two hours past." She raised her brows and offered Edouard a conspiratorial half smile. "He wants musicians for the wedding feast. And better wine."

"Now, why does that not surprise me?" Edouard laughed softly and placed her hand on his forearm. He pressed her fingers and felt her answering squeeze.

All the while, he congratulated himself again on his decision to wed this woman. Upon first glance at her the day before, he had known he would have her. She stirred his blood rightly enough, but her appeal extended beyond the obvious. He detected a remarkable strength, that inner calm, and a bold decisiveness surpassing any he had yet beheld in a woman. All that, without any evident aggressiveness. He wondered how she managed it.

She did resemble Hume's daughter, Honor, somewhat. Only Lady Anne's lovely gray eyes shot no sparks of hatred and fear when they met his own. Her inviting lips, which he had pressed for as long as he dared in their kiss of peace, offered only smiles and sweet words. Her musical voice did wondrous things to his senses, soothing and exciting at the same time. He could just imagine the gentle purr of it when he...

"When will we meet your son, my lady?" Henri dared ask. Edouard should have chastised him for speaking without leave, but he wanted the answer, as well. He added his questioning look to Henri's.

She bit those rose-touched lips together for an instant before she answered. "Later today, I trow. Robert went a-hunting with my steward. I fear we did not expect your company yestereve and today found our meat in short supply. You will forgive him, won't you? Rob does feel so responsible for Baincroft's hospitality."

"He has recovered from his illness then?"

"Illness?" The lady appeared confused for a moment and then fixed a bright smile. "Oh, aye, he is well enough to hunt! He seemed determined to go."

"That is admirable of him," Edouard assured her. He had noticed a small break in her poise and wished to restore it. She must be concerned about her son's reaction to the news that she would marry. "Lord Robert must provide you much comfort since you lost your husband. When he returns, I must commend your son for his thoughtfulness in seeing to our needs."

The lady merely smiled, nodded and indicated they should sit down. This time he motioned for Henri to join them at board. There were hands enough to fill the cups and the food already lay on the table before them.

Edouard had hardly touched his ale cup when a heavyset man, one he'd seen in the stables, rushed in at a lumbering run, gasping, "Lady—come quick—our laddie—north wall!"

Lady Anne issued a sharp little cry and leapt up from her seat. Abandoning all grace for speed, she raced across the hall and out the door. Edouard followed at a run, as did Henri and the rest of the hall's inhabitants.

When they rounded the keep itself, there were already a number of people staring up at the small figure atop the corner merlon, arms raised to the sky. A large hawk circled above him and the boy looked set to leap toward it.

"Mon Dieu!" Edouard whispered as he started for the steps to the wall-walk.

Lady Anne grabbed his arm and hung on as he rushed past her. "Wait! There's no time!" Then she released him and put the fingers of one hand to her lips, emitting a sharp, earsplitting whistle. Then another.

The lad turned. For an instant, he wavered, arms windmilling before he finally caught his balance. Edouard's heart stopped. He envisioned the broken little body lying in a heap on the other side of the wall.

Anne beckoned frantically and the agile little fellow scrambled down. No one in the bailey moved as they watched the boy tear heedlessly along the open wall-walk, a narrow path of rough wooden planks protected on one side by the stone wall to which they were attached. On the other lay an unguarded drop of some sixty feet. A collective groan emerged from the crowd as he reached the steps and clambered down.

Lady Anne sank to her knees in the dirt. Edouard marched forward and grasped the boy by his shoulders. He could not stop the flow of harsh reprimands. "Do you see what you have done, you reckless lackwit? Look at your lady! She is nigh in a faint with worry you would break your foolish neck!"

He shook the little beggar sharply and then dragged him before Lady Anne by the scruff of his neck. An old hound rushed forward, growling, but the boy silenced him with an upraised palm. Ignoring the dog, Edouard forced the boy to his knees in front of her. "Apologize at once!"

Edouard could not bear the pale fright that stole Anne's calm, the leftover terror in her soft gray eyes. Neither could the lad, apparently. With a look of absolute contrition and the most gentle of gestures, the grubby young hands cupped her face and patted. When he removed them, there were streaks of dirt along her cheeks, mingling with the wetness of her tears.

Her lips firmed and her eyes narrowed. "To my solar with you! Go!" she demanded. She did not shout, but clipped each word distinctly in a low tone that did not bode well for the little daredevil's backside, Edouard thought. The boy and the old hound trudged off as ordered, heads down and contrite.

He took her arm and raised her up. "You are extremely overset, my lady. Shall I deal with him for you?"

"No!" she exclaimed with a lift of her head. "He would not comprehend you—your French."

Edouard raised his brows at that. "I know my English. But I had no mind to do much speaking. The rascal is incredibly heedless and he needs be taught a lesson."

She pierced him with a look of the purest hatred he had ever seen. "Beat anyone who belongs to me and I will kill you!"

Before her shocking words registered, she had whirled angrily away from him and followed the boy around the side of the keep.

"Father, did you hear? She threatened you!" Henri whispered in awe.

"Yes, I heard. Apparently Lady Anne is very protective of her people." A good thing to be, Edouard supposed, but her vehemence seemed unwarranted. "Go along, Henri, and finish your meal. You have sword practice in half an hour."

Sir Gui approached as Henri left. "My lord, I need a private word with you."

"What's amiss, Gui?"

The knight fell in step with Edouard as they walked

slowly back to the keep. "I overheard the lady. You should take her threat seriously, you know."

Edouard laughed. "And why is that? You think her able to follow through?"

Sir Gui hesitated only briefly before speaking. "Yes, my lord. The people here are different than we are used to. Rough, not quite civilized, I think, and more prone to violence. Her first husband died under very peculiar circumstances. By her own hand, they say."

Edouard halted. "Who spouts such rumors? I would have his name. His tongue, too, if he cannot keep it still."

"I cannot give his name, for I do not know it. Last eve I slept in the stables instead of the barracks. My mount seemed ill and off his feed, so I took the empty stall near his. I awoke late in the night when I heard two men speaking together in low voices, as though secrets passed between them. One laughed and asked the other if he thought the French count might also succumb to the old lord's *ague* in due time."

"And the answer?" Edouard demanded.

"Most likely, so the other man said, for the lady suffered too long before discovering the solution to her problem. Now she had found it, the man declared, and it would be no great trick for her to solve this one. If that means she killed her first lord, she might have the same plan for you!"

The silence drew out between them while Edouard considered the probability of truth in the exchange. He knew well the power of gossip. When anyone died in a manner that left doubt as to the reason, the remaining spouse always became suspect. Never mind that there was no motive, no proof, no shred of evidence.

Edouard himself had been a victim of that particular occurrence, not once but twice.

But the fact remained, Lady Anne had just warned him

outright that she would kill him if he usurped her power to discipline her people. A strong reaction for the mere shaking of a stable lad.

The look she wore when she said it spoke of passion far more intense than he had suspected she possessed. He could direct that surprising fervor, however, and make it a positive thing between them. Despite that intensity, he could not believe Anne capable of murder.

"Speak to no one of what you heard, Gui. I doubt me there is reason to put any credence to it."

"Doubt if you must, my lord, but do not discount it altogether, eh? She thinks this place and these people are still hers, not yours. Even the tamest bitch grows dangerous when you manhandle her pups."

"You court death yourself with that comparison!" Edouard warned, his hand automatically gripping his sword.

Gui backed away, hands up. "No disrespect! I but meant to make a point. A poor choice of words. I apologize."

Edouard knew he had overreacted. "Very well, then. Take charge of Henri when he comes out. He needs work on his parry."

"Gladly, my lord." Sir Gui paused and risked another warning. "You will have a care? Finding another such generous lord would not be an easy task."

Generous? Edouard wondered what had fostered that compliment. Gui had not yet proved himself worthy enough to gather any special rewards. Nor was he likely to, given that loose tongue of his. "Of course, Gui. I am ever aware."

Chapter Three

Edouard climbed the rough wooden steps and entered the hall. The reckless stable lad, the hound, a priest, and Lady Anne were just exiting the solar. She rushed forward to meet him as the others headed toward the kitchens. "My lord, I must apologize for my hasty words. There is no excuse—"

"Do not trouble yourself, Anne. I understand how worried you were about that boy." He smiled down at her, feeling again that powerful need to restore her quiescence. "If you have the same concern for all your folk, I should imagine they adore you."

For a brief instant, he could have sworn she wore a look of fear. Perhaps because he had just reminded her of the incident outside, he decided.

She made no answer to his comment, but changed the subject entirely. "I spoke with Father Michael. He agreed to perform our wedding on the morrow so that you need not delay your travel."

Edouard reached for her hands and brought them to his lips, kissing each one in turn. "I applaud your efficiency, sweet lady. What a lucky man am I to find such a treasure." He felt the stiffness of her reaction to his gesture melt slowly into acceptance. Taking advantage, he turned her hands and kissed the palms.

Then he released one and trailed his fingers over her cheeks. "The little ingrate made mud of the tears you wept for him," he said softly. "For that alone, I could thrash him."

She yanked her hand from his. The blast of sudden fury turned her eyes to molten silver. "Not whilst I live!" she snarled.

"No, no, my sweet! You mistake me!" he caught her arm as she spun to leave. "But a figure of speech! I only meant that I hate to see you weep for any cause. Come now."

Edouard handled her heaving anger gently, determined to soothe her. "You have settled the matter and it is forgotten, eh? Over and done and we will think on it no more. Come, sit and have wine with me now, for we have much to learn of each other."

Her shoulders squared defensively and she refused to look at him. "Forgive me, no. I must go and wash my face. Then I must see Father Michael's wife and plan the—"

"Wife? Your priest has a wife?" Edouard demanded.

In her confusion, she seemed to forget the anger. That was something, anyway. "Aye, he does. What of it?"

"Priests should be celibate. 'Tis church law!"

"Bother!" she said with a wave of her hand. "Many priests are wed here in this country. Yours as well, I'd wager. 'Tis better than keeping a woman and children hidden away, do you not agree?"

Edouard closed his mouth. He knew better than to argue anything further at this point. The wedding was tomorrow. Afterward would be time enough to establish his control over foolhardy villeins and wayward holy men. He was no stranger to discretion, and that was certainly called for at the moment.

"As you say," he said mildly, adding a bow.

He watched as she took herself off in the same direction as the priest and the boy. Then he turned slowly and went out to observe Henri's progress with the blade.

Sir Gui might not be far wrong about the primitive nature of these Scots. After encountering Anne's startling bursts of rage, priests who took wives, young lords who shunned guests, and peasants who thought to fly, Edouard considered that his knight might have the right of it.

Despite all of that, mayhaps even because of it, Edouard liked this place. And he fully intended to stay.

Anne swept into the kitchens where she encountered Robert and Father Michael engaged in wolfing down bannocks. Rob's old hound, Rufus, scratched behind one ear, whining for Rob to share the food.

"Father, tell Meg I need to see her in the solar immediately after the noon meal."

Then she grabbed Robert's chin between her thumb and fingers. "Go to my room. Do not let *him* see you."

Robert nodded, grinning merrily around a mouthful of the doughy bread. He slid off the worktable where he perched and skipped off toward the hall, Rufus the hound in tow. Anne watched as Rob halted, peeked around the archway, and then dashed for the stairs.

Anne went to the solar for her sewing basket, found her sharpest scissors and followed him up.

"Sit here," she ordered her son once she had arranged the stool in front of her chair beside the window. "And be still."

She held a section of his shoulder-length hair between her fingers as she clipped it. Once she had shortened all of it considerably, she ordered him to undress and get into the tub. They laughed together when Rufus disappeared beneath the bed.

Rob screeched and shivered as he entered the water which had grown cold since her morning bath. "Mama," he began a protest, which she quickly squelched with a meaningful look.

"Scrub!" she warned him, ruffling his newly shorn waves. "Or I shall do it for you."

Anne watched sternly while he complied. She dipped and poured water over his head to rinse off the soap, laughing with him as he sputtered and giggled. It brought to mind his babyhood and the first bathing experience they shared. He was her very heart, this lad.

When he had finished, she held out a length of linen and wrapped it around him. Then she directed him to sit near the brazier where she rubbed dry his wheat-colored locks.

Though he had MacBain's coloring there, his eyes were like her own. She thought he had the looks of her own father, rather than his. His disposition was his own, however.

Merry Rob, friend to all. Yet he was canny, too, not quite as all-trusting as he seemed. He must regret that he missed the sounds everyone else took so for granted, but he never seemed to brood over it. Even during those worst of times with MacBain, it had been Rob who boosted her flagging spirits, who reassured her all would be well. She envied his self-confidence and wondered where in this world he had acquired it. A compensation from God, no doubt.

How handsome he was, all clean and scrubbed. She pulled a long-sleeved tunic of saffron wool over his head and handed him smallclothes and brown *chausses* to don for himself. When he had done so, Anne offered a belt of burnished leather with a gold buckle, one she had refashioned from his father's things.

He grimaced as he took it, probably remembering its former owner. "Uggy bet," he muttered, but obediently cinched it around his middle.

The way he looked now, Trouville would never realize Robert was the lad on the parapet this morning. She had transformed the long tangle of his dust-coated hair into a silken, sunlit cap. Gone were the threadbare, homespun clothes he always wore for his morning hunts. He looked a proper lordling now. Nay, the comte would not know him. She would barely recognize him herself did she not see him clean and dressed so at supper most nights.

Rob returned to his stool and sat. His expressive eyes, only a shade darker than her own, regarded her with questions. *Why the bath before evening? Why must I dress so fine before midday? What is afoot here, Mama?*

She knelt before him so that they were face-to-face. "You are to meet Lord Trouville today," she explained.

Rob's brows drew together in a scowl. He had not liked that shaking Trouville had given him. "Nay!"

"Aye!" she declared. "You will. Now you must heed me, Rob."

Rebellion had him closing his eyes and turning away, but she firmly tapped his knee, her signal that she meant business and he must attend.

When he finally faced her, his resignation apparent in the sag of his shoulders, she continued. "I must marry this man," she said, clasping her palms together.

He studied them for a moment, sighed loudly, and then gave one succinct nod.

"He wants to meet you. You must watch his words. Say only 'aye, my lord' or 'nay, my lord.'"

Rob chewed his lip and lowered his brows. She knew he was considering whether he could do as she demanded with any success. The French accent would be a great obstacle. Rob must have noted the problem when Trouville threatened him earlier.

"I shall be there. Look to me," she advised, touching

her finger to his eye and then to her lips. "Now for speech practice."

He clamped the back of one hand to his brow and rolled his eyes, groaning dramatically as he slid to the floor. Anne laughed at his foolery, for the moment forgetting her fears.

Later, as she left Rob in her rooms, perfecting his bow before old Rufus, Anne's apprehension returned. He had to meet Trouville, there was no getting around that. Pray God the man would be too caught up in the excitement of his impending wedding to pay much mind to a mere stepson.

Her new husband would be gone very soon. Of necessity, Rob must appear at the ceremony, but there would be no time for discourse between them then, surely. If only they could get through this evening's confrontation without detection, she would keep Rob out of sight until protocol demanded his presence.

If worse came to worst and the comte discovered the truth about Rob, she would have no recourse but to plead mercy. If she pled prettily and often enough, he might permit Rob and her to live on as supplicants. But Anne knew, as surely as she knew her own name, that Trouville would never grant her Robert all that was his by right of birth when he reached adulthood.

Many things could occur between now and that time, however. Her uncle would not be around to observe Rob in the years to come. He had a home and his duties in France. Trouville might make infrequent visits, but she could keep Rob away from him. If fortune smiled, neither of the men should guess until Robert was a man grown, if even then.

By that time, Anne hoped she would have taught her son enough to hold his own. By that time, she would have installed a wife for him with wits enough to supply what he lacked when he needed help. Meg and Michael's daughter, Jehan, had a good head on her shoulders. Rob would have a young steward, as well. Thomas, his brother-by-marriage, would protect and serve out of love for his lord. Their training was already well underway. She had done all she could for the present.

If not for her all-consuming worry, she could turn all her energies toward making certain Trouville departed the day after the wedding a complacent man. Anne knew she must still give serious thought to how she might send him home satisfied, assured that she would see to his interests here without any further supervision.

The ceremony and small celebration would present no problems in and of themselves. Then she must endure the wedding night, of course.

MacBain had never required anything other than her submission whenever he had come to her. Anne needed no further lessons concerning the futility of resistance.

Mayhaps performing her marital duty would not prove so ghastly this time. No woman could call Trouville loathsome to look upon. And she could not envision him as rough-handed when it came to wooing. The comte did not seem inclined toward brutality unless provoked, and she certainly knew better than to incite a man's anger.

Meg would assist her in avoiding another pregnancy just as the old herb woman, Agatha, had done in the years following Robert's birth. Another child must be prevented at all costs. Trouville should not question her future barrenness, given her advanced age. He had his heir, so that should not present a problem.

Her main concern must be in seeing Rob through this day and the next without mishap. Anne simply had little time to dwell on the minor inconvenience of contenting her new husband's carnal expectations. By the time she counted the twenty cherubs stitched on the bed's canopy, it would all be over and done, anyway. She would yield the once, and right gladly, to get him out of their lives in short order.

A small shiver of apprehension tingled through her. Surely it *was* apprehension, was it not?

"Lord Edouard Gillet, comte de Trouville, may I present my son, Baron Robert Alexander MacBain, Lord of Baincroft," Anne announced. She stepped forward and turned so that she stood to the side and slightly behind Trouville.

Anne had decided to introduce Rob to her betrothed just prior to the evening meal. Planning this night's repast and the nuptial feast for the following day had provided her the excuse to avoid the comte all afternoon.

She had kept Robert in her chambers practicing his words and his bow, in hopes of keeping him clean and out of mischief. Thank goodness he had left Rufus above stairs as she ordered, for the sight of the faithful old hound might give the whole thing away.

Now had come the moment she dreaded.

Robert bowed perfectly and straightened, looked directly into the comte's eyes and smiled winningly. He did that so well, she thought. Her son knew his assets and used them to full advantage. That smile ranked foremost among his talents. No one save his old father could ever resist it.

However, here might be another who could. She had the distinct feeling that the comte, at Robert's age, probably exercised that very same guile in like fashion. He used a more worldly form of it even now.

"Lord Robert," Trouville said formally. "I am pleased to meet you at last." He spoke French.

With an economy of movement, Anne gave a quick twist of her fist and pointed at her chest.

"And I," Rob said clearly.

Anne almost fainted, with relief that Rob had answered at all, and in dismay at his inadvertently poor manners. He had replied in English, because he knew no other way. Too loudly, as well, but that could be attributed to the tension of their first meeting. She hoped.

Even hereabouts, nobles always conversed in French with each other, using the English or Gaelic with lesser ranks. However, if Trouville took offense in this instance, he was too polite to say as much. In fact, he readily switched to English as he introduced his son to Rob. Neither boy said anything, merely bowed simultaneously and regarded each other with great interest.

Anne's heart leapt when she realized she had completely forgotten Henri and what he might make of Rob. He would not be so distracted as his father tonight, and might even make an overture of friendship toward her son. If not that, at least he would attempt conversation.

She hurriedly gathered them all as if herding unruly sheep and directed them toward the dais. She indicated Henri should sit to his father's left. She reminded Rob with a brief gesture that he was to stand behind and pour for their guests and herself.

Trouville insisted on holding her chair for her himself, and Anne thanked him for his courtesy. Then his long fingers subtly caressed her upper arms and shoulders over the fitted velvet that covered her. A chill rippled along her spine, though it did not seem an unpleasant sensation.

How forward he was, touching her so. Try as she might, however, Anne could find no will to reject the gesture. No good reason, either, since he would certainly dare far more than this in the very near future. *Please him,* she reminded herself.

Before they settled well enough to be served, her uncle arrived. Fortunately, his delight over acquiring several minstrels and a hogshead of French burgundy prevented his noticing Rob at all. Far be it from her to tempt fate with further introductions unless it became absolutely necessary.

With concentrated effort, Anne kept up a constant flow

of conversation, encouraging her uncle's suggestions for the morrow's festivities. Trouville seemed mildly amused by her chatter and drolly added his own thoughts when asked.

She managed to turn more than once and reassure Rob with her smile that all had gone as planned, and that he had performed admirably. If only he would make himself scarce immediately after the meal as she had ordered him to do. But Anne could feel his fascination for these strange visitors, especially Henri.

What if his tremendous curiosity outweighed his fear? Come to think of it, she had not even noticed any fear in his expression. None at all.

At the thought, Anne looked over her shoulder and shot Rob a frown of warning. He rewarded her, not with his angelic smile, but with the devilish grin he saved especially for her. The one he employed whenever he decided to act on his own initiative.

He stepped forward and held the flagon over her wine cup. "Mo, Mama?"

"*No* more, Robert! Thank you, that will be *all*," she replied, her brows lowered as if to threaten him. *Do not go against me on this or we shall both regret it!*

If the thought did not go directly into his head from hers, it was not for lack of effort on her part. If only she could explain the danger to him more clearly than she had done, her fear that he would lose everything, be cast out, lost to her and without her.

Rob chuckled low in his throat, a nearly inaudible sound, but meaningful enough to set Anne to gulping what was left of her wine. Now they were in for it.

Robert stepped to the far side of Trouville and held his flagon forward. "Mo, miyowd?"

Anne's gaze rolled upward, seeking assistance from heaven.

"Yes, thank you," the comte said, turning his head slightly to regard Rob as the lad poured his wine.

Anne could not see his expression, but she could imagine it well enough. He would wonder at Rob's speech, which never included *l* or *r* unless he took great care. She did not sense any trepidation on Rob's part, so his lack of attention to his words must be due to excitement. *Think, my lad! Mind your tongue!*

The comte was speaking. "You have mastered this task to perfection, young man. And your mother tells me that you also take it upon yourself to provide meat for your kitchens. A laudable enterprise for one of your years. Is this hare of your morning's quarry?"

Rob's eyes flew to her. Though the comte had spoken flawless English, her son had not understood one word. The accent had thrown him off as she knew it would. Even under the best of circumstances, Rob only gleaned about one word out of three, barely enough to gain the gist of one's meaning.

She made a swift up and down motion with her fist, like a small head nodding.

"Aye, miyowd," Rob answered with enthusiasm. "Aye."

"A tender treat," Trouville commented. "Why not hunt together one day, the three of us? Henri has not had much opportunity while we attended his majesty. King Philip mislikes the sport of it, and there are many others to provide for his board. Tell me, what sort of bow do you use?"

"No bow!" Anne interrupted, frantic to distract Trouville from his conversation with Rob. "He uses but a sling, with which he is very adept. And a tercel. He has a special affinity for birds. All animals, in fact. Do you keep hawks, my lord? I suppose not, since you say that you and Henri have small chance to hunt."

She knew she babbled. Her son now regarded her with

delight, as though they had made a game of this and it was her turn.

With a brazen wink behind the comte's head, Rob moved down behind and to the other side of Henri's chair. "Mo wine, you?"

Anne's breath caught. Henri grinned up at Rob and nodded. Rob poured expertly and stepped back with a satisfied lift of his chin. He obviously believed he had spoken as well as they. She had been all too generous with her praise. He had not a whit of self-doubt.

Trouville looked at her, the question in his eyes, but he did not ask. Anne knew he expected some sort of explanation. She whispered under her breath in French, as though she feared Rob would overhear. "Forgive him, my lord. 'Tis just that his first tongue was Gaelic. I fear my lad has no gift for languages."

The comte nodded and pursed his lips, apparently satisfied. "Nothing a proper tutor cannot repair. We shall see to it."

She prayed with all her might that neither Trouville nor his son would ever ask Rob another direct question that required more than an aye, nay or thanks. Even then he only stood one chance in three of giving the correct response.

Praise God, her uncle remained altogether oblivious to Rob's presence.

The rest of the meal progressed without incident. When the food had been cleared away, Anne's uncle announced the minstrels who, for lack of a gallery, sat to one side, just beyond the dais. As they tuned their instruments, he left his chair and approached Anne for the first dance.

With no just cause to refuse, she allowed her uncle to lead her around the table to the circle that was forming.

Sir Guillaume had appropriated pretty Kate, one of the young weavers, as partner. Simm, the steward, led out his wife, and young Thomas escorted his mother, Meg. Four other couples formed another circle, and the musicians began to play a lively *bransle*.

Though unschooled in aught but reels and flings, her people watched her steps with Uncle Dairmid and followed with only a few stumbles. Ineptitude only added to their merriment as the dance progressed. Only Sir Guillaume remained serious, executing the dance as though he had been ordered to the dreadful chore.

Bracing her lips into a forced smile, Anne glanced toward the table. Her knees almost gave way. Trouville, his large hand encircling Robert's elbow, frowned darkly as he spoke to her son. Her uncle whirled her again and she nearly fell.

As soon as she recovered, she looked back frantically at the two on the dais. Rob was nodding and smiling as sweetly as ever while the comte held his cup aloft for another refill.

Then Rob set the flagon on the table and scampered away with Henri. Jesu, they had been found out. Now all was lost.

The dance came to a rousing finish as her uncle lifted her by the waist and set her on her feet with a thump. Hearty applause mocked the futility of her evening's plans. Anne abandoned both her smile and her hope. She stared down at the scattered rushes and heaved a huge sigh of defeat.

"Dance, my lady?"

She felt Trouville's fingers capture hers, and slowly turned, expecting an angry denouncement of her duplicity, a promise of punishment for the truth she had sought to hide, and a threat to toss Robert to the four winds to fend for himself.

Instead, her betrothed smiled down on her. The lyre and

gittern struck a soft, slow *pavane* and he lifted her hand, turning this way and that as they slowly circled the floor.

He did not know yet! He did not know. Anne swallowed a sob of relief and focused attention on her feet.

How she wished to lose herself in the music, to be fifteen again and all-trusting. Trouville looked divine in his dark velvet and silver. The softness and shine did nothing to mask his formidable strength and hardness. His exotic scent enveloped her, stirring fantasies of sumptuous spice-laden feasts and unknown pleasures.

"Grace needs a new name," he said in a voice as velvety as the softness of his sleeve. "I shall call her Anne."

She sighed deeply in spite of herself. Here was a man who might have stolen her heart as well as her hand. A maiden's dream, a bride's illusion. She wished she had been allowed that in her youth, even for a brief interval. A chimera to cherish.

Would that he had come here years ago, before MacBain. Everything would have turned out the same after the birth of a child, of course, but she might have at least enjoyed the pretense of happiness for a while.

Anne shook herself smartly. She dared not afford even a moment's lapse in her guard tonight, certainly not to re-capture her long-lost girlhood and entertain romantic dreams. Her wits must remain sharp.

The comte did not know yet, even after speaking directly to Robert. Or mayhaps he did. He might well know every-thing, and only played this courtly game of his to increase her dread. Did all men enjoy baiting women?

Chapter Four

The dance provided Anne more dread than pleasure. The comte smiled down at her as though all was right with the world. She braced herself for what would surely come.

How long must she endure this before he would announce plans to seize everything her son owned? Until the music stopped? Nay. She suddenly realized that he would have to postpone that until after he had her safely wed for fear she would cry off. Aye, that must be the way of it. If she refused to marry him, then her uncle, as Rob's only male relative, would take Baincroft for his own. Dairmid Hume would have done so already if he had realized Rob's impairment.

Anne dared to look Trouville directly in the eye then, searching for the streak of cunning. All she saw was benevolent concern.

It could be that he had not guessed after all. Had Rob managed to bluff his way through an entire conversation without revealing himself? Anne had to find out.

"My son angered you tonight, my lord?" she asked tentatively.

"Angered? No, not tonight. I am afraid I did admonish him once more for his acrobatics on the battlements this morn. However, he solemnly promised me never to repeat the feat again. You should have told me earlier that he was your son, though I do understand why you did not.''

''You do?'' Anne held her breath. He had recognized Rob, after all, despite the changes she had wrought with the haircut and clothes.

His low laughter rippled along her jangled nerves. ''Of course. You feared I would take him to task for it again, only the second time as a father might do a son. Forgive me, for I did that anyway. I thought we should begin as we mean to go, Robert and I.''

She stopped dancing and stepped away from him, glaring. ''You are *not* his father! You have no right—''

He clasped her hands firmly and squeezed. ''Robert will be my son, Anne, as near to one as he will allow. Or as near as *you* will allow.'' His dark eyes locked on hers, soft with a glow of patient good humor. ''You know what you need, do you not?''

''Need?'' she asked, suddenly lost in his all-encompassing gaze. She nearly forgot his question.

''You need more children! You *coddle* that boy!'' He forced her to move again, resuming their dance. ''Perhaps coddle is not the correct word, but you hold him too closely. He should be working, preparing to squire, not teetering on merlons, courting an early death. The rapscallion's nimble, though. I will grant him that.''

She could not form words, her heart beat so frantically.

Trouville continued, ''He attends well, that one. Never once did he let his attention wander as boys are like to do. I swear he hangs on every word. Can you not see he craves guidance?''

''I give him guidance!'' she declared in defense. If he only knew the guidance required for a lad like Rob. Daunting.

''Of course you do,'' he replied soothingly. ''But all

boys of that age seek adventure. I would put a small sword in his hand and teach him skills to defend what is his when he comes of age. He needs the discipline of serving a firm master so that he will learn to give orders of his own one day.''

All too true. Anne admitted that. But how? Trouville spoke as if he would teach Rob these things himself. How could she allow the man who might be his worst threat to apply that instruction? She could not.

"I would keep my son by me, my lord. I insist he remain here. At Baincroft.''

For a long moment, he said nothing, advancing elegantly to the music. "I agree. He should remain here. Do not worry more over it, my dear. It was simply a thought.'' The music ended and he led her back to the dais.

Both his son and hers had joined the others around the musicians, waiting for the next dance. Rob tugged at Jehan's braid and took her hand, while Henri edged his way between his father's knight and young Kate. At least while they danced, she could breathe more easily.

There was nothing for it now but to wait and see what happened. Apparently, Trouville must have asked only questions which Robert had somehow answered appropriately.

Rob's poor speech might have seemed only a matter of difficulty with a language other than Gaelic. A jest there, for he only had command of a half-dozen words in the old tongue. But Rob did have a gift for appearing to listen intently even if he did not understand a thing. Or even if he was not at all interested. That was another tool he wielded with efficiency, as he did that celestial smile of his.

Exhaustion threatened to overcome her as the night wore on in an endless progression of songs and poems by her uncle's entertainers. She rested one elbow on the table and propped her chin on her hand. Not a dignified position for a lady, but it kept her from nodding off.

"Did you not sleep last night?" Trouville asked as he captured her other hand and teased her fingertips. "I admit that I lay awake for hours on end. How unfair of you to have had your lovely face engraved on the ceiling."

Anne's sudden laugh surprised her as much as it did him. "What foolishness is this? What can you mean?"

He leaned toward her and touched his nose to hers. "You were all I could see, lying there awake. And when at last I slept, you invaded my dreams. Mayhaps it is on my heart you have etched your sweet likeness." His lips brushed across her own, a whispery touch that sent heat coursing through her like a sudden fever.

She drew back and stared at him. Never before Trouville had anyone other than her son teased her into laughter. And no one had ever paid her court in such a way. What point to all this? she wondered. Whatever did he hope to gain by this play?

The thought formed words and escaped her mouth, "What do you want, my lord?"

He nipped her bottom lip gently and then looked directly into her eyes. "You were to call me Edouard, my sweet. And for now, I want only to see you smile again."

Her only option was to please him, to keep him content until he went away and left them alone. And so she smiled.

Lord, how he loved the taste of her. He loved the sight of her. And he loved her gentleness. Even the too gentle heart that allowed her son a child's way when he was nearly ready to become a man.

Edouard vowed he would soon make her see how dangerous was this path she allowed the boy to travel. With no formal training at arms, little language other than the heathen tongue of MacBain's ancestors, and a marked lack of discipline, the boy would turn out worse than useless as lord of his own keep. Robert badly needed the firm hand of a strong father figure. MacBain must have grown too old to care before his death, or perhaps too caring.

Not that Anne's son had acquired no attributes in his ten short years. He possessed a sturdy body, even though small for his age. He was a strong and handsome boy. Agile as a tinker's monkey, too. Robert loved his mother, politely respected his elders, and had grown adept at some duties required of a page.

Wonderful mother that she was, Anne had taught her son all that she possibly could within the realm of her experience. Now Robert's education must fall to him, Edouard decided.

He marveled at the good fortune that had led him to this place. Who would have guessed he would find a woman so perfect, one who would give him her son to foster and, God willing, more children of his own in the near future?

Even more wondrous than that, he was gaining a beautiful, willing companion who seemed set on his every pleasure. He admired how her fiery spirit, banked beneath her gentleness, blazed high when anything threatened one she loved.

No woman had affected him this profoundly, but most of the time he rather welcomed these new and deeper feelings. His heart warmed at the very sight of her. Other parts of his body grew considerably heated, as well, he thought with a shake of his head.

Contentment of the soul mixed with the heady excitement of lust ought to make theirs an enviable union, indeed. She would provide the first, of course. And that second commodity, he could bestow full measure upon her. It would be almost akin to the love they had jested about last evening. Unique, and quite satisfying.

"I wonder, Anne. Do you also believe we shall suit?"

he asked softly, almost unmindful that he had spoken his
thoughts aloud.

She lifted her lashes and regarded him serenely. "I
cannot think why we should not."

Edouard thanked the saints he had found Anne. He had
not wanted a young and frightened bride to initiate. Nor
had he desired taking one of the women at court to wife,
well versed as they were in pleasuring a man. He wanted
a woman he could trust. And everyone who knew him
would be shocked to learn that he would like to have a
woman he could love.

As he had said to Anne, only half in jest, he did believe
in love, though he had been offered precious little of it in
his thirty-two years, certainly never by a woman. His
mother had considered him a duty, presented him to his
father at birth and promptly forgot his existence. His father,
glad enough to have an heir, did not wish a child underfoot.
Consequently, Edouard had been relegated to the servants
until he reached seven years, and then sent to court as a
page.

Fortunately, he had met Lord de Charnay there. Edouard
had served him as squire, and eventually received his spurs
from the man. During his time with de Charnay, Edouard
also gained a glimpse of the happy home life and affection
the man enjoyed with his lady wife. He held those mem-
ories dearer than any others.

That couple had not loved him, of course, but they had
shown him by example that love could flourish between a
man and woman. When his father arranged his marriage at
seventeen, Edouard had been fully prepared to bestow all
the love within him on his new bride. Only she had wished
to be a bride of Christ.

Daunting competition, indeed, but Edouard had tried. He
had his parents and hers as allies. Poor Isabeau. She had
died blaming Edouard for taking her innocence and making

her like it. He would always think of her kindly, however. She had given him Henri, ultimate proof that love existed and that he possessed it.

His second wife, another of his father's choices, doused his hopes at the very beginning. Helvise had already loved another man, one unsuitable in her father's estimation.

But this wife, his Anne, would not die and leave him with only guilt, regret and a motherless infant as Isabeau had done. Nor would she betray him the way Helvise had. This marriage could fulfill his secret dream if he nurtured it carefully.

It confounded Edouard a little, the way his hopes soared. Never before, with Isabeau, Helvise, or even when he had believed himself in love with the Lady Honor, had he let down his inner guard this way. Always, he had kept in mind the strong possibility of a marital disaster. But now, with Anne, there was this meeting of two minds, this mutual affection, this shared hope for happiness.

How perfect she was. Yes, he could love her well, and she would love him. He would see to that. In time, she would realize that he had couched his deepest wish within that repartee they had shared about a loving marriage.

People were taking their leave now and seeking their own homes, or retiring to the alcoves and buildings in which they slept.

"You should go above and rest now," he said as he saw her eyelids drop. "Tomorrow will come soon and last long, I trow."

"No doubt," she agreed, rising to her feet with his assistance.

He delighted that she now seemed fairly comfortable with his touch. His plan to set her at ease, at least in that respect, seemed to be working. Though she had been wed before and knew what to expect, Edouard knew it could not be an easy thing to admit a veritable stranger into her bed.

"I trust you will sleep well tonight? Should the ceiling taunt you, then you must turn your face to the pillow," she ventured shyly.

Edouard pressed his lips against her delicate ear to whisper, "Ah, but I will allow you in my dreams, my sweet one. How else shall I endure the wait for the morrow's eve?"

With that he ushered his lady toward the stairs and wished her good-night. He decided he would return to the hall for a while and have another cup of wine. The bare walls and rough furnishings there challenged his imagination, a sorely needed distraction this night. Yes, he could turn this old fortress into a splendid setting for the jewel that was his Anne.

Living here appealed to him. Living here with *her* appealed to him. The gilded French court seemed a tawdry and dissolute place by comparison, and he missed it not at all. It was as though he had thrown off his heavy cloak of guile, woven of the pretense necessary to survive in a world of politics and intrigue. Here was a freshness, a new beginning, and simple contentment. Yes, he would stay and right gladly.

Anne collapsed on the chair before the brazier, infinitely relieved that she had found Rob already asleep on his pallet in the anteroom. Much as she wanted to find out what had passed between her son and Trouville's Henri, she knew it would prove fruitless to try and waken him. Rob slept like the dead.

"My lady?"

"Meg! Where have you been? I asked Father Michael to send you to me this afternoon."

"Tending young Dora. Her babe came tonight, a fine

lad,'' Meg said, smiling through her worry. ''Are you not feeling well?''

''Aye, well enough, but I need some herbs and right soon. The wedding is tomorrow,'' Anne reminded her. ''Will they take effect this near the bedding?''

Meg cocked her fair head to one side, her green eyes glinting in the firelight. ''Which herbs? You mean to render the Frenchman incapable?''

''Nay,'' Anne admitted, feeling her face heat with embarrassment. ''I doubt me he would believe it of any natural cause, virile as he appears. He will only be here for the wedding night and then he returns to his home in France. I dare not refuse him.''

Meg laughed and clapped her hands. ''Dare not or do not wish to? A braw one, that count of yours. I've seen him myself, and he is one to stir the blood! Stirred mine, right enough, and me married with two bairns!''

''Meg, hush!'' She could not meet the other woman's eyes. In truth, she did find Edouard handsome. And charming. A part of her trembled with avid curiosity about what could take place between a woman and a man of young years and comely countenance. ''I must not quicken with his child. You know well the reason.''

Meg sighed and fiddled with the bag she wore tied round her slender waist. ''You fear bearing another such as the young lord?''

Anne stiffened. ''Nay, I do not *fear* it! I could not ask a finer son!''

Then the anger drained away. Meg knew the problems involved as well as she. ''Aye, that. I must admit it,'' Anne said on a sigh. ''Aside from that, a child would bind his lordship closer to this place and might cause frequent visits. I want him gone from here and content to live in France with the profits from my lands. You know what will surely happen if he learns of my Robert's deafness. You heard of

Lord Gile's son, the one who was blinded and lost everything to his brother because of it?''

Meg nodded. ''Such is the way of things. Might rules. But our Rob's a mighty one, mind you, or he shall be once he's grown.''

Anne grinned at her friend. ''Aye, he will be that. Until then, we must hold what is his by any means we may. Now, have you a potion to aid me or not?''

''A pity our Old Agatha's long gone, and I am so new to this. Birthing, tending the sick, cooling fevers and such, I have learned to do right well.'' Meg shook her head. ''We can but try the only thing I have heard of that works. Seeds of lettus did well for Angus's Moraig. Only the one bairn in some twelve years. Agatha gave that to her to prevent her bearing again. '''Tis all I know that won't poison you to the bargain.''

Anne frowned and rubbed at the pain spreading through her temples. ''Nothing more certain than that?''

''Nay. Still, his having only one night's chance at you is better than a constant planting, eh?'' Meg asked, brightening.

''One time is all it takes, as I recall,'' Anne retorted.

''We'll try the seeds,'' Meg declared as she headed for the door. ''I'll go and grind them now for the potion. You had best begin taking it tonight.''

Meg would do all she could to help. She and Father Michael had remained her truest friends these past years. A handsome couple they were and happily wed despite the circumstance that caused it. Their wonderful children provided hope for her Robert's future success. Father Michael's pragmatism and wealth of intellect combined well with Meg's sunny disposition and loyal nature. They had produced two exceptional offspring whom Anne loved nearly as much as her own son. She felt herself blessed to have this family with her.

They had given her much needed support when she was wed to MacBain, and would again when she became wife to the comte. With their help, she would prevail in her plan to enforce Robert's rights. And she would survive this marriage.

Anne undressed herself and crawled naked between the soft linens topped with her fur coverlet. She brushed the downy rabbit pelts, gifts from her son, which she had sewn together to form it.

Tomorrow night she would spend in the lord's chamber and rest amidst silks and rich marten furs which had traveled with Trouville from France. If, indeed, he allowed her any rest. The thought made her shiver, and Anne almost wished it were due to dread. She felt a bit guilty over her curiosity and her lack of horror over bedding with Trouville. But he was far from a horrible man, so far as she could tell.

Longings buried since girlhood crept out of their hiding places and pricked at her like little demons. What would it be like to give herself up to these wicked feelings Edouard engendered? Dare she risk it for the space of a few short hours? Might it not be wise to do so, since her sole aim was to distract him fully until his departure?

Anne snuggled into her pillows. Of course, she should. Why not? He would be gone with the next sunrise.

The restless night Edouard had expected finally gave way to dawn. He rose the moment sunlight invaded the window.

No doubts troubled him on this day. He whistled softly while Henri prepared his bath. He endured a shave, always risky when Henri remained half asleep. An hour crawled by and then another as he and his son performed their morning rituals with exaggerated care and little exchange of words.

Damn, but he wished they could just go below and get

on with it. He hoped Anne did not suffer similar anxiety or they would both appear forced to the match.

He sat by the window, dressed only in his smallclothes and hose, waiting while Henri dragged on his own clothing.

"It is near time," Henri mumbled, flinging a hand out toward the candle marked to show the hour as it burned.

"As though I have not watched the damned thing like a hawk marking prey!" Edouard snapped.

He dressed so quickly, he hoped he had not forgotten anything important. Henri made only token attempts to help before Edouard shooed him away.

Once they reached the hall, further waiting commenced. An entire hour of it. Edouard readjusted his jewel-hilted sword, shifted his weight to his other foot and tugged the neckline of his finery with one finger. His black velvet jupon fitted uncomfortably and proved too warm for the day. He only wore the thing to please Henri. The boy assured him this was his most flattering and would please the bride. Edouard suspected it made him look as villainous as a tax collector.

How he loathed waiting. In most cases, he only tolerated doing so when a king was involved. Again, he figeted, rolling his shoulders forward and back. Then he forced himself to be still, clasping his hands behind him.

"She is late coming," whispered Henri impatiently.

Edouard raised his chin a notch and shot the boy a warning look. "I believe we came early."

"Everyone else is here," Henri remarked as he eyed the crowd of castle folk gathered in the midst of the hall. "Mayhaps she changed her mind and ran away."

"Not unless she climbed the wall," Edouard replied dryly. "The portcullis is so old and rusted, its creak would have been heard all the way to the coast. Think you she's a climber, then?" He smiled down at Henri's attempt to squelch a giggle.

Even as he watched, the boy's eyes widened with wonder and his mouth dropped open. Edouard glanced up to see what had elicited such awe.

The sight of the bride struck him so, he almost mirrored his son's expression. The vision she made evoked a collective sigh from all assembled for the ceremony.

Her flowing hair surrounded her shoulders like a dark, silken cape. With her every movement, its rippling sheen reflected light from every taper in the hall. A narrow, chased-silver circlet crowned the glory of it.

Her overgown appeared woven of finely spun, silvered threads, regal in its simplicity. The snow-white sleeves and neckline of her samite chemise bore an elegant embroidered design of silver thistles. The silver and white of her garb and the fairness of her skin only served to emphasize the natural rose of her soft, expressive lips.

Edouard's hands reached out for hers before he even thought what he was doing. He, who always maintained an attitude of polite disdain, knew he had revealed too much eagerness. For some reason, he did not care at the moment.

The slight tremble of her fingers against his own fostered a fierce longing in him, a compelling desire to comfort, protect and reassure.

Her priest spoke. As though in a dream, Edouard moved with Anne to a nearby table where the prepared contracts lay ready for signature. She might have offered him nothing more than her sweet person and he would have signed away every sou he owned and borrowed more to give her.

How humbling to lay himself open in such a way, Edouard thought. How foolish. However, for Anne, he seemed to have cast away all doubt and suspicion. She might prove him wrong to trust so, but today—and tonight—she would be his alone. An incomparable woman. An incomparable wife.

Reluctantly he released her hands. Edouard hardly heard

the priest enumerate his properties and declare the dower portion. He barely glanced at the documents, and scratched his name with a hurried enthusiasm that, at any other time, would have appalled him.

When he turned, Hume had drawn Anne away. The two now stood near the priest beside the door to the small chapel that adjoined the hall. Flanking them were Henri, Robert, Sir Gui and a lovely maid in simple dress.

Edouard used the time required to cover the short distance regaining what he could of his decorum, but he knew Anne's spell still held him in thrall. It likely would until they had passed a night together. Perhaps two nights. Or more.

The fact that he felt so besotted suddenly annoyed him. Certainly, he wished to love Anne, but he could not allow himself to lose all control. It was undignified to behave the way he was doing.

He frowned as he listened to the priest's verification of nonconsanguinity and consent. He accepted Anne's hand with alacrity when Hume offered it to him. At the proper time, Edouard stated his vows in a clear, brusque voice.

Only when Anne, in her soft and sincere tone, vowed to honor and obey him for the duration of her life, did he feel his poise return full measure.

He realized then that he had held some small fear she would change her mind. Now why would he have thought such a thing? Had she not agreed quite readily to the marriage? Edouard banished the foolish imaginings as common to bridegrooms, and beamed down at his new wife.

When Sir Gui prodded his elbow, Edouard removed the ring he always wore on his small finger. No one had ever worn it save his mother and, after her death, himself. He felt a small stab of sadness that he had never really known the woman who bore him.

The gold-set emerald felt warm in his hand. Following

the priest's incantations, he slipped it on the first joint of Anne's forefinger, then her middle finger, and then finally settled it on the one with the vein leading straight to her heart. Anne belonged to him now. Forever.

Her upturned face invited kissing and he did so, trying to restrain his fervor. They did, after all, have the Mass to get through. And a celebratory meal likely to last the day. He almost groaned thinking of the long hours they must abide before the bedding. Even thinking the word stirred him nearly past endurance.

Edouard ushered Anne before him as they entered the chapel proper and took their places beside one another for the nuptial mass. The priest droned on and on, the liturgy endless, the Latin barely intelligible, while Edouard allowed his mind to dwell on the night to come. So there he stood, erect and shameless, ignoring mass and thinking lascivious thoughts.

He could almost laugh at the torture he worked upon himself. Not once did he seriously attempt to quell this unprecedented, public randiness of his. He desired Anne and he wanted her to know it. He wanted everyone to know. Therein lay the difference in this and his other marriages. This time he was more than willing. This time, *he* had chosen.

Yes, theirs would be a love match. Edouard had decided now, and no jest about it. He could think of absolutely nothing that would prevent their loving each other.

Chapter Five

Anne drew in an anticipatory breath as they exited the chapel and made for the dais where they were to break their fast in splendor. Meg said the cook and staff had outdone themselves, given the short time for preparation and supplies available.

Uncle Dairmid had helped them along by procuring various delicacies such as anise and almonds, along with the expensive wine. He had even purchased lampreys, which she could not abide despite their worth. But the French adored them, so said her uncle.

The trick here would be to avoid the disgrace of penury before her new husband, without impressing him enough to warrant frequent visits in future.

"What a pleasant ceremony," she observed as the comte seated her and took his own chair. "Far preferable to my first, though I do recall little of that day. I was so young then."

"As you are still," Trouville said. Nay, *Edouard* now, she reminded herself. She must call him as he wished, even in her mind. Do everything as he wished.

"Ah, here are our sons, come to wish us happy!" he said, turning to greet the lads.

"Felicitations, Lady Anne, Father," Henri offered with a formal bow.

"Many thanks, Henri!" she exclaimed, smiling at her stepson.

"Appy Day, Mama," Robert said, and with a hesitant look at the comte, added softly, "Fathah."

Anne knew if she lived to be a hundred, she would never forget the look on her husband's face. His usual *savoir faire* deserted him for a mere instant, and she could swear he looked humble. Either that, or Robert's outrageous presumption had rendered him speechless.

She hurried to concoct some explanation. "Forgive us, my lord, but I am afraid Rob misunder—"

"I am honored," Edouard interrupted, his eyes locked with her son's. "Deeply honored. Son."

Henri chuckled. "Then may I call you Mother, my lady?"

"No!" Rob interrupted, cuffing Henri on the shoulder.

Edouard frowned at Henri and looked about to chastise him when Rob interrupted.

"Say *Mama!*" her son explained with wide-eyed reproof and repeated, "Mama."

"Mama!" Henri repeated, laughing and poking Rob playfully in the ribs.

Anne watched the boys scramble for the bench at the far end of the dais. Edouard ignored their unseemly behavior and faced her with hope in his eyes. "Do you mind?"

She placed her hand on his sleeve without any consideration for propriety and smiled. "Nay, I do not! Henri is a fine son."

"Then you would not object if I should leave him here with you when I go?" he asked. "I vow I have never seen him so content. He has had few true friends near his age and no mother at all."

Now what? Anne searched about in her mind for a reason

to deny him this. She liked Henri, but it bode no good for Henri and Robert to become attached as friends and brothers. Henri would have no secrets from his own father, after all. He would tell Edouard all about Robert. 'Twas a wonder he had not already discovered the truth. The fact that lads of their age spent most of their time in physical pursuits and little conversing was probably the only thing that had prevented it thus far.

"Will he not miss you?" she asked.

"I think not."

Edouard clutched her hand and raised it to his lips. "You do realize that a son's disposition ought to be the farthest thing from our minds at the moment? By right, we should be dwelling on each other."

The double entendre could hardly go unnoticed with that wicked light in his eyes. Anne found herself responding with a heated blush, amusement twitching her lips. "Indeed?"

"Yes, indeed!" he affirmed with the raising of a brow. "I should like nothing better than to get on with this day and have it over and done."

"You are eager for the morrow, then?" she teased.

He grinned and nipped the end of her forefinger. "For the night!" he exclaimed.

Anne blushed yet again, but not with embarrassment. The lingering heat of his teeth and tongue against her finger made the blood pound in her ears. She could feel the rush of it throughout her body.

She finally admitted that evening could not come too soon for her. Why shouldn't she look forward to this? Why not explore the pleasures to be had in the marriage bed, if only for this one night?

She knew from her observation of the happily wed couples among her people, that bedding was not always the frightful duty she had endured with the MacBain.

This man would seek to please her. Anne had no illusions about his purpose in that. Her own pleasure would increase his own. Meg assured her this was true for a man with enough intelligence to realize it. Edouard seemed truly wise in this respect, she thought with a smile.

Knowing this, Anne almost wished he could stay for a while, impossible as that would be. He tolerated nothing less than perfection. His men and his son seemed to have no faults at all. His own manner and appearance were without blemish. Even his clothing bore not a wrinkle.

Had he not already assumed he could correct Robert's words so that they did not offend his ears? How would he react should he realize he could never mend this? He could hire all the tutors in the known world and Rob would still be deaf. There would be worse complications than simply dealing with her son's speech impediment should Edouard discover that.

Anne could only imagine the disgust her husband would feel at Rob's imperfection. And then the real truth would dawn. Then he would consider the very source of her son's flaw. Herself.

No doubt, he would turn them both out and take Rob's birthright as compensation. And the king, Robert Bruce, would uphold the claim, no matter that her son was his namesake.

She admitted the risk was great in taking this man in marriage. But the surety of losing Rob to her uncle if she had refused made taking that risk necessary. Chances were fair, however, that she could keep the secret from Edouard if he left Baincroft tomorrow morning and stayed away as he obviously planned to do. This could work. It had to work.

Edouard danced attendance on his bride. Rather than finding that tedious as he had with women in the past, he discovered joy in it now. Her open admiration of him fed his vanity, of course, but more than that, he enjoyed her shy laughter and ready wit.

He saw beneath her beauty a strength of spirit and a rare intelligence. There, also, lay that passionate nature he felt certain no man had tapped as yet. Though he might not be the first to touch her body, he hoped with all his might that he would be first to touch her heart.

The day wore on endlessly. To satisfy tradition, Edouard endured the morning hunt with Hume, Gui, and the two boys. He took down a large roe to prove his skills at providing sustenance for his bride's table, and then persuaded Hume to call a halt. They returned to the keep where they bathed and donned their finery again for the afternoon's entertainment.

At long last, the numerous courses of the evening meal had been cleared away. The musicians and acrobats Hume had hired looked to be tiring of their exhaustive tasks. As was he.

Edouard had waited as long as he intended to wait. He stood and offered his hand to Anne, who looked every bit as restless as he to get on with matters. That prompted a huge smile, which he shared with those assembled. "Time to retire," he announced.

With whoops of glee, several of the maids at the lower table rushed forward, led by the older one who had attended Anne at the ceremony. They surrounded her and hurried her off and up the stairs.

As soon as the women disappeared, Hume rose and offered a long and wordy toast. Sir Gui's followed, somewhat restrained. And then Henri's. Edouard acknowledged each in turn.

Then Robert held up his cup of watered wine and beamed. "Appy night!" he sang out. Everyone roared.

Edouard stared at the boy, wondering how much a ten-year-old would know of what was about to take place. Not a thing, he decided, judging by the beatific smile on the boy's face. He returned the expression with gentleness, knowing Robert to be wholly sincere in his good wish.

It did not surprise Edouard when the men did not hurry forward to carry the bridegroom up the stairs. In the first place, he was too large for them to comfortably lift, even had they not been flown with wine. In the second, his own demeanor prevented it, he was certain. No one dared touch the comte de Trouville without his leave to do so. His carefully constructed reputation enhanced by constant aloofness stood him in good stead this night. He surely had no wish to be hauled up to the marriage bed, stipped naked and dumped on the mattress next to Anne.

An inglorious beginning *that* would be to his planned seduction, he thought wryly. It certainly had proved so on his first wedding night. The sight of him naked had so shocked the innocent Isabeau, he had been three weeks convincing her that all men were made so, and that he was not somehow deformed! He had managed to avoid that fright for Helvise, but that woman had never welcomed his attentions no matter how gently offered. He had simply been the wrong man.

Not so, this time, however. Anne would welcome him to her bed and to her body. He had seen the desire sparkling in those eyes of hers, turning them almost silver. That knowledge excited him. Warmed his heart. Heated his blood. She was waiting.

With a deep sigh of anticipation, he strode to the stairs and took them two at a time, outdistancing his merry followers.

"Out with you!" he ordered the women as he entered the master chamber. He softened the command with a wink at the older of the maids. "And clear the stairs on your way down."

He herded them out and shut the door, quickly dropping the bar in place.

Purposely, he had waited to look upon Anne until they were alone. He turned slowly and regarded his bride. If he had thought her a feast for the eyes on her wedding day, he now saw the confection to complete the meal.

She leaned back on the huge pillows propped against the headboard. The ivory sheets barely concealed her breasts and clearly revealed the shape of her slender form. In one hand Anne held a silver chalice which she offered him. "Wine, my lord?"

"I fear my hunger outweighs my thirst," he admitted suggestively. "By far."

"Then we must see your needs are fed," she whispered in kind as she set the wine aside.

The languorous look Anne sent him drew him to her like a silken lead. One moment he had stood against the door and next he found himself beside her, leaning over her, his mouth devouring the sweetness she so eagerly offered.

He employed all his powers of restraint to end the kiss and draw away from her to undress. Edouard found the delay almost welcome, for he did not wish to spend himself too soon. Certainly not while still fully clothed and before he had even touched her intimately.

He took a deep breath to fortify himself, determined to stretch out their pleasure once they commenced in earnest. Edouard quickly shed his jupon and the chainse beneath it. Though he did not dare to look up, lest he abandon his task, he felt her eyes on his bare chest. Her hum of appreciation almost undid him.

She laughed a little when his fingers failed in their first attempt to untie the hose points attached to his waistband. Not mocking laughter, but an empathetic sort that told him she would love to aid his cause. He stepped closer and she did.

He watched, growing harder and heavier by the instant, as her small hands worked the ties loose and pulled them free. The soft linen of his loincloth did nothing to hide his size, and he feared she might feel threatened.

"Ahh," she commented softly, but she might as well have shouted, "Hurry!"

Edouard chose to do just that, abandoning all his good intentions. With one motion, he yanked loose the belt of his last garment and slid into bed beside her.

Ready arms surrounded his neck as he drew her flush against him. The feeling equaled nothing he had felt before in his life. It was near to reaching the warmth of home after months in the frozen north. Only greater than that, indescribably better. Nothing had prepared him for this. He had not known such fulfillment existed.

"Love me," he whispered desperately into her ear.

"Yes," she answered, but more than with words. She opened herself to him as naturally as though they had always lain together. Such trust. Such faith.

Edouard sank into her warmth with a deep groan of ecstasy. The sensation filled his very soul. Her wordless plea allowed no regrouping of his senses, no delay to regain control. He simply gave what she wished, and gave more, thrusting into her depths until she screamed softly with surprise.

Her body quaked beneath him, rippling with intense waves of pleasure that encompassed his whole being. He stilled for an instant to absorb the almost painful sublimity and then, unable to contain himself longer, filled her with his own release.

Totally spent, his mind submersed in a cloud of drugged contentment, Edouard held her. Dimly, he felt her small struggle to breathe more deeply and rolled to one side.

When he left her body, he heard her small, wordless

sound of regret. His heart leapt inside his chest and he brushed a hot kiss across her shoulder. "In a while, love."

She cradled his face and settled her mouth over his. Soft at first, her kiss grew more demanding as tongues played and teeth nipped and hands grew bold. "Now," she ordered as her slender fingers trailed down his chest, seeking.

His body jerked to life as she found her answer. And this time, he surrendered all hope of control at the very outset. Since he had neglected prayer that morning in favor of trying to imagine this very occurrence, Edouard now formed a fervent prayer in his mind. *Please let this last forever.*

Anne awoke first. She stretched her arms above her head and yawned. Edouard slept on and she turned to watch as the shadows of his features gave way to details. Relaxed in sleep, his face wore the open innocence always present in his son's visage. Though she knew him to be a bit past thirty years, he wore few worry lines. 'Twas that world-weariness in his eyes that made him seem older while awake.

She wished she could keep him. La, the night had passed all too quickly. Mayhaps she should not have thrown herself into this consummation business with such great relish. Now that she knew what a marriage could be, she would spend many sleepless hours regretting that theirs could not continue in the normal way. She would miss him. For nights such as the one they had just passed, of a certainty, but also for his gallant company.

Her protracted sigh woke him and she watched him smile. "Good morn, my love," he whispered, his voice gravelly with sleep. He reached over to brush away a strand of her hair that covered one eye. "My treasure."

Anne took his hand in hers. "'Tis time we arose," she said with regret. "You must break fast before you leave for the coast. Your mounts must be packed, and Henri will want to—''

"Stay where you are!'' he commanded as he got up and crossed the room to his clothes chest.

As he did so, Anne allowed herself to study the body that had so pleasured her own. A shiver of longing stirred her so soundly, she crossed her arms and clutched her shoulders.

He removed a small jewel casket from his belongings and opened it, drawing out a small linen-wrapped parcel tied up with a scarlet riband.

When he returned to the bed, he took her hand and placed in it the thing he had retrieved. "Your morning gift,'' he explained.

"But this is not necessary,'' she said. "I have nothing for you! There was no time after you—''

"You are the bride, love. You have given your gift,'' he said as he plucked at the riband. He raised one fine brow. "Well, do unwrap it. I unwrapped yours.''

She did so and exclaimed with awe as she revealed a necklet of gold set with emeralds that matched her wedding ring. "Oh, Edouard! I have never seen anything so beautiful!''

He took it from her trembling hands and fastened it round her neck. "Nor have I,'' he said softly. "All bare and inviting, tousled from your sleep and draped in jewels. What a vision you are. When I return, I would see you just so.''

Anne laughed nervously, embarrassed by his extravagant praise. "And how should I arrange that when neither of us know when I may see you next?''

He planted a kiss on her lips and smiled that wickedly intimate smile of his. "Thursday next. Less than a sennight. Expect me just as darkness falls. And I want you here, exactly as you are now.''

Anne gasped. "But—but you are to sail! You told me you must meet your ship! Your home is in France!"

All the time she spoke, Edouard kept shaking his head slowly side to side. "My home is here, my love. Here with you and our sons. I meet the ship to collect all that my factor has sent from my estates. How could you believe that I would wed and then leave you?"

Anne gave no answer, for she felt speechless. Speechless and terrified.

Even the concern evident in his words did nothing to reassure her. "It is small wonder you are surprised," he said, "but I never realized you had so misunderstood me. Are you not happy that I am returning soon, my sweet?"

Returning? Oh, God. Oh, God. What now?

Anne forced her lips to curve upward and nodded. Edouard wanted to know if she felt happy? What she felt was totally undone! What was she to do? How was he to live here day after day without knowing all there was to know? She gripped her hands together until her knuckles turned white.

"What's this? Tears?" he chided gently. "I sincerely hope you weep for joy!" Though he tried to make it sound a jest, Anne heard the undertone of suspicion beneath his words. Or was it hurt?

She must not give the game away just yet. He would be gone in a few hours or less. Once he left, she would have several days in which to form another plan before he returned. For now, she must reassure him somehow. That small decision made, she reached up for him.

Once in his arms, Anne felt some of her calm returning. How could Edouard be the ogre she imagined? She certainly had never met anyone quite like him before. Was it possible that she was wrong about how he would react to Robert's deafness? If only she could determine that without actually telling him about Robert.

"Edouard?"

"Yes, love?" He ran his large hand up and down her bare back, tracing her spine with one finger.

"Could we simply lie here and speak of small matters for a time? I cannot bear to think of your leaving just yet. Might we pretend you do not have to go anywhere, that we have the day to idle away? Just for a little while?"

"And love again?" he asked with a soft laugh and a kiss in the curve of her neck.

Tempted, Anne put a little distance between them. "Mayhaps, but first, I would like ask your opinion on certain issues. That will help me to know you better than I do. Now we are man and wife, I do hope we are to share even more than this," she said honestly. "Though *this* is quite heavenly."

She brushed her hand over his forehead and smoothed his brow, an innocent gesture such as she might have offered her son. "What say you?"

He sighed and moved farther onto the bed so that he lay comfortably beside her. "What issues are these? Are you troubled about something?"

"Oh, nay." Anne grasped for a subject that would not give away her purpose. Something general and unrelated to begin with.

"I merely want to understand how you view…things. How you are used to living. What you think. You are, after all, more worldly than anyone else I know, and yet new to our ways here. For instance, what do you think of our king, The Bruce?"

Edouard worried the dark morning stubble on his chin with the tips of his fingers. "A man born to politics, I believe. A natural leader. I admire his ability to organize an army out of undisciplined and untrained men, I can tell you. Though I have heard his father leaned more toward craftiness than honor, I do think he bequeathed your king a healthy measure of ambition.''

She nodded emphatically, now seeing exactly how she might twist the conversation to suit her needs. ''Aye, and a rich inheritance that was to add to his wealth. Speaking of that, what say you to laws of primogeniture? It is the law in France, is it not?''

''Yes, of course. And as one who benefits from that institution, I must say that I do favor it,'' he admitted, grinning. ''Such weighty issues! Are we agreed on this one?''

Anne could see that he was humoring her, being not a little condescending while he was about it. Dared she risk asking what she really must know? ''Elder sons should always inherit, no matter the circumstance, then?''

He drew his brows together in thought before answering. ''Well, I suppose there might be occasions where that would be impossible, but in general, yes.''

She pursed her lips and looked away from him so that he would not see the importance of his next answer. ''Madness of the elder, for instance?''

''*Certainement*. A madman could hardly manage properties or serve the king and his people well.''

She nodded. ''And what of blindness? I know such a one who lives nearby. The heir lost his sight suddenly and the younger brother assumed all that he owned. That one took his lands, his birthright, everything. That seemed wrong to me.''

Edouard pondered that for a moment and then shrugged. ''As I see it, the second son had little choice there. It would be nigh impossible to handle all of the responsibilities without one's sight. Also, such a man could not defend himself. What has happened to that elder son, the one gone blind?''

Anne sighed. ''He lives upon his brother's charity.''

''A shame, but life is seldom fair, Anne. Why all these questions to do with inheritance? Does this trouble you for other reasons? Is this man a friend of yours?'' A small note of jealousy crept into his tone, she noticed.

"Nay, I have never met him or his brother. 'Twas merely idle conversation.'' Anne had her answer. Not one to her liking, but there it was. "Let us speak of something else,'' she suggested.

For some time they discussed the cost of living in Paris as opposed to that in Edinburgh and the inner reaches of Scotland.

Eventually he grew impatient with the inane questions she posed to cover her real purpose, and glanced yet again at the window to note the position of the sun. "The hour grows late, my love. I should prepare to be away, else I must travel past sundown. I promise you we shall have years to compare our ways and beliefs.''

She granted him a tight smile. "Of course. My thanks for your tolerance. I admit that I only wished your company for a bit longer.''

His hand brushed along the curve of her hip. "You had only to ask. I might tarry half an hour yet.''

"And put yourself late in the night arriving? The risk would be too foolish! I have kept you too long as it is.'' She pulled the sheet close around her, intending to get up.

With his hand on her shoulder, he kissed her again, a tender husbandly kiss that tasted of farewell. "I shall remember you thus while I am gone. Will you promise to meet me here in six days, Anne?'' he asked, patting the bed beside them.

"Of course,'' she said. While she dressed herself, Anne found her eyes straying to her husband, noting the grace with which he moved. He donned his travel clothes and packed quickly. Now and again, he would turn to her and acknowledge her perusal with a heated look that said he did not like to go.

Her own feelings warred within her like two well-matched adversaries. The wifely part of her wanted him to stay, to repeat what they had done these past few hours, to learn his likes and dislikes in that respect, give him more children and be a good helpmeet as she had vowed to do. But her motherly instincts and those of self-preservation wished him gone with all speed, never to return.

Chapter Six

An hour later, Edouard marshaled his sleek Arabian, Bayard, toward the steps of the keep and accepted the stirrup cup from Anne's slender hand. He quaffed the wine, handed down the chalice, and then smiled at her upturned face.

Such a lovely bride, even rain-wet as she was. Most women would have said their goodbye in the warmth of the dry hall, but she had come out to the bailey to wish him well on his journey. The concern evidenced by her expression moved him to reassure her. "Do not worry for me, little wife. I shall return before you have missed me."

"I do not doubt that," she murmured as she clutched the silver vessel to her breast.

He beckoned the two boys to come closer. "Henri, Robert, see to your lady mother's well-being. You are excused from training with weapons until I return, but not from lessons of courtesy. Apply yourselves, both of you, and prepare for some strenuous exercise once I am come home."

"Yes, Father," Henri replied. "We shall not disappoint you." He nudged Robert with an elbow.

"Aye, Fathah. Umm...chichapont you," Robert added with a succinct nod.

Edouard tempered his frown. Robert's English was atrocious. The very thought of what he would do to French made Edouard wince. However, the lad seemed willing enough to learn. Henri would provide the main source of that instruction, simply by being with his new brother. Once Robert had constant discourse with other than the Gaelic-speaking locals, he would soon become proficient. Or hopefully, at least understandable.

"See you stay out of trouble. I want no cause to correct you. Robert, keep you off the ramparts. Henri, no dicing."

His son nodded and Robert followed suit.

"*Bien.* I bid you adieu," he said at large to Lord Hume, the boys, and several of the men-at-arms who had come to see him off. Then he directed his full attention to Anne, to receive her blessing. "My lady?"

"Fare thee well, my lord husband. God keep you and see you safely returned."

How formal. How correct. How absolutely beautiful she was, both without and within. What other wife would feel such sincere worry after knowing a husband so brief a time? No feigning there. He could see dire imaginings reflected in those lovely eyes. She feared for his safety on even so short a trip. Shaking his head in wonder at his good fortune, Edouard forced himself to rein Bayard toward Baincroft's gate and take his leave.

Anne stood there watching as the gates closed behind Edouard and his knight. She felt, more than saw, Meg's approach from behind her. Her friend's soft Scots barely broke the silence. "He returns Thursday next. I just heard."

"God's own truth, I know not what I shall do then! If he means to train both lads himself, he is certain to discover Rob's lack of hearing," Anne replied in Gaelic without turning. She drew in a deep breath of foreboding as she watched the lads race toward the stables. They seemed oblivious to the drizzling rain or the mud under their feet.

"What is this, then?" her uncle demanded. "You fear he will find out—"

Anne jerked around, stunned. She had not even noticed her uncle's proximity. "Naught! 'Tis nothing to fret on." Meg flew from the courtyard, leaving Anne alone with him.

His eyes narrowed as he halted toe-to-toe with her, his hands braced on his hips. "Do not lie to me! I have ears, and do not think I have forgotten the language of my youth! You said *lack of hearing!* Your lad is *deaf?*"

She thought of lying, but knew it to be useless. "Aye," she whispered, head bowed, unwilling to see the condemnation in his eyes.

"How can this be? I heard him speak. The deaf are dumb!"

Anne stepped away from him, away from the angry countenance so like her father's. "Not always so, Uncle Dairmid. I have taught him to speak."

He huffed out a curse. "A foul job you've done of it! I thought him merely cursed with a twisted tongue. I saw him dance last eve. He answers when you speak! How is this if he cannot hear?"

Her shoulders slumped with defeat. The game was up. Her uncle would broadcast this to the four winds. Everyone who did not already know, would soon enough.

She offered what explanation she could. "Rob feels the music somehow, watches others and mimics their movements in the dance. I get his attention and he watches my lips move. He can see the words as I speak them, and understands most of what I say. Also, we have made a language of gestures between us."

Her uncle spat in the dirt, rubbing his forehead with one hand as he began to pace. "Dire," he muttered. "Dire news indeed. Have you any notion what Trouville will do to me? 'Tis I who insisted on this union of yours! I, who will suffer his wrath when he finds himself shackled to a woman who bears useless animals instead of the fine sons I promised!''

Anger stiffened her back, set her shoulders square, and raised her chin. "He is no *animal!* My lad should make any parent—or any kinsman, for that matter—prouder than most would do! Besides, Trouville already has his heir."

His bitter laughter made her skin pebble. "Aye, he does have one, but what of a second to doubly ensure his line continues, eh? What of that? And what man alive wants to produce an *imbecile* from his loins, even though it clearly be the fault of his wife?''

Anne whirled around, unable to face him any longer lest she strike him. "We shall find out when you tell him, I suppose!"

"Tell him? Are you mad? He will slay you outright! Me, he will want to suffer, no doubt. God only knows!''

Hope blossomed in her breast. He would not tell. "You will help me keep the secret, then?''

Again he laughed without humor. "You may count on that, I assure you." He pounded his fist in the opposite palm. "But what to do with him? I certainly cannot take such a lad on. We must find a place to secret him away. There is an abbey at Kelso, and for enough coin, you could—"

"Nay!" Anne all but screamed. She took several breaths to calm herself as best she could. "You will never send my son from me. Rather, I would tell Trouville all and let him cast us out together."

"You little fool! He will kill you, I say. 'Tis rumored he slew his first wife for producing a sickly bairn that was not like to live. Never mind that it did so. He did not even wait to see whether it would!''

She halted in her pacing and stared at him, dumbfounded.

"Aye," he continued, his voice lowered to a grating whisper, his eyes narrowed to mere slits. He shook two fingers in her face. "And the second wife, she bore no child at all. Took lovers to try to increase her odds, but Trouville found out. She suffered a knife through her heart! See you how he rewards deception in a wife?"

Anne wept silently, wanting desperately to disbelieve her uncle. But she had witnessed a mild form of Trouville's anger. Even then, his threats toward Robert after the incident on the castle wall had made her blood run cold with fright. Never mind his gentle, courtly manners or those winning ways beneath the blankets, the man had never been crossed since the moment he arrived. No one had given him cause for a truly murderous rage. This news well might give him that cause.

But she could never send Robert away. He would never understand why, and would believe himself unloved. Thrown away by the one person he trusted most, his own mother.

"Do not speak on this more, I beg you," she whispered, hoarse with tears. "Not now."

Her uncle blew out a long breath from between clenched teeth and looked skyward at the emptying clouds. He stepped toward her and laid a hand on her trembling shoulder and squeezed. "All right, as you say. Standing out here in the cursed rain and arguing about it will get us nowhere. I need time to consider what must be done. We will talk more later."

Anne left hurriedly, wanting nothing more than to be quit of him. Her self-serving uncle would keep quiet about Robert out of fear for himself. He had promised she might depend on that fact. But she still had to worry about Trouville's own powers of observation when he returned. And, more currently, Henri's.

The mizzling rain lasted for five days and finally gave way to a bright sunny morning. Robert abandoned his bed early, dressed himself and went to the master chamber to see how his mother fared. He and Henri had promised to look after her, but Henri was too ill to do that.

He knew most people could hear footfalls, so he took care not to wake her as he tiptoed into the room. She seemed downcast about something and needed her sleep. She must feel sad because his new father had gone away. After his hunt, he would look in again.

Rob paid little attention to the castle folk who were rising to begin their day when he passed through the hall. His doing so was a common enough occurrence. For four long days, however, he had remained indoors, feeling hot, then sniffling and coughing. Today he felt himself again. Henri had the same malady, but had not recovered so quickly.

The hunting would be good this day with all the hares out to see the sun. His trusty hound, Rufus, would enjoy that, but Rob saw him nowhere about this morn. He adjusted the sling he had stuck through his belt, pretending it was a sword. Soon he hoped to have a sword like Henri's. He had his old father's sword, of course, but it was far too heavy to handle well.

When he figured out how to do it, he would ask this new father to give him one. Why not forget choosing words and simply point to Henri's blade, and then to himself? Unlike his old father, this one seemed to have a brighter wit. He ought to understand that simple request.

But Mama had told him these new people were not to know he was special, with keener eyes than anyone else in the world. They would not like it if they found he could understand and make himself understood without using words. Above all, she feared his new father would not like it.

He must pretend he could hear. Thus far, he had fooled them, and would continue to do so if it kept Henri his friend. Their eyes told him they knew he was different, but he also knew that none had guessed why.

Rob especially liked that his new father treated him better than the other one had. There were no beatings or hiding now. He wondered if his pretending so well could be the reason for that.

Old Nigel and Tiernan ignored him as they struggled to raise the portcullis to allow the day's traffic in and out of Baincroft. Robert leaned against the stone wall, waiting. He could have left by the postern gate, but was in no hurry.

He marked two of the men who had arrived with Mama's uncle. They stood near the smithy's, looking at Rob and talking behind their hands so he couldn't see what they were saying. Rude of them, he thought idly.

Not that he could make out many words these new people spoke anyway. Mama said they came from another place where all the words were strange. She had taught him a few, but since these people formed most of the sounds in their noses, she warned him theirs would not be easy speech to learn. He shrugged and dismissed the thought.

When he turned back, the gates swung open and Rob scampered through, eager to check his snares and ply his sling. Nothing better than roasted hare, he thought with a happy grin.

The sun rose higher, almost directly overhead, by the time he arrived at the location of his third snare. He found it sprung open and empty just like the first two. Rob shook his head, despairing of ever getting the hang of setting them properly.

When he bent to reset the thing, all light suddenly vanished. Madly he clutched at the rough sacking held over his head. Pulling and tugging furiously, Rob sucked in deep breaths and roared again and again, as hard as he could. He kicked desperately at whoever pinned him to the ground until his boots connected.

Just when he thought he might wriggle away, more than two hands grabbed him and Rob felt thongs tighten about his wrists.

They tied his hands securely and set him on his feet, pulling the sack down over his shoulders to further bind him. Rob abandoned his useless struggles and set to thinking. Mama always warned him not to panic if he got frightened. He must keep his wits and think, she said.

She had also taught him that the sounds he made would not go far in the air, and he was almost half the day away in the midst of the forest. He doubted she would hear him in the keep, no matter how he roared.

Why would anyone do this to him? Robbers, who wanted his snares and his sling? Poachers who feared he would tell Mama he saw them hunting hereabouts? Why had they not killed him, then? They covered his face so that he could not see them, so he must know who they were.

They grabbed his arms then, and pulled him along between them as they walked. Rob found he could breathe easily enough through the loosely woven cloth, so he let them do as they would, thinking they would likely tire soon and stop. Then he would get away.

They did cease walking, just as he hoped, but only to heft him to the back of a horse behind one of the men. Rob applied himself even more diligently to the bindings at his wrists.

He did not need to see their faces or to watch their words to know his captors had no intention of taking him home. If he did not get free before they left his forest, he would never find his way back. If they let him live to try.

He sniffed hard, determined not to weep, even when the

rough thongs cut into his wrist and drew blood. If the leather got wet, it might stretch, Rob thought. Again he twisted his hands and felt the raw stinging increase. He would not give up. Mama said one must never give up. She never had, and neither would he!

Edouard rode alone as he approached Baincroft's gates. Gui and the men hired to escort his treasures from France to his new home would be another ten days arriving, traveling slowly as they were with a score of baggage wains. Edouard had left them to it.

This dull gray keep with its unimaginative square construction held no candle to the meanest of his other properties, Edouard thought. But that was so only if one counted the appearance of the place. Already he held Baincroft dear because of what it contained.

For nigh a sennight, dreams of his lady had urged him to hurry his business and return. Visions of her naked in their bed, waiting open-armed and eager for him to arrive, drove him to abandon all caution and rush to her side. Hence, he traveled alone at breakneck pace. Now he was here.

The gates stood open, the portcullis raised. Beyond it he saw a crowd gathered in front of the steps to the keep. Something must be amiss. He nudged Bayard to a trot and rode inside, reining in at the edge of the group. It parted immediately as Anne came tearing through, shoving her way toward him. Edouard quickly dismounted and caught her up as she stumbled into his arms.

"Anne, what has happened?" His first thought ran to Henri, but she gasped Robert's name.

He held her a little away from him and shook her gently. "Calm yourself. Tell me. Is Robert hurt?"

"Gone," she groaned as she shook her head. "He is gone since early yestermorn. I—I sent searchers out when he did not return. Oh, Edouard, where could he be? The men have combed the forest, searched the banks of the burns. He is nowhere to be found!" She wilted against him. "Find my son. Please find him!"

Edouard offered words he thought might soothe her, while his mind examined and discarded possibilities. Robert had either wandered off Baincroft land and gotten lost, or someone had taken him for ransom.

In the first case, they must find him as soon as possible so that he did not suffer the weather or hunger. Edouard did not believe the boy would starve unless he had injured himself past the ability to hunt.

Should he be the prisoner of someone seeking to sell him back, however, Edouard knew it would be fruitless to do anything other than wait until they were contacted.

Even as he thought that, he knew very well that Anne would never countenance waiting. He certainly would not if it were Henri who was gone, and should not with this new son of his.

He cradled Anne with one arm as he pointed to several of her men whom he thought would be reliable. "You, you and you, ride to each of the keeps nearest by and ask everyone if they have seen anything of Lord Robert."

A timid voice intruded. "Pardon, my lord, but they would not know him."

Edouard looked down to see the modest maid called Meg who sometimes attended Anne. "Why not?"

Anne herself answered, firmly brushing away the tears that wet her cheeks. "Because MacBain hid him away whenever anyone visited." She sniffed.

"His father *hid* him? But why would he—"

Hume rushed to interrupt, looking rather wild-eyed, and rattling on about the search that had already taken place. "It is very likely he fell into a burn and washed miles downstream into the loch, my lord. He will never surface should that be so. We do fear this is what happened.''

Anne turned against Edouard's chest, shaking with uncontrolled grief.

"No!" Edouard nearly shouted the word. He held her tightly and reaffirmed his denouncement of Hume's supposition. "No, Anne, that cannot be. Robert is not such a fool that he would fall into rushing waters!" But he recalled that same little fool balanced precariously on the parapet, arms outstretched in simulated flight.

"Anne, be calm!" he whispered. "I shall go on the instant and search for him myself. Be calm. Here now," he said as he peeled her off his surcoat and dried her tears with her sleeve.

"But you do not understand," she sobbed. "Rob cannot—"

Edouard hushed her. "Oh yes, he can. He can look after himself until we find him. Go and see to the evening meal. Have something tasty for our Rob when I bring him home, eh? You know he will be hungry as a hound." Edouard handed her off to the waiting Meg and turned to remount Bayard.

The men he had instructed to travel to the nearby properties stood immobile. He flicked a hand toward the stables. "Go! Saddle your mounts and be on your way. Describe the young lord to those you meet. Tell them I offer a one-hundred pound reward to anyone who will offer up his whereabouts. If you gain any word of him, pursue it with all speed. No one at Baincroft rests until Lord Robert is returned!"

With that, he wheeled Bayard toward the gates and rode toward the nearby woods.

Edouard soon realized that tracking the boy would prove impossible. Hundreds of footprints littered the forest floor where the searchers had passed through. If only he had been here at the outset, he could have avoided that obliteration of clues.

Hours later, when darkness fell, he finally turned back to the keep, weary and frustrated.

If no new word of Robert awaited him there, then he would set out again at dawn to find Anne's son. She had entrusted the boy to him, and Robert had accepted him as father. Edouard knew without doubt that his wife would never forgive him, did he not succeed in this. Nor would he forgive himself. No one under his protection could be allowed simply to disappear.

The evening meal held no appeal for Anne, concocted as it had been for her son's enjoyment. He was not there to eat it.

Edouard tried to distract her, thanking her profusely for her good care of Henri, who still lay abed. Though Robert had recovered quickly from the ague the lads had suffered this past week, Henri remained ill with a sour stomach and slight fever.

She pictured Rob sickening again from exposure to the chill of the night, hungry and alone. Did he lie in a dark and dangerous place, hiding from forest predators, or huddled in some bastard's dungeon awaiting ransom?

The latter seemed unlikely since he never went out finely dressed, and none outside Baincroft knew him by sight. Still, that would be preferable to his facing wolves or wild boar.

Edouard encouraged her to eat, murmured his reassurance, but Anne marked well the new worry lines about his eyes. She saw fierce determination in the set of his broad shoulders and the firm line of his mouth.

Her stomach turned over when he offered her a bite of honeyed pear. With a tortured sigh, she turned her head. "I cannot."

Uncle Dairmid hovered on her other side, badgering her with pleading looks and frequent squeezes to her arm and hand. He entreated her silence, she knew, for she had almost blurted out the truth about Rob to Edouard this afternoon.

She still thought it might be necessary to tell her husband everything. Would it affect his search? Of course it would. Did he know the truth, he might consider Rob not worth the trouble. Certainly not worth the huge reward he had offered. 'Twas as great as the ransom for a full-fledged knight.

Uncle Dairmid was right in this. She reached out and laid her hand over his where it rested on the table, signaling silently that she would defer to his wish and remain quiet about Robert's deafness. She decided, at this point, her silence on the matter would be best for all concerned.

Edouard rose the moment he had finished eating, "Come, Anne, I would retire now so that I might go out again at dawn. Also, we must speak of Robert so that I may know his habits and his skills. Have you knowledge of these, or is there someone else I must ask?"

At least she would have some small part in the proceedings. "I can answer." She followed him up the stairs and into the master chamber.

There she allowed him to disrobe her while she stood immobile and uncaring. He tucked her into the bed and covered her to the shoulders with furs.

Anne almost wept, remembering the last time they were here together and her promise to meet him clad only in the jewels he had given her. How she had dreaded his return then, but now she thanked God he had come back. If anyone could discover what had happened to Robert, Edouard would. Whatever came later, they would endure. But for now, all she wanted was her son safely by her side again.

For a time, Edouard questioned her gently about whether

Rob could make a fire, if he knew edible things within the forest other than the game he hunted, what weapons he owned, and if they were missing as well. In this way, he did reassure her somewhat, for she soon realized from her own answers that Rob was not as helpless as she had feared.

"I thank you, Edouard," she whispered when he grew quiet. "Whatever happens, I do thank you for your concern and for your determination to restore Robert to me."

"How could I do less?" he asked, as he lay propped on one arm looking down at her. "Have you not tended Henri like a devoted mother? He was nigh well of his ague when I looked in on him before we supped. Though he is as worried as we are about his brother."

Tears overcame her again. "Oh, Edouard, I cannot bear this."

"You can and you will," he murmured as he drew her into his arms and held her.

How long had it been since she had leaned on anyone? Ages, she supposed. But now, she let it happen, fully expecting to pay the price for it. He would want her body as reward for his kindness, and she would comply.

Only, after quite some time, Anne realized he asked nothing of her, made no move to entice her into pleasing him. He simply kept her enfolded in his warmth, her ear against the beating of his heart. The steady, reliable rhythm of it lulled her and eventually she slept.

When she awoke, Edouard stood by the fire pulling a padded gambeson on over his lambskin shirt. The fitted wool hose displayed legs heavily muscled from constant exercise. He looked a man quite capable of any feat, however challenging. Simply looking at him bolstered her hopes.

How she wished she could confide in him, that he would offer understanding and assurance that Rob would retain his birthright. But she feared Edouard's demand for perfection in all things.

Even as she considered this, she saw him carefully lift his hauberk and examine it for damage. Not a thing out of place in his attire, she noted when he had finished dressing. No flaws whatsoever in his garb or in the man himself. How could she expect him to tolerate a major shortcoming in a lad he would call son?

At the moment, however, this worry had plummeted in its importance. She had to get Rob back.

He glanced her way, saw her awake, and smiled. "I am off now, love. Keep busy this day. Try not to dwell on what might be."

"Bring him to me, Edouard," she whispered, tears spilling before she could contain them.

"As soon as may be," he agreed. Then he crossed the room and pressed a kiss of promise on her lips. "I do vow I shall do all within my power to find him. No rest until I place him in your arms."

Anne believed with all her heart that he would do all he could. She only hoped that it would be enough. With a nod and a forced smile of encouragement, she bade him godspeed.

Chapter Seven

Anne remained in her chamber well into the day, lost in dark thoughts and fervent supplication. She promised God all manner of things if only He would watch over her Robert.

Several times, someone scratched upon her door. "Word of my son?" she called out, and a voice would answer nay. "Then leave me be," she demanded and returned to her prayers.

Finally weary of confinement and anxious to do something—anything—physical, Anne rose from the cold floor and rubbed her aching knees. She brushed her hair and had just begun to braid it when a sharp knock interrupted.

"Niece? Let me in! I must speak with you ere Trouville returns this eve."

She threw open the door and found her uncle shifting impatiently from one foot to the other. "What is it? Has he been found?"

"Nay," he admitted, and pushed past her. He set up a pace before the fire, looking at her and accusing, "You almost told him!"

"But I did not. And I shall not. Must we speak of this now?" She sat down on the chair near the hearth and continued plaiting her hair. "All that matters now is finding Robert."

He shot her a quelling look. "It is God's will the boy is gone, you know. Best thing for everyone. You, me and Trouville, of course."

"Best for *all?* God's *will?*" Anne demanded, aghast, as her hands stilled at their task. A niggling suspicion formed and grew. She regarded her uncle carefully, searching for anything that might proclaim his guilt. He avoided her eyes and his pacing became hurried, almost erratic.

"Uncle Dairmid? What do you know of my son's disappearance?" she demanded.

"I?" he croaked, pivoting toward her, appearing dumbstruck. "You believe that I—?" He poked his massive chest with one thumb. "His own great-uncle?"

Anne leapt up and rushed at him, slapping frantically, screaming, "Beast! What have you done with him? Where is my son?"

He grabbed her by the shoulders and shook her so hard her neck nearly snapped. "Calm yourself, woman! Hush, afore you bring everyone in the keep!"

She gulped to contain her sobbing fury, knowing of a sudden this would get her no answers. With a determined effort, Anne drew in one deep breath after another until she had herself controlled. He let her go and she stepped back.

Then she locked on his stern countenance and assumed that same look herself. "You will tell me, Uncle. Tell me where my son can be found, or I promise you Trouville will have the whole of it. Ere he has chance to unarm himself when he rides in, I shall confess all. How you forced this marriage of mine, how you meant to use his influence with the French king, and how you are trying to cover your mistake at my lad's expense."

He glared. "You'll never dare that. Trouville would cast you aside. If not worse!"

Anne meant every word. "As he will do anyway when I am mad with grief! Tell, or be damned, and 'twill not be the devil who damns you! Did you send Robert to Kelso? To the monks?"

His faltering gaze answered the question. Anne groaned and threw up her hands. "Get out of this chamber! I must dress and be off."

"Wh-where do you think you are going?" he asked, his fear now apparent.

"To Kelso, where else? To find my child."

He reached out one beefy hand in supplication. "But you cannot! Pray, wait, and I shall go myself, in secret. I promise to bring him back. And unharmed, Niece, I swear it. My men had orders not to frighten or misuse him. When I return him, we shall forget this ever happened."

Anne rushed to the door and flung it open. "Get out of my sight!"

Her uncle nodded, all false contrition now. "You'll not tell him, then? I could say you went out to search for Robert yourself, and—"

"Tell Trouville whatever you will. I mean to go and find my son. Now, get out!" Anne repeated.

"Aye, I'll go," he agreed, stepping out to the landing, still speaking furtively. "Only mind you follow my lead when you come home. Your lad was merely lost, eh? Trouville need never know—"

She slammed the door in his face. After a moment, his bootfalls clattered out of earshot. She wished she'd had strength to kick him down the stairs, the cursed wretch.

Anne yanked off the bedgown and drew on a fresh chemise and overgown. Donning her most practical surcoat, a plain woolen mantle, and sturdy boots, she prepared to travel the twenty leagues necessary to set her heart at ease.

Her poor Rob had best be in his finest state of health when she reached him, or Uncle Dairmid would pay for this foul trick of his. He would most surely pay. Even if it meant their giving up Baincroft, her own dower lands, and any prayer of a future with Edouard of Trouville.

Edouard urged Bayard to a full gallop as he approached the open gates. He had found Anne's son. Or rather, Robert had found him. The boy had stepped from behind a large oak, held up his arm and cried, "Fathah!" He seemed hale as ever, though certainly weary from his adventure in the woods. Edouard meant to speak to Robert of that folly, but later, after the joyous reunion at Baincroft. A great smile creased his face and his shout rang out to all and sundry. "Ho, there! Fetch my lady!" He spotted her then across the bailey. "Anne!"

He quieted his prancing mount as he watched her run full tilt from her path to the stables. Robert wriggled against him and threw one leg over the pommel, attempting to slide off his high perch.

Edouard held him fast until Anne arrived, sobbing and laughing, speaking incoherently as she reached up. Only then did he allow the boy to slide from his grasp into her waiting arms.

The backs of his eyes burned as he looked down on the two embracing. Anne's uncommon love for her son amazed him. Would that his own mother had held him in such high regard. Would that *all* mothers felt so, but Edouard knew Anne to be unique. True that she coddled her son, and disregarded the more important elements of his training, but love him she did.

It warmed Edouard to see it, though it made him feel his own loss more than he ever had. He prayed she had a spare corner in that heart of hers for Henri. Mayhaps even a small space left for her husband, as well. The thought made Edouard smile.

When she looked up at him, Edouard felt her gratitude

wash over him like a sweet, warm tide. "You kept your promise," she whispered. The words formed on her lips like a benediction. Though he could not hear her voice, what with the joyful noise of the crowd surrounding them, her message came clearly to him.

"Yes," he answered without sound. "I always will." Her trembling smile told him that she heard in her heart, as he had meant her to do.

When the cacophony subsided a bit, Edouard dismounted, handed his mount's reins to one of the stable lads, and followed Anne and Robert inside the keep.

Instead of stopping in the hall, they made straight for the solar. Edouard closed the door behind him so that the three of them were alone. He spoke directly to Anne. "I found him in the woods. Worn down as he was, I asked no questions save whether he was injured. He says not."

He then addressed Robert. "Tell us what happened, son," he said softly. "You wandered too far and were lost?"

Robert nodded, his eyes drooping with weariness.

Anne pressed the boy's fair head to her breast and kissed the top of it. "We should wait until the morrow, husband. He must eat something and sleep first."

Edouard agreed, rather eager for some food and rest himself. *Rest beside his Anne who would most likely wish to show her thanks.*

"Very well. However, we should ensure that nothing like this happens in future. You, my boy, may look forward to company when next you hunt. And every time thereafter. Understood?"

When he had no answer, Edouard thought the boy might have fallen asleep whilst standing and leaning against his mother. "Shall I carry him up to his bed?" he asked Anne.

"Nay," she said softly. "Leave him to me, my lord. Why not go to our chamber and unarm? I will have someone bring you food and wine. When I have Rob settled and made certain Henri is still improving, I shall join you.''

Edouard would have cheerfully walked through hell to do her bidding in any matter, such was the glowing promise in her eyes.

Anne's overwhelming relief at having Robert safely home eclipsed any other emotion for a while. Only after she had seen him fed and tucked him in for the night, did she begin again to consider their future and what it might hold.

Henri slept peacefully when she looked in on him. His fever and persistent coughing seemed to have abated. Meg assured her that he had eaten well and had begun to complain of staying abed. Soon the lads would resume their budding friendship.

She had warned Rob not to reveal what had happened to him, especially to Henri. If Edouard ever discovered that her uncle had ordered her son's abduction, he would not rest until he found the reason for it.

Uncle Dairmid knew her husband far better than she did, having observed his activities for years. Anne did not doubt her uncle's word when he said that Edouard's wrath would encompass them all. He would feel duped, cheated of his chance to produce more children, and possibly angry enough to do murder. He could challenge her uncle and slay him without any trouble, given Edouard's reputed expertise with weapons. As for her, no one would offer her any defense, for a man might dispose of a wife as he saw fit. If Uncle Dairmid spoke truly, Edouard had done so before. Anne shuddered. He would not kill her son, of course. The law would frown on that, should it be reported. He could easily oust Robert, however. What had happened to MacGuinn's heir could well happen to MacBain's.

Rob could never defend his right to Baincroft if Edouard

removed her first. There would be no one of sufficient rank who would stand for him. She could not bear the thought of Robert living the life of a beggar, alone and friendless, bereft of family.

Anne leaned against the wall outside the small chamber she had assigned to Henri. Her gaze traveled down the short corridor to the door of the master chamber. Could she enter that room, smiling and ready to offer gratitude for all her husband had done today? Could she do that, knowing he might be the instrument of her destruction and the one to condemn her only child to a life of poverty?

She did not want to believe Edouard a vengeful man. How could one so skilled at loving, so caring and solicitous in all other ways, turn vicious enough to slay two women because they displeased him? It hardly seemed possible. But she did know that he had enjoyed his way in all things since his birth, born to wealth, power and privilege, and related to the royal family. Edouard might very well eliminate anyone who thwarted his wishes. He certainly could do so without recriminations of any kind.

She clasped both hands to her heart. It beat so rapidly, she feared she would collapse right there and need to be carried where she feared to go.

Stop this! Anne ordered herself to halt these dire imaginings before she did something foolish. In this state of mind, she might well blurt out everything, fall to her knees and beg for his mercy the instant she entered the room.

Heavy footsteps on the stair distracted her and she straightened, prepared to face whoever it was.

"Uncle? What do you here? I was about to retire," she said.

He approached and leaned toward her, his voice but a low whisper. "I meant to reach you before you did so. I watched for you to leave the lad's room so that I might.

You will not reveal anything to Trouville this night or any other. Mind what I say!''

Anger swept through her, obliterating her unease. Here was the cause of all this turmoil. Here stood the one responsible. She wished with all her might he had never come here, that she had never looked on his face. Getting rid of him would alleviate at least a part of her problem, and she knew exactly how to do so.

"I want you gone from Baincroft! Be out of here at first light. If you do not, I shall admit your part in Robert's disappearance before we break fast!''

She halted his response with her hand raised in a fist. "Trouville might cast Rob out. He might kill me as you said he did his other wives. But you, my lord, will suffer worse! You have said so yourself."

He lowered his gaze to the floor, as though repentant. She knew better. But when he spoke, he did sound more sincere than she expected. "Anne, I know I am partly to blame for all that has happened. Had I kept in touch with you all these years, had I known about your son, you must believe I would never have brought all this about. Pray, listen to me now."

He dared to take her fisted hand and hold it between both of his. "Let me take the lad with me. Nay, hear me out!'' he insisted quietly. He increased his grip on her fist as though to prevent her running away. "If you will allow, I shall take him to Byelough Keep when I go there to visit my daughter. Her husband is a good man, though he be a highlander. He loves children, even the wee lassie Honor bore her first husband. Allow him to foster your son, I beg you.''

"Never! I do not know this man, and I scarcely remember my cousin. This is my only child, Uncle, the only one I shall ever have. Were he a bit older, and if I thought you had Rob's well-being at heart, I might consider it. But you worry only of your own fate, not Robert's or mine. You are a selfish old man and I want you away from Baincroft. I mean what I say. Go tomorrow, or suffer the consequences.''

He released her hand and sighed. ''As you say.''

She turned away from him, arms crossed over her chest, and waited for him to leave.

''God be with you, Niece,'' he said sadly. ''Please believe that I did mean well.''

Anne leaned her forehead against the stone wall and listened to his retreat. When all grew quiet again, she braced herself for the coming night.

Unwilling to give in to despair, she weighed her advantages. Edouard did desire her. And, despite all the reasons she should not, Anne admitted that she desired him as well. They had made a good beginning in that respect. Were it not for this secret she must keep for Robert's sake, her inability to give Edouard more children, and the horrid occurrences of Edouard's past violence, she might have welcomed the match.

Anne decided she must use whatever means she could to delay the inevitable. If nothing else, what passion he felt for her might prove a distraction to him. Who knew what miracle might happen in the interim? The French king would surely recall him to France before long. Uncle Dairmid had said that her husband served in a important advisory position at court. A man so accustomed to wielding power ought to tire very quickly of life in a secluded keep in a strange country.

If only she could keep Edouard's mind and body occupied with other interests, he might scarcely notice her son's presence at all. She could not afford to consider the situation hopeless just yet. A woman must use all the weapons afforded her, especially if she lacked any other alternative.

The main thing that troubled Anne about this was the

fact that she did not mind using her *weapons* at all. Every time he looked at her, or she looked at him, her heartbeat thundered and she would recall their one night together. His hands on her body, his lips, the spicy scent of his skin, the feel of him inside her. She wanted him again. Her desire grew so great at times, she had to forcibly remind herself why he must be made to leave here.

Should she not feel repelled by such a man as would slay two women when he could simply have set them aside, immured them in a religious house to live out their days? But he did not repel her. Not in any way.

Anne realized now that she seriously doubted Edouard's guilt in this. Despite her uncle's insistence that her husband had committed these dark deeds, she could not, in her heart of hearts, believe it true.

But there existed the possibility that she was wrong. His winning ways and her passion for Edouard might very well have distorted her perception of him. For safety's sake, she must act on the assumption that, given reason, he would be capable of the ultimate violence.

In any event, she fully intended to try to keep him so enthralled he would have little time for anything else until his king sent for him. To that end, she smoothed the wrinkles from her gown, moistened her lips with her tongue, and marched toward the master chamber.

Edouard leaned forward in his high-backed chair and stoked the fire again, a useless act to pass the time. His inner fire increased without any stoking. What the devil kept her? It seemed he had been waiting for hours.

All those fantasies he had entertained all the way to the coast and back again had come to nothing after all. Anne had not awaited him naked, jewel-bedecked and eager for his touch. Instead, he'd found the whole of the household in turmoil, the lady in tears, one son ill of a fever, and the other missing.

Everything considered, however, he thought the incident of Robert's disappearance had wrought a better understanding between Anne and himself. He now knew the depth of her ability to love and that pleased him more than any physical act could have done. And she had learned that he would always keep his word to her, no matter the cost.

Tonight would provide all he had missed on arrival. If she would only get herself to their chamber.

He turned at the sound of the door opening. When he saw her, Edouard immediately revised his plans for seduction. She smiled sweetly enough, but the expression appeared forced. Her eyes held nothing save signs of exhaustion. The small shoulders beneath her robes looked a shade too square for natural carriage.

He did not rise to meet her, but remained where he was. "Come," he invited, stretching out one hand to her. She came without hesitation and laid her palm against his. "You are tired to death from these two days, are you not?"

She began to deny it, but he paid no mind to that. Instead, he drew her down onto his lap and encouraged her to lie against him, her head on his shoulder. Her long sigh told him the truth.

He caressed the length of her back until his hand reached her neck. Sliding his fingers beneath her heavy braid, he kneaded the small muscles there until he felt her relax against him. "Rest, my love. A poor husband would I be to expect more from you this night. Just be still."

With practiced hands, he unlaced her overgown. He reached down and tugged off her sturdy leather boots and tossed them aside. She hardly moved when he raked her skirts above her knees and unrolled her woolen hose. "My God, what has happened to your knees? Did you take a fall?"

Slowly, reluctantly, she sat up and glanced down at her bare legs. "Oh. Prayer," she explained. "'Tis nothing."

Edouard shifted her a little so he could get up. Then he lifted her in his arms, carried her to the bed and set her upon it. "What you need is a good night's sleep."

He undressed her as rapidly and impersonally as he could manage, ignoring her protests that she could do it herself. He yanked back the covers and ordered her underneath.

She clutched his hand. "But before you left, I promised—"

"To obey me," he said firmly. "And you shall do so. Now close those eyes and I'll hear no more." He tugged the coverlet up under her chin and kissed her lightly on the forehead.

"Edouard?" she murmured. "Will you come to bed?"

"In a while," he promised, touched by her need of his presence. "I shall join you soon."

Though he had need of her tonight—a different sort of need than hers for him—Edouard wished her comfort above his own. To his mind, this spoke of his growing love for her and he welcomed that.

Anne would have succumbed as gracefully to his advances as she had done on their wedding night had he demanded it of her. There would have been no whining, no impatient sighs, no denial in thought or speech, had he done so. He knew this much about the woman he had wed. This indicated that she might feel more than simple acceptance of him as a mate.

His body might go wanting this night, but Edouard's heart felt full of satisfaction. He and Anne were well on their way to making this arranged marriage of theirs into the loving union he intended for them.

Contentment settled over him as he returned to his chair beside the fire and stared into the gentle flames. In them he pictured a happy future that stretched over many years, years in which they would laugh and love together. They would watch their sons grow into fine young men who would take their own places among the nobility of France and Scotland. Their daughters, once they arrived, would grow in gentleness and grace, small versions of their lovely mother.

After Anne slept and Edouard had joined her in bed, he continued to build hopes. He could envision it all, a future woven with the caring he had never experienced as a child. None of the cold, calculating self-indulgence of his parents. None of the infidelity and deceit of his former wives. This new life would be perfect in every way.

Later in the night, Edouard wakened, stirred by a dream more vivid than any he had endured the past few nights. Anne's hands roamed his body, stroking, soothing, then arousing him to fever pitch. Even now, as sleep released him, he imagined the heat of her palm caressing him. His own hand brushed down his body and came to rest over hers. No dream, then, he thought as he groaned with anticipation.

He squeezed her fingers over himself, reveled in the sharp jolt of pleasure, then abandoned her hand to return the favor. He wished for light. The fire had burned out now, and no moon shone through the window. The stygian darkness of the room lent an unreality to this loving, and he needed all his senses to believe it real. How he longed to see her hunger, even as he felt it.

Her breathing quickened as his hand found the fullness of her breast, the tightness of her nipple. He leaned to draw it between his lips to taste her. Her grip on him tightened almost painfully.

Dwelling on her obvious inexperience might have provided the distraction needed to prolong this joining, but Edouard merely delighted in all that it implied.

In the recesses of his mind where reason had retreated, he understood that she had not suffered her first husband's amorous attentions in any great measure. The old man had taught her nothing of pleasuring and had likely not offered much of it himself, given her innocent clumsiness. An ineptitude that was driving him toward completion faster than any well-practiced maneuvers had ever done.

His blood raced in his veins. A heady dizziness enveloped him as he reached for her leg and drew it over his body so that she lay atop him. "Take me inside you," he gasped. "Now, love. Now!"

He felt her guide him, a frantic grasping, a greediness that he encouraged heartily by arching up and into her until she was fully seated. He relished the scent of her, the softness of her skin, her small cries of surprise as he moved beneath her.

His hands closed over her hips and guided, first gently, then forcefully as the rush of ecstasy overtook him. Inner muscles tightened rhythmically around him, drawing him deeper into a vortex of mindless reaching. His harsh groan rent the night as he poured himself into her, thrust after thrust, until he could no more.

He released her hips and slid his arms around her, pulling her flush against his body, replete and full of sweet appeasement.

"I love you," he heard himself say. He had not thought to utter the words. They simply issued of their own accord. So he repeated them against the soft pulsing of her neck, just to taste them on his lips more fully. To have her hear them, feel them, know they were true and straight from his mind as well as his soul. "I love you."

She snuggled and sighed. And slept.

Edouard remained still, loving the closeness of their bodies joined and sated. No rolling away, no crawling out of bed to wash or hurry away somewhere. Their holding each other so seemed inexorably right somehow, as though something had ordained it from the beginning of time. He loved her. With his whole heart, he loved. And she must love him as well.

She *must*.

Chapter Eight

Anne pretended to sleep. Only the fact that her entire body felt like melted butter prevented a reaction of shock to Edouard's words.

Twice he had said it. Only once, and she might have attributed it to the moment. Had she not felt the same stirring to speak? To say something to glorify what had just happened between them? But for him to say it twice?

She sighed again and shifted her face a bit, so that her lips brushed the pillow instead of his silken hair. An unthinking kiss to his temple might signify that she had heard, even that she returned his feelings. Assuming that he had voiced true feelings. Surely not. They had known each other so short a time, how could he *possibly* love her? No doubt men said that sort of thing all the time in like circumstance.

Still, the way he held her—in an almost desperate embrace, even after he had satisfied them both—made her think he needed something more. Something he wished her to give that she had not. Should she have returned those same words? Was that what he expected? She could say them. Who would it hurt?

Indeed, she did feel something she could not quite define.

She certainly admired Edouard, and not only for his wondrous body and handsome features. He had shown her nothing but kindness, a willingness to please, and a genuine effort to make theirs a happy union. The ugly tales Uncle Dairmid had repeated about her husband could not be true. Why should she believe the man who had blackmailed her into marriage, threatened her and abducted her son?

At the moment, she felt she could unburden herself to Edouard and he would show her compassion and understanding. Surely this loving man would never harm her or her Robert.

Uncle Dairmid must have lied. But to what purpose would he blacken Edouard's name? Her uncle's fear of Edouard seemed genuine, certainly real enough to send him running.

Dared she wager the whole of her son's estate and her very life by trusting this husband she scarcely knew?

She owed Edouard compliancy, had vowed to give it, and so did not feel any guilt at meeting his husbandly needs. Nor did she have many qualms about using those needs to draw his attention away from Robert in the days to come. But to utter words of love to him, when she knew in her heart what she felt was only keen desire and admiration? Aye, that would trouble her. At least in this, she would give him full honesty.

Hearing that declaration of love from him did give her great hope, however. In that, she would be honest with herself. She wished with all her being that he spoke the truth, that he did well and truly love her. Would that not solve all her problems?

She must wait and see. And in the meantime, they could… Anne shivered with surprise. He grew inside her even as the thought crossed her mind that they might love again. Her hips arched down of their own volition, drawing him deeper. She sighed with pure delight.

"I adore the sounds of your pleasure," he whispered. His tongue traced the shell of her ear and his lips drew the lobe into his mouth. The soft nip he gave her elicited a cry.

He seemed to leap inside her. "Edouard?" A plea for more.

His low, growling chuckle vibrated through her body. "I am glad he taught you nothing."

"Hmm?" Anne murmured, her senses as filled with him as was her body.

"MacBain. Forget he existed. As of this moment, forget," he mumbled through a hot wet kiss. His mouth seemed to devour her, his words delicious food interspersed with the drugging wine of passion. "For you are mine now, my angel," he rasped. His hands encircled her waist controlling, thrusting slowly upward, then withdrawing when she would hold him fast. "Ever…and always…mine."

"Always. In all ways," she promised, returning his kiss and clinging to him with all the power she possessed.

When the rush of ecstasy threatened to consume her, he lifted her away. "Oh, nay!" she cried out in sharp protest.

He soothed her with another kiss, another promise, "This way," he suggested, turning her to her back. She felt him drag a pillow down beside her and lift her hips to tuck it underneath.

Her body pulsed almost painfully, wept for him, as he placed his palms on her inner thighs and opened her fully. "My flower," he crooned. She felt his breath upon her. "Sweet petals," he whispered with a slow circle of his tongue. "A bud to treasure—"

Anne cried out as the storm took her. He moved over her with all haste, filling her with a force unlike any she had ever dreamed. His powerful thrusts increased in depth and speed until she thought she might die of the pleasure. His sudden shout and eruption within her sent her soaring yet again.

Even as he lay motionless, she felt his stirring tremors inside her.

She might have spoken then, had she breath to do so. She might have offered him her soul if he did not already have it. The rest of her being, he had claimed for certain.

With what seemed an exhaustive effort, he pushed himself up on his elbows above her. "Breathe," he gasped, "if you can."

She detected wry humor beneath his order. Obediently, she drew in air and released it.

"The little death," he explained. "Will you live to die again, or have I crushed you beyond hope?"

He shifted again, withdrew from her body and lay beside her. One long-fingered hand swept her form lightly as though to inspect for damage. It came to rest on her left breast. "Ah, a heartbeat! A rather rapid one." He pinched her nipple playfully and leaned down to kiss it. "Welladay, your first lesson. What think you of this tutor? Too French?"

Anne laughed. She had never expected this side to the man. Though he offered the questions in jest, she did not miss the anxious note behind them. He feared he had shocked her. And he had. She thanked all goodness for the concealing darkness.

Not in her wildest imaginings had she thought such things possible. "I think the French may lead us out in more than fashionable garb," she offered. "Our bucolic ways must seem rather backward."

He toyed with a lock of her hair, drawing it over her chin and down her chest. "You may have noticed, I am not dismayed."

"Umm. I did observe that you take your teaching rather seriously. Have you had many students, then?" La, she had not meant to ask that, even lightly phrased! Now he would think her jealous of his former lovers. In all truth, she was.

Why that should be so, she could not imagine. The man had been twice wed, after all, and likely no saint when unattached.

"A few," he admitted. "But none so entrancing as you. Why is it that MacBain left you so innocent? You were wed ten years. I cannot feature any man who would waste all this inborn...adaptability." His finger circled her navel and dipped inside.

Anne shivered, both from his touch and from his question. Edouard approached a dangerous subject. How could she tell him that her husband despised her even as he came to her bed? "You asked me to forget MacBain. He is forgotten," she replied, more curtly than she had intended.

He cupped her face and kissed her lightly on the lips. "Do not think for a moment that I would wish to embarrass you, love. I but asked out of curiosity. There should be no secrets between us. I promise there is nothing you cannot say to me. Let us talk of the past and then we may put it behind us for all time. Tell me of MacBain."

"And will you tell me of your wives?" she asked, stalling him so she did not have to answer. "What makes you think I wish to hear about them?"

He tapped her on the nose. "Because you are curious as any cat. Do not deny it!"

"Then tell me, if you must," she said grudgingly, for he was right. "Go first. And include the lovers as well, if you like." Mayhaps by the time he had finished, he would have forgotten his question to her. Or run out of breath, considering the number of women he must have had. At least, she would have time to conjure some reason why MacBain had avoided her bed.

He drew her closer. For the sharing, she supposed. "My first was a dairymaid," he announced, a smile in his voice. "Comely, plump, and reeking of cheese. No need to enumerate the others until I turned seventeen and married. They made little impression."

"Oh, thank you for sparing me. And the wife?" Anne asked reluctantly. She wasn't certain she wanted to hear this if what Uncle Dairmid said was true. Rumor was that the woman had borne him a weakly son and he had slain her because of it. Surely not.

"Ah, Isabeau. An arranged match. My father brought her to me and we were wed. She did not care for marriage much, but neither of us had a choice in the matter. Shortly after she bore Henri, she died."

"In childbed?" Anne asked carefully.

"Loss of blood," he equivocated. Or it sounded so. Anne certainly heard no sympathy or sorrow in his voice. She dared not ask him to elaborate, for fear what he would say.

He remained quiet for a moment and then resumed his listing. "I had a mistress for two years. A widow."

"Did you care for her?" Anne demanded. She had not meant to.

"Yes, I liked Marie very well. When she decided to wed again, I helped her choose a suitable husband. She has two strong sons now and seemed very content when last we met at court."

"Convenient for you," Anne retorted. "Why did you not wed her yourself?"

"I was betrothed," he said. "To Helvise, my second wife. I do not like to speak of her, but I will this once, so you will know everything. Unbeknownst to me, her father forced her to the marriage. She loved another." He sighed heavily. "And she continued to love him at every opportunity thereafter."

"Wh-what happened?" Anne whispered, dreading the explanation.

"She died for it," he stated in a flat voice.

Anne would not ask if he had killed the woman. She heard the hurt in his voice, the betrayal he had suffered. He might have slain this unfaithful spouse in a fit of rage. To enrage him anew with questions about it did not seem prudent. She still did not quite believe that he had done so, but was afraid to find out for certain. Best to let the matter rest, for there was nothing she could do to right the wrong if there was one.

"I see," she said simply. "Is that all?"

"All who are worth discussing. Now take your turn. I would know everything about you." He searched for one of her hands and played with her fingers as he waited.

"I wed at sixteen. MacBain was a friend of my father's. He perished from a fever six months past. Surely my uncle has told you all of this," she said.

"Was it a good marriage for you? Did you get on well?" he asked gently.

"No, in truth, we did not." Anne stopped with that, hoping it would satisfy him. She should have known better.

"You gave him a fine son. I am surprised he required no more of you."

"MacBain was an old man," she said. "And not much given to bedsport or to children. Must we continue this? It makes me feel disloyal, speaking of him here."

"Hmm. Disloyal to him, or to me?" Edouard asked softly.

"Both of you, I suppose," she snapped. "Leave it be, Edouard. He is dead and gone. I would he were forgotten, as well."

"As you will, then," he said, evenly. "What shall we talk of now? Our sons?"

Anne squeezed her eyes shut and prayed for guidance. *What now?* Whether divinely inspired or otherwise, she turned to Edouard and pressed her lips against his cheek. "Must we talk at all?" she asked, as she slid a hand down his side and raked one nail along his slender hip. "Must we?"

All conversation ceased immediately, as was her intention. But even as she abandoned herself to the all-consuming flames Edouard ignited once again, Anne wondered how she would redirect that curiosity of his in the light of day, outside their bedchamber.

For the next seven days Edouard devoted himself to enhancing Baincroft. Since Sir Gui had not yet arrived with the baggage wains and the others who were coming here from France, there was no one with whom Edouard could hone weapons skills. Henri seemed well enough, though a bit too weak to wield his sword. And Robert seemed too exhausted by his adventure to begin any training.

In lieu of that activity, Edouard rode out to discover how he might improve the holdings hereabout. He met with tenants, examined the fields, deciding which might be planted and which to use for pasturing. With him went Anne's steward and sometimes the lad, Thomas. The outings proved pleasant and rewarding, but he grew more curious each day as to what troubled his wife.

Today, needing solitude to consider the matter more clearly, he rode alone.

Though Anne laughed readily and seemed always ready to accommodate him in every way, something bothered her. He only hoped she would soon trust him enough to reveal whatever problem trammeled her thoughts. He hated that lines of worry etched her lovely brow. Edouard wanted nothing to mar the flawlessness of either his new bride or this new life he had carved for himself.

Their abode would rival any in Scotland soon, if not in size, then surely in rich appointments. Even now, hired workmen carefully patched and limed the outer walls in shining white. He had ordered a new portcullis built, as well as gates of richly carved oak. Soon his goods would arrive from France to grace the inner keep.

Edouard intended to create a setting beautiful enough to grace this jewel of a wife he had chosen. That done, he would begin to build an even finer castle upon her lands adjoining these. Then, when Robert came of age to assume his inheritance, the new and grander property would be prepared for Anne and himself. And their future children, of course. The perfect home for his perfect family.

He wondered why Anne grew agitated whenever he spoke of all this. Edouard often reassured her that he did in no way diminish Robert's profits or beggar himself. His own wealth amassed daily from his investments and income from his estates.

Living so frugally must be a way of life difficult for Anne to abandon. Had she ever known any other way? How had she borne it all these years? Baincroft needed much restoration, simply to make it properly habitable.

In his experience, when something was broken, one immediately fixed it. If beyond repair, then it should be discarded. This idea made Anne wince every time he voiced it. Only that which was without blemish would do to keep. He must teach her that she need not hold to things that had no use or beauty, for they could easily be replaced with those that did have those qualities.

She was, after all, the comtesse de Trouville. Only the best would serve, for he wanted her happy in every way. He loved her.

She had never said the words, but he hoped to hear them any day now. Or any night. That thought brought a smile to his lips. These incomparable nights. At least he could banish her troubles, whatever she imagined them to be, when he plied her with kisses and all that followed. Another child would surely result and Edouard could scarcely wait. A daughter, this time. One just like his Anne.

A sudden and related thought occurred. Might Anne fear barrenness since she had quickened the once with Robert and never again? Could that be what bothered her?

He would tell her tonight the reason for that. MacBain had been too old and probably too infrequent in his attentions to her to get another babe. Not too infrequent to suit Edouard, however. Though he was glad she had borne Robert, who obviously gave her joy, Edouard wanted to be the one to fill Anne's house with children.

And so, he would. With that delightful task in mind, he turned Bayard toward home.

Anne stood on the roof of the keep looking down over the bailey and past its crenellated wall. She watched Edouard ride past the cottages that lined the road leading to the gates.

Each day that passed, her guilt distressed her more. Each night he held her in his arms and made such sweet love to her, Anne felt worse about her mistrust. He had given her no reason at all to conceal such important facts that affected his life as surely as it did hers and Robert's. Her chest ached with the need to unburden herself and stop living this lie.

Edouard had said that he loved her so many times and in so many ways. She knew that he expected her to return his affection and say as much. In truth, she feared she had already grown to love him. What else could she call these feelings that swelled her heart to bursting? Lust? Nay, for her ardor increased once that was satisfied. Admiration? Certainly that, but more. She had come to respect Edouard, and she felt an overwhelming need to please him in all things.

The truth, if she told it, would certainly not please him, but she owed him that as surely as she owed him the compliance and obedience of a good wife.

"A fine figure, that man of yours," Meg commented as she joined her and leaned her hands against the protective wall that surrounded the roof.

"He is that," Anne agreed. "He is nothing like I thought him to be when first he came here. His fierce looks were deceiving."

"Seems of easy temper," Meg mused aloud.

"I hope you are right." Anne pursed her lips in thought as she saw him dismount, pat his mount on the neck and hand off the reins to young Tobe.

"Meg, I am considering telling my lord about Robert. He is sure to notice Rob cannot hear when they begin the training. His anger will be worse if he finds I meant to deceive him. Rob is so eager to begin, I do not think I can stall much longer."

She sighed. "I only hope my husband will receive the news without flying into a rage and doing one of us harm. Remember MacBain's reaction when he first learned of it?"

"Not likely we would forget it!" Meg exclaimed. "The old wretch was fit to kill. We had to hide you both."

Anne needed someone to advise her before she made a final decision. "There have been no incidents of violence since I wed Lord Trouville. In fact, he has been nothing but kind and good. Everyone here seems to accept him as overlord."

Meg nodded sagely. "Aye, his judgement is good. He is a reasonable man, they do say."

"Pray God that is so."

She turned to Meg and laid a hand on her arm. "I have decided. Tomorrow eve, I wish to serve him all his favorite foods. After he is well-fed and we have retired for the evening, I will content him as best I can in every way. Then I will confess it all. Mayhaps he will not banish Rob and me, especially if I appeal to his chivalry and vows to protect those weaker than he. What think you, Meg?"

"I'll wager that he will soon know, whether you tell him or no. 'Twill go down better should you prevent his having to guess, or hear it elsewhere." She bit her lips and then expelled a weary breath. "Will you bring up the issue of more children?"

Anne looked down at her husband, who was addressing several of the village lads. "Nay, I'll not have to. Once he understands that Rob was born the way he is, there will be no question of more babes. He will want none of mine. And even should I assure him I will not bear again, he would still want none of me. I am resigned to it. Our marriage will be over and done. The very best I can hope for is his mercy, a place to live, and his promise not to hold Baincroft from Robert when he comes of age. Mayhaps he will grant me that, if his behavior toward us holds true to form."

Meg pushed away from the wall and headed for the small circular stair that led below. "I shall pray he does."

"And so shall I," Anne answered. "But I do have great hope that I am right in this. Edouard is not a cruel man. I have no right or reason to withhold the truth from him any longer."

Secretly Anne wished that he would vow undying love and promise everything she asked, but she was nothing if not realistic.

She would savor this night and hold it in her memory, for it was like to be the last she spent in Edouard's bed. He might abandon her and return to France. Or else he could set her aside, remain here, and send her to her dower lands to dwell in one of the cottages there. There was no proper keep, only a ruin, so she'd been told.

Rob would go with her, of course, if that happened. Hopefully, Edouard would grant him leave to return to

Baincroft when he had reached the age to inherit. That was Rob's only chance to hold what was his.

Even could she conquer her guilt-ridden conscience, this secret could not be kept much longer. She had no choice but to trust Edouard.

Chapter Nine

The next morning, Anne threw back the covers and hurried to dress herself. Edouard had left her abed and gone about his business quite early. The unforgettable night that had quite exhausted her must not have affected him so.

She smiled when she recalled lying there listening to his almost inaudible whistling while he donned his clothing and armed himself. He had kissed her softly and bade her rest, tucking the coverlet close around her as he did so. Anne had snuggled back into the downy warmth of sleep for a while, inviting dreams of their night's loving.

Should she live to be one hundred, she would always remember the night she had just passed with him. Anne tried to put out of mind her plans for the coming eve, when she would tell him of Robert. That would come soon enough, and likely end any hopes of repeating the pleasures she had come to crave. But even more than their physical joining, she knew she would miss Edouard's teasing laughter, his tenderness and caring, the friendship that had begun to blossom between them. The love.

Tears wet her cheeks and she sniffed, allowing herself a moment to mourn all that she would lose. She almost wished she had admitted how she felt about him while she had the chance. But then, when she made everything clear to him this coming night, he might believe she had lied. He would think she said it only to try to spare herself and Rob his wrath.

She could not imagine Edouard's wrath. Not directed toward her and her son. But the possibility was certainly there that it would be, and she would face it if she must. His anger would prove a certainty if he found out some other way. Her mind was made up. He must know everything.

She met Meg on the stair. "Where is my lord? Have you seen him?"

"Hunting with the lads, my lady. They took out early with Thomas and the hounds." Meg grinned at her. "Oh, and good news, my lady! Sir Gui rode in just after they left to hunt. He came on ahead to tell us the wains will arrive tomorrow. I have been ensuring that the storage chambers are made ready."

Anne thanked her and continued down to the hall. Edouard would be glad to have his things about him, she supposed. He had seemed restless this past week with the waiting.

A day's hunting might do all of them good. Henri was certainly recovered enough now for a brisk ride and a bit of excitement. Lord only knew Robert could use some activity.

His riding out with Edouard and Henri did not worry her overmuch. There would be little time for conversation while plundering the wood for game, an activity in which Rob excelled. Young Thomas would be there to cause a diversion should Robert run into trouble understanding Edouard. He understood the problems involved as well as she. In a way, Anne felt relief that she had to uphold the charade for only one more day.

Keeping her son secluded in her old chamber these past

days had been a chore. He had needed rest after his ordeal, but not the week she had forced on him.

Robert had told her with signs, drawings, and what words he knew how the men Uncle Dairmid commanded had taken him while he was at his traps. Without old Rufus by his side to warn him, Rob said he had been easy game.

Though Rob had tended himself well following his escape, his poor wrists still bore scabbing from his struggle with the bonds. Thank God that was his only hurt, and also that he had been too proud to reveal the injury to Edouard or Henri. Everyone still thought he had simply wandered too far from home and became lost.

Rob had wriggled out of his bindings and slipped off into the forest when the men had stopped to eat and rest. He had climbed a tree and hidden himself, watching the men until they finally gave up looking for him and went away.

Thanks be, his uncanny sense of direction had brought him within several hours' ride of the keep. Had Edouard not found him, Anne had no doubt Rob would have walked through the gates next day.

Her wee, braw Rob. How could anyone not appreciate that quick mind of his? For all that he lacked hearing, his other senses should be the envy of full-grown men. Agile as a rope dancer and quick as a flash of lightning, he was. He would excel with weapons once trained, if his self-taught skill with a sling was an indication.

Though she refused to allow him to ride without company, Rob did control a mount as well as any man. He had a way with beasts of all kinds and trained them with ease.

His precious hound must have returned the favor and trained that nose of Rob's, for her lad seemed to sniff out quarry in the wood. Why, he could tell her what Cook was preparing for supper before they descended to the hall to eat.

And Rob's eyes never missed a thing. He could communicate his thoughts to her with just a look most times without having to speak or sign them. His judgement of people had proved infallible many a time. He could sense guilt or treachery in a person and ferret out a liar before she could. These were the traits which would stand him in good stead once he became lord.

She would point them out to Edouard when she told him of Rob's deafness. If only he would give her the chance. How she hoped he would heed her words. Mayhaps he would not ignore Robert's talents, but would enhance them with the instruction he needed.

Anne strolled past the women who were busy scrubbing down the trestles to prepare them for the midday meal. She intended to inspect the cheeses which were ripening in the dairy and send someone to fish for dinner. The moment she reached the bailey, she heard a commotion at the gate.

"They come home early!" someone on the wall shouted. "Look there! Something's gone afoul!"

Anne rushed toward the entrance to meet the hunting party as they rode through. Simm, Sir Gui and several others joined her.

"What has happened?" she questioned as the riders halted. She marked all the long faces and Rob's barely stifled sobs. "Is someone hurt?"

Rob kicked out of his stirrups and slid off his palfrey. Before she could reach for him, he dashed away toward the keep. Never in his life had Anne seen her son abandon a sweat-covered mount with no thought to its care. She started to whistle him back, but caught herself in time.

"The old hound," Edouard explained. "He is dead."

Anne jerked her gaze from the fleeing Robert and looked up at her husband. "What?"

Edouard dismounted. Then she saw the hairy body of Rufus draped across the back of his saddle. Several other dogs slunk around the hooves of the mounts as if they feared a like fate.

"Why?" she whispered, stepping closer to run a hand over the head of Rob's dearest old friend. Blood crusted the fur beneath his neck and soaked part of the blanket in which they had wrapped him.

Rufus had come here with her uninvited when she had wed MacBain, the only living thing from home that remained with her after her marriage. She felt tears roll down her face before she even knew she wept. "Why is he dead?"

Henri started after Rob, but Edouard stopped him. "Leave him be, son. He would rather mourn in private. You and Thomas take the mounts to the stables. Clean up the hound and rewrap him for burial. We will see to that task when Lord Robert rejoins us."

Anne brushed away her tears, dreading to hear what had happened to her old friend and Rob's protector. "Tell me."

Edouard ran a gloved hand down her arm and grasped her hand. "The old fellow ran too hard today. He collapsed and could barely catch breath. I had to put him down so that he would not suffer."

"You killed him?" Anne shouted angrily, jerking her arm out of his grasp. "You *killed* our Rufus?"

"There was little choice about it, Anne. He could barely see or hear, and his lungs were used up. He must have seen fifteen years or more. What good is a hound in that condition?"

Her horror knew no bounds. "You slew this poor, faithful beast? Took a blade to his throat because he could not live up to the great comte's idea of perfection?" Her voice rose on every word, outrage shaking her right down to her boots. "How would you like it should someone do that to you? Damn you to hell for this, Trouville! I could kill you for it!"

She whirled around and ran for the keep to comfort Robert. He would be devastated by this. Inconsolable. Even as she hurried to see to her son, Anne realized the implications of the act. Trouville could not bear anything—or mayhaps any*one*—who exhibited any faults. Oh, he would never slit Rob's throat, of course, but he would surely see no use for a lad who fell below his standards. He would get rid of him as soon as he could.

Before she reached the stairs, Edouard grabbed her from behind and pushed her toward the solar. She batted at his hands, sobbing out her grief for Rufus and her grave disappointment in Trouville.

She hated that she had come to love this man. It frightened her that she had almost placed her total trust in his compassion, when he had absolutely none.

Once the door was closed, he forced her to a chair and pushed her down. "Now you will calm yourself, madame!"

Anne clenched her teeth, her breath rasping in and out with the urge to do him harm. "I loathe you!" she ground out, shuddering with the emotion.

He knelt before her and shook her gently, then grasped her face between his palms. "Listen to me, Anne. I did what I had to do. Would you rather Robert had to do it? He understood. I told him what must be done and he agreed it was necessary."

She pulled away from his grip and shook her head sharply. "He did not understand you! He had no idea what you meant to do, you fool! He cannot—"

"He did, I tell you! We discussed it and he fully understood."

Anne buried her face in her hands. "Oh, leave me be! Just leave me be."

He stood up and backed away. "Very well. I shall send

someone in to tend you. Do not go to Robert now while you are upset.''

''I shall go to him as I please, and you have nothing to say to it!'' she declared.

''You will remain here in this solar, Anne. The boy is nigh a man. He will hate having his dam see him reduced to tears. Why do you think he ran? Trust me, he will recover himself and come to lay the hound to rest. You may come, too, if you can leave off this unseemly tantrum.''

''Unseemly?'' she shouted. ''You murdering lout! How dare you judge me *unseemly!*''

He met her heated glare with one of deadly determination. His voice came softly, but it bore warning. ''Stay you here in this chamber, Anne. I command it.''

Then he left her there, weeping like a child and wondering what she would do now. By giving vent to her outrage, she had forgone any hope of softening his heart toward Robert's plight. If, indeed, she could have done. It appeared that her husband would not tolerate faults in any who lived beneath his hand. Not Rufus the hound, not her, and surely not her son.

She barely had time to compose herself before the door opened again. Henri came and knelt before her, head bowed. ''My lady mother, I beg leave to speak to you of Robert. I must say what I've come to say ere Father finds me here. He would ask why I came to you and I cannot lie to him.'' He ducked his head guiltily. ''Leastways, not outright.''

''What is it, Henri? What of Robert?'' she asked, reaching forward to touch his shoulder.

''We must hide the fact that he cannot hear! Father must never know.''

So, Henri had guessed. She supposed his finding out had been inevitable. As it would be with Edouard once he began spending more time with Robert.

He rushed on. "I have been able to cover the truth of it when we are all together. My own chatter distracts Father so he does not notice. And I tell him things that Robert confides to me." He looked a bit shamefaced. "I sometimes make them up, of course, but it leads him to believe Robert can speak well."

Anne nodded, amazed at the boy's resourcefulness.

"Jehan and Thomas know already," he said. "They are teaching me how to understand Robert. I thought at first my Father should be aware of it, so he could help somehow. But now I have changed my mind, and am glad I did not tell him."

He wiped his nose on his sleeve, shot her an apologetic look for it, and continued. "Father killed Rufus. That poor old fellow did nothing wrong save grow tired, but Father killed him." He clutched his neck and swallowed hard. "Just cut his throat and then bled him out."

Anne felt a strong pang of sympathy for her stepson. He could not abide cruelty. She brushed a hand over his head and cupped his cheek in one hand. "I am sorry you had to witness such a thing."

He shrugged. "I have seen things slain many times. 'Tis just that, well, I had not grown to like them first. You know?"

"Aye, son. I do know. You must not hate your father for it. He insists he only did what had to be done." Anne knew Edouard did not view his slaying of Rufus as a cruel act. He truly believed that the hound was better off not living, given the age and disabilities.

"I know," Henri said. "Father is a hard man at times. He expects too much. It is so difficult for me to measure up, my lady. How much more of a task will that be for Robert, I wonder." He gulped. "And what will happen if Robert is not able?"

Anne clucked her tongue. "Surely you do not think your

father would harm him!'' She noted the indecision on Henri's face and felt her blood turn to ice. "Do you?"

Henri shook his head slowly. "I have never witnessed him visit a serious injury on any person who did not threaten him first. Only the hound. But it cannot bode well for Robert, does Father discover the truth. He might send him away somewhere."

"Aye, I admit I had the same thought. Do you believe we could keep Robert's secret, then? Will it be possible?"

"Yes. Father always requires more listening than talking. With all of us working together, I think we might," Henri said, his expression as fierce as his sire's could be at times. "Given the day's happenings, we had best try." He sighed. "I do not like this feeling of disloyalty, my lady, but I must protect my brother as best I can. 'Tis not Robert's doing that he is as he is. Though he does right well, for all that. Do you not think?"

Anne smiled and leaned forward to embrace him. "I am forever in your debt, Henri. Whatever happens with this matter, I am very glad that you are now my son. And, for whatever it is worth to you, I believe you have the very best of your father within your heart."

"Thank you, my lady. I pray it is so." He worried his bottom lip with his teeth and met her eyes directly. "I would not wish you to think him an evil man. He can be quite kind. It is only that he cannot abide—"

Anne smiled sadly as he struggled for a fitting word. "We are agreed, Henri. I know what you mean. Why don't you go back to the stables now before you are missed?" She laid a hand on his shoulder. "I do thank you for your concern and for your help."

Henri disappeared as quickly as he came and Anne sank down onto the window seat to ponder what she should do. Informing Edouard about Robert was now out of the question. That much she knew. Rufus was dead, and there was nothing to be done for that. Heaping accusations on Edouard's head would change nothing except his feelings for her. More hope lay in keeping his mind on things other than Robert until he went away.

She would curb her temper, bury her grief and act the perfect wife. Edouard would make no allowances for her if she were not all that he expected her to be.

Her disappointment in him was her own doing, Anne reasoned. She should have learned her lesson with the first husband. Aye, and also with her father and her uncle. Tolerance and tender feelings were merely pretense, all too brief in duration, and quite leeched out of a man ere he reached adulthood. So, she would welcome Edouard's pretending when he deigned to offer it, and he would have hers. She was a fool to have thought things could be any other way.

Robert bore his grief well. Edouard watched his stepson shovel dirt into the hole in which they had placed the old hound. Though his eyes were red from weeping, the boy seemed well over the worst. Henri assisted in the burial, looking more distraught than anyone else attending. His son refused to meet his eye or even to speak to him since they had returned from the aborted hunt.

Anne stood stiffly by, her face a mask showing no feeling whatever. Edouard felt the greatest sorrow he had known in some time for performing that necessary act of mercy. She had obviously held great love for the old dog.

Even had he known that at the time, he could have done no differently, however. The poor beast had fallen in the path and was gasping pitifully, a liquid sucking sound Edouard had heard before. A horrible death would have followed in a few hours, the animal suffering miserably in the process. Robert had sensed that, Edouard knew from the look in his eyes.

"Shall I end his agony, Robert?" he had asked the boy. He had offered the blade, should the lad wish to do it himself. With a simple shake of the head, Robert had declined. Edouard thought none the less of him for that. He remembered well having to destroy a favorite destrier which had broken its leg in a melee. Would to God he had found someone willing to do that for him.

The boys had the grave covered and were now piling rocks upon it in the tradition of the Scots. Their cairn, to which they would add a stone each time they visited the departed.

When they had done, Robert dropped to his knees beside it and simply stared at the mound.

"Let us leave him for a while," Edouard suggested, ushering Henri and Anne away. When she resisted slightly, he insisted. "Come away, Anne, and return later if you will."

She moved smartly then, taking long strides ahead and leaving him behind to walk with Henri.

"Son, I know this troubles you."

Henri finally looked up at him, squinting. "Does it trouble you, Father? To kill, I mean."

"Of course it does. No sane man *enjoys* it," he answered, surprised that Henri thought the question necessary.

"You have killed men before," Henri stated.

"I have," Edouard admitted. "But only when I had no choice, in a kill-or-be-killed circumstance. You may have to do the same one day. That is why I wish you well trained."

"Old Rufus offered you no threat!" Henri hotly accused.

"He was dying and in pain—" Edouard began to explain. But Henri had dashed away, tearing across the bailey at full speed. With a curse, Edouard stopped and watched them run from him. Henri, toward the stables, Anne toward the keep.

For the first time in his adult life, Edouard regretted that

others considered him hard and merciless. He had labored
ceaselessly to make people think that he was that. In truth,
he could *be* that. But in most instances, it was unnecessary.
In countless situations his reputation had probably saved
his life, or at the very least, prevented his having to engage
in a contest of wills that would leave someone dead or
maimed. Few challenged him nowadays. Those who did
were forewarned.

He had become unused to defending his actions. As far
as today was concerned, he had explained more than once
why he had put the dog out of misery, and damned if he
would do so again. Both Anne and Henri were willfully
misunderstanding what he had done. So be it, then. Let
them think as they would.

"Were I you, I believe I would sleep with one eye open
tonight," Sir Gui said as he approached.

"I saw you earlier. When did you return?" Edouard
asked, still watching Anne's retreat.

"Soon after you rode out this morn."

"All's well with the shipment?"

"Arriving tomorrow." Gui assured him. He followed the
line of Edouard's vision. "I do hope she lets you live to
see it."

"Get gone from me, Gui. I am in no mood for your dark
levity," Edouard growled.

"No jest intended, my lord," Gui said. "I was deadly
serious. I heard what she said to you about the hound. So
did everyone else. Our lady is none too shy about voicing
her hateful thoughts, is she?"

Edouard glared. "Thoughts she is certainly entitled to,
as you are to your own. Though I do wish you would go
and have yours somewhere else!"

The knight sighed, nodded and ambled away, shaking
his head.

For half a moment, Edouard wondered whether Anne did

truly hate him enough to seek retribution. Such vehement temper belied the serenity she usually maintained, and that which he always associated with her. Twice now she had threatened his life. Should he beware?

Was his wish for abiding love and a good marriage blinding him where she was concerned? Anne had never said she loved him, or even that she liked him well. Not with words. Her body loved his, he knew without doubt. But lust could certainly exist without involving the heart at all. Or the mind, for that matter.

Mayhaps *he* was the one mindless in all this. He had not lived this long by ignoring any threat, however subtly offered. And Anne had not been subtle in hers, not by any man's measure.

But the thought of Anne killing him for performing an act of kindness to a dog seemed ludicrous. If she intended to do so, surely she would be wise enough not to shout aloud her intentions.

His stomach had begun to roil. It must be the heat, he thought. Or the day's events. His head now ached so fiercely, he could scarcely think. Nor did he *want* to think more on this particular problem, he decided. To clear his mind, he took himself to the small barracks where Gui and Anne's few guardsmen resided and ordered up a bath. Afterward, he appropriated one of the empty pallets and fell asleep.

The day wore on as Anne remained secluded in their chamber. She alternately prayed for guidance and cursed her inability to control her temper. She would gain nothing by angering Edouard further. It could lose her everything, even if he never discovered the secret. He could banish her to a convent, Rob to a monastery, and be done with the both of them for no reason at all if he wanted. And she continued to provide him with reasons like the veriest idiot.

Anne summoned the cook at midafternoon and ordered up all of Edouard's favorite foods. She had originally planned to do so when she told him about Rob. Now she did it to pretend atonement for her behavior.

Anne thanked providence that he had avoided her after the burial, not even coming to the chamber to change for the evening meal. She wore her favorite blue camlet gown and had dressed her hair becomingly. Now all she had to do was go down and face him, smile and act as though nothing untoward had happened.

"Good evening, my lady." He rose and greeted her without expression, holding her chair out with studied care. His movements seemed too deliberate, as if he had imbibed too much wine and wanted to conceal the fact.

"My lord," she replied in kind and took her seat, arranging her skirts just so.

"Our sons requested their meals in solitude. I hope you do not mind that I gave my permission," he offered politely.

"'Tis your prerogative to give your leave where you will, my lord," she said softly.

"Just so." He said nothing else until the soup had been served and consumed.

Edouard looked down as one of the servants placed a trencher before him and another heaped it with succulent slices of lamb. His gaze shifted quickly to her place where another had been set and half filled with small slivers of roasted partridge. "We do not share?"

"I do not care for lamb, but I know that you do. I had it prepared especially."

"Ah." He poked at it with his knife and then glanced down the table at the others. "For me alone?"

"Aye. 'Tis all for you," she said, wearing a wide smile, though it felt frozen on her lips. "My way of making amends for my hasty words this morn."

Slowly he dragged his gaze to the lower table where Sir
Gui sat watching them intently. The frowning knight lowered his eating knife and opened his mouth as though to
speak. Edouard looked back at her, holding her captive with
his eyes as he lifted a piece of the meat to his mouth.

Bite after bite, chewing thoughtfully, maintaining his
piercing regard of her, Edouard ate every morsel on his
trencher.

"Delicious," he said in a curiously determined voice.
He raised the silver cup and watched her over the rim as
he drank.

Anne hardly tasted the piece of partridge she had taken.
"Would you care for more?"

He did not answer. Instead, his eyes widened and his
face grew pale as death. Beads of sweat popped out upon
his brow and his hands clenched in the table linen, over-
setting his wine. The muscles of his throat worked in
spasms as he swallowed again and again.

"Edouard?" she questioned, "What is wrong? Are you
ill?"

With a gut-wrenching groan, he shoved away from the
table and half-ran, half-staggered toward the nearest door
which happened to be the solar.

She jumped up to follow, but Sir Gui had rounded the
dais and shoved her aside in his haste to reach his lord. By
the time she reached them, Edouard had emptied his stomach and lay prone on the floor of the solar. His back rose
and fell with harsh gasps for breath.

"Go and bring Meg! Quickly!" she cried to Sir Gui as
she knelt beside her husband.

The knight dragged her upright and shoved her away so
hard she stumbled against the wall. "You will burn for
this!" he cried.

A crowd had gathered around the solar door, mouths
open in shock. Sir Gui raised a fist in her direction as he

addressed them. "Your lady has poisoned my lord. Take her to her chamber and lock her there. I will deal with her later. You, woman!" he spoke to Meg. "If you know any remedy for this, apply it now or die with her!"

Meg flew to Edouard's side, shooting Anne a questioning look even as she crouched. Surely Meg did not believe she would do such a thing?

Edouard groaned and tried to rise, but the knight and Father Michael eased him down again, making soothing noises. Meg sent someone for her herbs and then requested that the men help her to turn Edouard onto his back.

Anne gasped and ran forward when she saw how lifeless he looked. His breathing came in short, irregular gasps and the line around his lips looked white. "Edouard!" She ran a trembling hand over his face. He felt so cold.

Sir Gui elbowed her aside and yelled over his shoulder. "Get her out of here, else I'll kill her now!"

Her steward came forward and grasped her by her arms. "Come away, my lady."

Though Anne struggled to stay, Simm clasped her against his beefy body and dragged her out of the solar. He quickly rushed her up the stairs and put her into the master chamber. "You had best remain here until we see what happens, Lady Anne. Did you—"

"Poison him? How can you ask such a thing?"

He ducked his head, looking up at her from under his spiky lashes. "Sorry, my lady, but you were spiteful angry with him over the hound."

Anne heaved out a breath of frustration and worry for Edouard. "Not *that* angry! My God in heaven, Simm, he is my husband! My lord!"

Simm nodded, his expression doubtful. "Aye, that's so, but it's no secret that you fear what he might do when he learns everything about Master Rob." He sighed. "Best you stay here until we see what's what."

With that, he backed out, closed the door and went back down the stairs. Anne collapsed on the bed. She knew she was not locked in. There was no way to lock the chamber from the outside. Yet if she did go below, Sir Gui might make good his threat. She only prayed that Meg would do her utmost to save Edouard from whatever ailed him.

Surely it could not be poison. No one would do such a thing unless she ordered it, and probably not even then. The only thing she could figure was that the meat had been spoiled. Not likely, however, since the lamb was only just slaughtered.

She tried to recall if she had ever seen anyone afflicted such as Edouard had been. Nausea, chills, raspy breathing, deathlike pallor. The strange ague the lads had suffered two weeks ago carried those same symptoms, only the onset had been well into the night, not immediately after eating. By morning, their fevers had set in. Henri had been affected far worse than Rob and took twice as long to recover. Could it be that Edouard had an even worse case? No one else had sickened.

Hurried footsteps in the corridor drew her to the door. Before she reached it, a sharp pounding began. She jerked open the panel and interrupted Simm and two of the men who were attaching iron fittings for a lock. He shrugged an apology. "Best back away, my lady. Sir Gui's orders, y'see?"

Anne realized she must get word to Meg about her thoughts on Edouard's malady. "Listen to me, Simm. I believe my husband has the same ague our sons had. Tell Meg to use the same treatment. Crushed mint, and willow bark tea when his fever rises—"

"Don't think she'll need it," he said sadly. "It appears his lordship's past any help at all."

Anne gasped, covering her mouth with her hands. "Oh

nay,'' she moaned, leaning against the door frame to keep from falling. ''Tell me he's not—''

''I expect Father Michael will be up soon,'' Simm said, his tone sorrowful. ''When he's done with last rites for his lordship, you'll want to be saying your confession.''

Extreme Unction! Oh God, Edouard was dying! Or already dead! Anne's knees crumpled under her. She barely noticed the men still hammering away at the wall and the door.

Simm stepped across the threshold and lifted her to her feet. He guided her to the window seat and lowered her to it. Without another word, he left her there and closed the door behind him.

All fell silent for a few moments. Then Anne heard the lock rattle into its new fittings, closing her in with her fear and grief.

Chapter Ten

Edouard drifted in and out of consciousness, unable to distinguish between feverish dreams and reality. He ached all over and could not stir himself or open his eyes.

Dimly, he heard the drone of Latin and imagined himself at Mass, kneeling beside Anne, holding her hand. But the hand felt too loose, too cold. It released him. Then cool, wet fingers touched his lips, his eyes, and ears.

"...*et Spiritus Sancti. Amen*," a low voice murmured. Edouard sighed and tried to sink back into the comfortable darkness and escape the heat.

A woman whispering drew him back. "What do you think, Michael? This fever rages despite everything I've done. He cannot swallow. Ach, I have no experience with poisons!"

Someone grunted. "Well, neither have I. But Sir Gui must have. He guessed right away that is what this is. Who are we to gainsay him? The man spent nigh his whole life at the French court, which must be rife with this sort of thing. Would he not know?"

"Aye, I suppose. But who would think to murder Lord Edouard? You know very well Lady Anne did no such thing."

"She fears him, Meg. You know she does, and we all know why. Sir Gui means to hold court on the morrow and charge her with Lord Edouard's murder."

The woman scoffed. "The man's not even dead yet! Besides, that French knight cannot impose sentence for that offense, even should it prove true! Who does he think he is?"

"He has sent for the sheriff. It will happen. Attempted murder of a husband holds the same penalty as the successful act. I am forbidden to go to her until her guilt is decided. I fear our lady will suffer the fire for this, Meg. I truly do."

Shock stole Edouard's labored breath. God in heaven, they were going to burn his wife! He forced a sound out through parched lips. He had to tell them it wasn't true. Anne would never harm him. The darkness pulled at him and he fought it with all his might.

"He stirs!" the woman said. She drew near enough he could feel her breath on his face. "My lord! My lord, can you hear me?"

"Oui," he rasped through the rawness of his throat. "Anne?"

"Sir Gui thinks she has tainted your food, my lord, but I swear she did not! She would not!"

"Non," he said. "Gui?"

But his knight did not come. With all his will, Edouard struggled to remain lucid to defend her, but fog drifted in and blocked out all awareness.

Anne wept until she could not. Father Michael did not come as Simm had promised. No one came. The hours drew out until the pink of dawn lightened the dark chamber where she mourned. Edouard was dead.

Weeks ago, when he had first arrived, she might have welcomed the news. Guilt for that left her desolate. How

had she come to love him this much in so short a time? He
had never given her real reason to mistrust him. She had
attached all the sins of man to him because of stupid rumors
and her own sad experiences. If she had been honest from
the first, he might well have offered Rob compassion.

Nay, she admitted with a sob. Now that he was gone,
she was only bestowing virtues she wished he had possessed. Henri could not be so wrong about his own father.
The boy had lived with Edouard nigh fourteen years. He
would know precisely how exacting the man was. How
strictly his father judged a person's infirmities. But even
so, Anne did not wish this end for Edouard. She would
rather have him banish them forever than to see him dead.

His face haunted her. That beautiful, exquisitely formed
countenance with a winged brow raised in question. The
finely wrought lips turned up slightly at the corners. The
eyes, long-lashed and dark as sin, boring into hers. *Did you
kill me, Anne?*

"Oh, nay, Edouard. I did not," she whispered sadly.

Why had MacBain's shade never appeared to accuse her?
There, she would have stood on less certain ground. Had
she tended him herself, she might have prolonged his life
for another few days, even weeks. Why had she not? Had
she thought it a kindness to allow death to end his suffering? Or had she feared his complete recovery and more
beatings?

"Bah, this is foolish," she muttered to herself. She had
no special gifts of healing, nor any particular knowledge of
medicaments. "Who is to say my attendance at his side
would have done any more than that of the others?" Not
likely that MacBain would have welcomed her presence
there any more than he had when he was well. The guilt
might remain a constant companion, but thankfully his
ghost did not.

Not like Edouard's. She could not dismiss his constant

image from her mind, nor did she wish to. Anne embraced it, considered it a gift, and planned to treasure it as long as she lived. Which might not be long now, in any case.

She would not care if it were not for Robert. What would happen to him now? Would Meg and Michael be able to maintain the deceit? Would they carry out her plans for him? Or would he become a beggar by the road, dependent on the charity of passersby?

Anne leaned back against the embrasure and stared out the window. The gates stood open and several riders were approaching the keep. Aymer Galbraith rode at the head of the party, instantly recognizable by his considerable girth. So they had sent for the sheriff. No more than she had expected of the good Sir Gui, loyal knight to Trouville, the faithful lieutenant. And now he would command them to burn her at the stake as he had threatened.

How could she defend herself against the charge of murder? Edouard had eaten, drunk some wine and immediately collapsed.

Meg would not guess the cause of it, for she had not been there when the lads first sickened that night. Anne had called her above stairs only when their fevers began to rage the next morning. If Edouard had passed before that stage of the sickness set in, Meg would never see the sameness of it all.

Anne watched as the sheriff and two of his men rode through the gates, somberly greeting all they passed. She noted Henri and Robert standing off to one side, watching the men go by. Did they, too, suspect that she had tried to kill their father? *Do not believe it, my sons.*

Robert suddenly looked up at her. He dragged Henri by the elbow until they stood directly below her high window. No one in the bailey paid them or her any attention. Everyone else was busy watching the sheriff and his party ride in.

I am so sorry. She signed, her palm rubbing her chest as it ached, her eyes tearing up yet again. She had thought her tears all spent. She watched Robert's lips as he tried to confer her message to Henri with his limited words.

Henri looked up and mouthed the silent words. "Did you poison my father?" Robert echoed the question with eyebrows raised.

Anne shook her head vehemently. While speaking the words of denial, she plucked at her midsection with her hand, Rob's signal for sickness, drew her forefingers together side by side, which to him meant sameness, and then pointed down at first Henri and then Rob. "No, He was sick, the same as you both were."

She watched them nod as though the matter were settled. She sniffed and wiped at her eyes, content that they, at least, believed her innocent.

"Now he is dead," she added in a grieved whisper. "Dead."

Anne sensed more than saw Robert's frantic waving. When she blinked away her tears and peered down at him, he smiled and signed broadly. *Father is not dead.* Henri mimed the words, grinning. "We saw him!" he added.

When she recovered from the joyous shock, the boys had disappeared. Could it be true? If Edouard lived, why had no one come to tell her of it? Why had the sheriff arrived if not to try her for murder?

Anne could think of only one reason. Edouard himself thought she had tried to kill him. He believed that she had poisoned his food and meant for him to die because he had killed her hound. He planned to have her punished for the attempt. How would she ever convince him that she had not?

Exultation over the fact that he lived eclipsed even her fear. Anne sank to her knees and thanked God it was so.

She also asked mercy for her own plight, and prayed Edouard would realize her innocent before it was too late.

Two hours later, Simm came to fetch her. She preceded him calmly down the stairs. She wore the same gown she had worn to that fateful supper. Though she had combed her hair and washed her face while she waited, Anne had been afraid to undress, knowing they would come for her soon.

Sir Gui, Sheriff Galbraith, and two strangers who had arrived with him sat on the dais.

Simm ushered her forth to stand before them. "The comtesse de Trouville," he announced in his gravelly voice.

Galbraith stood, his massive weight causing the boards of the dais to creak. "Were I not a fair man, fairer than the law requires, I should not permit you to speak today, my lady." With his fat and hairy fingers, he shuffled two loose parchments that lay before him on the table. "However, since we have no proper evidence, I would hear all sides of this matter ere I decide what's to be done."

He turned slightly toward the angry knight on his right. "Sir Guillaume Perrer levies a charge of attempted murder against you, your grace. He says that you did spitefully and maliciously poison your lord's food or wine last even, causing him to fall so gravely ill that he lies near death at this very moment. How plead you to this accusation?"

"Without guilt," she stated. "I poisoned no one. I believe my husband has fallen ill with the same malady that caused our sons to sicken two weeks past."

He raised one bushy black brow and hummed. "I do wonder. Word is that your first lord, MacBain, died in similar circumstance. What say you?"

Anne bit her lips together, realizing how damning the rumors were. "MacBain grew old, sickened and died. I did nothing to cause it." And little to prevent it, either, but she would never admit that here.

The sheriff nodded to Sir Gui. "Why do you believe the lady wished Lord Trouville dead?"

Sir Gui spoke through gritted teeth, his eyes narrowed to mere slits. "She threatened his life twice in my hearing. Once, when he offered to punish her son for her, and again when he dispatched a hound that had outlived usefulness. Both times, my lord only intended help. Both times, she warned him she would retaliate. And so she did. All saw my lord fall."

The sheriff glared at her and pursed his lips for a moment. He glanced down at the parchment. "Margaret MacBrus, come forth."

Meg approached the table. "Aye, my lord sheriff?"

"You are the healer here. Will his lordship succumb to this poison?"

"I do not know. His fever runs high. He is not conscious now, but he did rally once to speak."

"And what did he say?"

Meg cleared her throat and hesitated. "Well, he called my lady's name and then that of Sir Gui. Afterward, he fainted away again."

The sheriff leaned forward. "Were you present at the time of Lord MacBain's death?"

"Aye, I was."

"Did your lady offer him any food or drink? Did she ever ask you to provide herbs that might have caused him to sicken?"

"Nay, she did not. No herbs at all. The food and drink were prepared in the kitchens, usually brought by one of the maids."

"Fed to MacBain by her own hand, then?" the sheriff asked.

"Nay. She saw he was tended, but did not tend him herself."

Sir Gui interrupted. "She could well have added poison

while no one was looking. And even if they did see, they would never speak out against the woman who would rule them once MacBain was dead. The man hated her and she despised him. It is common knowledge hereabouts!''

''No one asked you,'' the sheriff stated in a flat voice. ''If I need your supposition, sir, I shall ask for it. This is a fair hearing, not an outright condemnation, do you hear?'' He acknowledged the knight's surly nod and continued. ''Go and tend his lordship, Mistress.'' Meg left quickly.

The sheriff sat down. He leaned toward the men on his left and they murmured to each other for a few moments. Then he turned again toward Anne. ''Your guilt cannot be decided with the information available. Lord Trouville ate and drank all of the food and wine supposedly tainted by the poison. Did we have any left, we could feed it to some beast and see whether it died. Lacking that, and discounting old rumors, it becomes Sir Guillaume's word against your own. He says you tried to do murder. You say you did not.''

His considering gaze traveled the circle of folk gathered round the hall. ''We must rely on trial by ordeal. God's judgement. Fire or water, my lady?''

A chorus of shocked protests erupted. She saw Henri, Rob and Father Michael draw aside, speaking together. She hoped the priest would give Rob comfort. The noise continued for some time, growing louder and more threatening until the sheriff finally silenced them with the pounding of his fist on the dais. ''Water or fire?'' he demanded when all grew quiet.

''Water,'' she said with a shudder.

He nodded and spoke to his cohorts. ''Shall we to the loch, then?''

''Hold!'' Henri's voice rang out.

''And who is this bairn that interrupts these proceedings?'' the sheriff asked.

"No bairn, my lord sheriff. I am Henri, heir of Trouville. And I demand the right to ascertain my stepmother's guilt."

He strode forward, every inch his father's son. He might be half the weight and lacking height, but the commanding presence was there, Anne thought. Did Henri think differently now that he had heard the sheriff's questions?

"You will not halt this trial, my young lord. I care not who you are!" the sheriff informed him.

Henri nodded once. "So be it, but I will stand for my father and see this done properly." He marched forward and dragged Anne's hands behind her, tying them together with a cord from his pocket. Anne recognized it as the small rope with which Henri practiced sailor's knots in his idle time. The pastime had made him most proficient. When he had finished, she could not stretch the bonds at all.

His voice sounded rife with sarcasm, like Edouard at his worst, when he spoke, just loudly enough for all to hear. "Look to your son, there, my lady. He stands twitching to see how you shall fare in all this."

"No need to be cruel, lad!" the sheriff admonished him. "Just get on with it!"

Anne's gaze flew to Robert. Solemnly and unobtrusively he signed the words, *Henri will help you.*

Anne nodded once. Left little choice since Henri held her on a tether, she trailed behind him as he marched from the hall. The sheriff and the others quickly rounded the dais and fell in step.

The crowd grew restive again as everyone trudged en masse the full league's distance to the loch.

Anne shuddered when she thought of the coldness of the water, but still believed it preferable to the trial by fire. Rob had walked on ahead of them, leading Henri and her to a bank where the loch was not so deep. Through the murky water, one could even make out vague shapes along the bottom.

Her son met her eyes with a stoicism and assurance she would not have expected from anyone about to watch his mother die. His thoughts reached out to her. *Courage, Mama. All will be well.*

Anne looked away, unable to bear up under her fear for him. What would happen to her son? Her handsome, all-too-trusting son. "Watch after him, please," she begged in a whisper, glancing first to Henri, then to Simm. "Please."

Simm returned her look. He knew who she meant, even if no one else did. Even if he thought her guilty of the worst of crimes, he would look after her lad. He and the others of Baincroft were already bound to Robert by oath. Anne took what comfort she could from that.

Father Michael approached then. Anne hardly heard the words as he hurriedly offered her absolution. He made the sign of the cross and pressed his crucifix to her lips. "Mind Henri," he said, and stepped away.

When the sheriff called for the bindings, Henri snatched the coil of rope from Simm before anyone could stop him. "I shall do this myself!" he announced. "You may examine my knots. I do not mean to make half work of them, I assure you."

Sheriff Galbraith looked at him askance and pursed his thick lips. "Proceed."

Henri pushed her down so that she sat on the grass, and ordered her to put her knees to her chest. He bound her so tightly in that position she could hardly breathe. He left a very long end of the rope to hold on to, so that he could drag her back once the water decided her fate.

The murmuring of the crowd that had followed them to the pond grew louder, but Anne held out no hopes that they would try to rescue her. No one would go against Galbraith, an appointed officer of the crown. Nor would they dare to protest the word of Sir Gui, their new lord's second in command.

When Henri leaned closer to secure the last knot, he whispered vehemently, "Force all air from your chest when you go in. *All* of it!"

Anne wondered if he meant for her to drown immediately. Was he trying to effect a quick and efficient death for her? He had taken a lesson from Edouard's dispatch of old Rufus after all. A mercy kill. Like father, like son.

Whatever his intent, Anne decided to mind his advice. She knew she would die here one way or another. God would have little to do with keeping her alive in this instance.

If she floated, that would prove her guilt. They would burn her to death for attempting murder of a husband. She supposed she ought to be thankful Edouard was French nobility instead of English or Scot. Then her crime would be treason and she would be hanged, drawn and quartered.

If the water claimed her for its own, declaring her not guilty of the accusation, she would drown down there. But then, at least, Robert, Henri and the others would believe she had spoken truly. She would pray for that end, and do as Henri had suggested.

Sir Gui looked down on her with smug satisfaction, likely picturing her in hell already.

Henri stood quickly then and nodded to the others. The men came and tugged at the ropes, declared them soundly tied, and stepped away.

Galbraith addressed the crowd. "Witness ye! Should the lady float, her guilt is certain. Should she sink, the accused is innocent as charged. Do you accept the judgement of this ordeal, Sir Guilluame?"

"I do," he announced in a loud voice so that all would understand him. "She will float."

"Then let us see if that is so," the sheriff said. "Into

the loch with her!'' He sounded all too eager for Anne's taste.

Henri grunted as he and Simm lifted her high and dropped her into the loch.

Anne expelled all the air in her chest just before she struck the water. Wound into a ball as she was, she sank immediately to the bottom.

When she looked up, she saw a number of wavery heads peering down at her. Her clothing billowed about her and her body shifted and started to rise. Just then her bound hands discovered a large stone half-buried in the mud beneath her. Anne curled her fingers around the edge and hung on for dear life.

Hours must have passed, she thought, struggling with the overpowering urge to draw something into her vacant lungs. Anything. Just as she gave in, the rope tightened. They were pulling her up! Her sluggish mind warned her of the surface. *Nay! To rise proved guilt!* Anne could not make herself release the rock. Water rushed into her mouth and nose and Anne panicked. *I did not, Edouard! Oh God, I did not do it!*

Henri and several of the others dragged her onto the muddy bank and began cutting the ropes. She flailed frantically as they released her, sputtering and coughing up the fluid, and sucking in precious air. Her nose burned horribly and her mouth tasted of fish and bile. Her limbs felt numb and lifeless, uncontrollable.

Glad cheers rang out among those gathered. Robert fell beside her, brushing her hair back from her face, rubbing her wrists, mumbling incoherent syllables of worry. She managed to smile weakly at him, and then at Henri, who stood above them looking as dignified as any proper judge.

Thank God for your interference. Anne sent the thought as directly to him as she always did to her Robert. To her surprise, he nodded and granted her the small ghost of a grin. She could see Edouard in his every feature, God love them both.

The sheriff turned to Sir Gui as though he had known the outcome all along. "Well, sir, are you satisfied? She is innocent, you see? She may, of course, bring a charge against you for witnessing falsely against her. Would you do so, my lady?" he asked, all business.

Anne was sorely tempted. But Sir Gui had only done as he thought right. Never mind that he could not have been more wrong, he was loyal to his lord, and all for seeing justice done. Now he merely looked aghast at what he had caused. Obviously, he held more belief in trial by ordeal than she ever had.

But then, mayhaps God *had* saved her, using Rob and Henri as His instruments. Who was she to question it?

"Nay, I will not charge him," Anne muttered angrily. She struggled to her feet with the lads' assistance. "Let us go home."

She pushed through the group of sheep-noggins who would have let her drown, and headed back to Baincroft to tend her husband. After enduring all this, she was damned if she would allow him to die.

Chapter Eleven

Despite the overly civilized dignity Edouard had exhibited during the first weeks Anne had known him, the man proved a beast of the lowest order when confined to bed.

Anne cursed the day he fell ill for more than one reason. True, it had nearly spelled her own doom, but that was the least of it. For two days after her acquittal, she had nursed him through the fever and remained at his side even when she could scarcely hold her eyes open to tend him. She had bathed his heated flesh, listened to invective wild enough to scorch her ears, and suffered several hard knocks when he thrashed about with night terrors. Now that he was out of danger and knew exactly what he was doing, his rantings annoyed her.

"Open your mouth and drink this, Edouard!" she ordered brusquely, holding the cup to his lips. "You'll get no pudding if you continue to refuse!"

"I am sick of the thrice-cursed *pudding!*" He shoved the potion aside. "And take this vile stuff away. It stinks like the pit of a garderobe! I am fine, I tell you."

"Child!" Anne accused, thoroughly sick of his petulance. She slammed the cup on the table with a savage thunk. "Die, then, and see if I care!" She plopped down in the chair beside the bed and covered her eyes with her hands.

To her horror, her entire body began to shake with great, gulping sobs. She poured forth all the anguish and misery she had not let loose in years. Unable to stop, she hugged herself and leaned forward, rocking, the keening sounds she made echoing through her head.

Suddenly arms surrounded her, holding her close. "Hush! Oh, Anne, do not do this! I will drink it! See? There, it is done. Delicious, I swear. For God's sake, will you stop weeping!"

Anne no longer cared that her wailing had gone beyond control, the release almost too heady to bear. Edouard shouted for Meg.

Through the blur of tears, she noted that he crouched beside her naked, his hands stroking her, trying to soothe.

"Cover yourself, my lord!" Meg ordered as she scurried in. "You'll catch your death and then what? We've six others down with your *poison* today, and all of them needing my attention."

"Oh, Meg, I am sorry," Anne moaned, now feeling foolish that her outburst had dragged Meg from her other duties. But even so, she felt lighter in heart for it.

"Put her to bed," Edouard ordered Meg sharply. "See she gets some rest. I do not want her in here again until she is completely well!"

Meg sniffed in disgust. "Until *you* are completely well, would be my wish! Will you return to your own bed or hang about naked, courting more fever? Men!" With that epithet, she practically shoved Anne from the master chamber and down the hall to her old room.

"You calm yourself now, my lady. I'll not have you sicken on us, too. That man of yours and the other sick folk below are trouble enough! I think I'd like to sit down and weep myself, come to think on it!"

Anne shrugged out of her wrinkled gown, grimacing at the soreness in her muscles. "Could you have someone bring a bath for me, Meg? I hate to ask it, but—"

"'Tis time you asked for something for yourself! I am heartily sick of seeing you wait upon that great hulk day and night! And him with that viperish tongue of his!" Meg retorted.

"Do not speak so of my husband!" Anne fussed, frowning, and then spoiled it all with a watery giggle. "He is awful, is he not?"

They laughed together, falling back against the high bed like giddy young maids. Anne threw out her arms, letting her legs dangle over the edge. "Ah, Meg. It makes no sense. Give me one reason why I should love that man."

Meg snickered. "He is rich?"

"And so arrogant about it!"

"Mannerly, then?"

"Oh aye, you see that!" Anne countered with a roll of her eyes. "So gallant I can hardly bear it!"

"And a devil in bed, I'll wager," Meg said with a sly grin.

"We have all witnessed *that* truth!" Anne said, chuckling.

"You know very well what I meant, and it wasn't his sickbed."

"Aye," Anne admitted. Then she sobered and sighed. "Oh, Meg, I am so afraid."

"Why, my lady? He is weak as a wee pup. For all his loud barking, there is no reason to fear him at the moment."

Anne turned her head so that she faced Meg. "My courses were due last week. I realized this morn that I may be increasing."

Meg sat up, her grin now a memory. "Oh *nay*! You did take the potion we prepared?"

"Aye, without fail. Well, *it* may have failed, but I did take it. Every day."

"But you have missed your time before, even when there was no chance you had conceived, when the old lord lay ill. Remember?"

Anne sighed. "So I did, but there was no other sign to worry me then. You saw how I fell into that fit of weeping just now."

Meg scoffed. "And small wonder at it. Look at all you have borne since that man came here! Aye, and even afore that with the MacBain. I trow, you've had great enough cause to greet for years now. And yet you rarely give way to it."

Anne shrugged and blew out a shuddery breath. "Not often. But remember when I quickened with Robert? Tears aplenty then. And I did feel ill when I woke today."

Meg groaned. "Oh, lady. What must we do?" She shifted restlessly on the edge of the bed and looked askance at Anne. "You would not—?"

"Nay," Anne said softly. "I would not. This child, if there is one, will be as cherished as my Rob. Even if I must cherish it beside the road while I beg for alms."

For a long time, they remained silent, each caught up in her own thoughts. Then Anne pushed up from the bed. "Go and see to my bathwater, would you, Meg? I must freshen myself and get back to my lord before he tosses his pudding out the window."

Edouard cursed the weakness and cough that continued to wrack his body on occasion. Otherwise, he felt well enough and was thankfully free of the fever and aches that had plagued him.

The near isolation would soon drive him mad, however. Were he able to give vent to his desire for Anne, he would enjoy having only her for company. Even though he could probably manage to pleasure them both, poor Anne appeared even more spent than he felt.

He needed some distraction. Some visitors. Other than his wife, few had been in to see him. Simm came and took care of his personal needs. Meg brought in her vile potions and his food, such as it was. Father Michael arrived each morning after Mass, offered a very brief prayer, and left.

As if in answer to his wish, someone scratched upon the door. "Enter, whoever you be!" he called out, desperate for conversation, a game, an argument, anything.

Sir Gui stuck his head through the opening as though he fully expected to be shooed out.

"Gui, come in, come in! God's nails, you are a welcome sight." Edouard pushed himself up against the pillows and held out his hand.

Hesitantly, Gui took his arm in greeting. "I thought you might not wish to see me, my lord."

"Do not act the fool, man, unless you have a proper jest," Edouard said in a hearty voice. "Sit down! Tell me all I have missed these past few days. Does Henri practice regularly? Has Robert begun yet? How goes the repair work?"

Gui avoided meeting Edouard's eyes. His voice remained wary. "The boys play at it, my lord. They do well enough from what I have observed. The walls are finished and the new gates up. All your goods arrived and are either in place or stored away until you are well enough to see to them."

Edouard sat forward, his arms resting on his upraised knees. "Are you turning ill as well, Gui? You do not sound yourself today."

Gui drew in a deep breath and expelled it. "I came to tell you what happened before someone else does." He sniffed, looking disdainful. "Though I'm certain *she* would prefer to be the first. Though she says not, it seems to me you are well enough to know now. And I would you heard all from me so you get the straight of it.''

"I take it you have had an altercation with my lady," Edouard said.

"I ordered a trial when you fell ill, my lord. I was certain she had given you poison."

Edouard stilled. So he had not dreamed that conversation. "And what sort of trial was it, Gui?" But he already knew.

They *had* meant to burn Anne. Nightmares about it had deviled him all during the fever. Since she had been here during his every waking moment but one, he had assumed it was but a feverish imagining. "Tell me," he ordered.

When the knight had finished the accounting and fell silent, Edouard dismissed him quietly. "Get out of this room."

Gui objected. "Even your lady does not hold me accountable. She knows very well I had good reason to suspect her! You cannot blame me for doing my—"

Edouard did not move as he leveled the man with a glare of hatred. "Go, before I kill you with my bare hands."

Now he understood why he had been allowed so few visitors, why the boys had not been admitted. Anne had thought to keep the truth from him so he would not be troubled. She must know very well that he would never have remained abed had he found out. Not until every last man jack who had the least to do with that travesty had been punished severely.

That bastard of a sheriff would hold that post no longer than it took Edouard to locate Robert Bruce. And sooner than that would Henri feel his wrath. To bind his new lady mother and throw her into a loch— To suspect her in the first place! He had never beaten Henri before. That would be rectified as soon as he could grasp a rod and find the little wretch.

No wonder that damned priest of hers had made himself so scarce! He would tear the man limb from limb for allowing that trial. Ordeal, indeed! None of them had seen the like of the *ordeal* they would suffer for this mockery.

"Aha! I see you have left your supper to grow cold!" Anne said as she swept into the chamber. "Do you wait for me to spoon it up? Very well—"

"Why did you keep the truth from me, Anne?" he demanded, swinging his legs over the side of the bed. He rose unsteadily and grasped the bedpost to keep from falling. "Why did you not tell me of the trial?" His head swam so, he had no choice but to sit down. His voice dropped to a grating whisper. "My God, you nearly died!"

She pulled up the chair and sat directly before him, her hands resting on his bare knees. "Sir Gui finally sneaked in and confessed, did he not? I could beat him for this!"

Edouard glared at her. "I will *kill* him for this!" He sighed with frustration. "As soon as I can."

She laughed. "That's a fine thank you for his loyalty! The man truly thought me a murderess. You looked dead after you emptied your belly and collapsed. Can you blame him for thinking as he did?"

"I shall do a damn sight more than *blame* him!"

Simm entered the chamber. "Sire, do you need my help?"

Edouard did, but he needed something else more. "Get my son. I wish to see him. Now!"

Anne placed her hand on his arm. "You are not to shout at Henri. If you only knew what he—"

"Silence! And stand over there. I will hear from his own lips what he did to you, not some pretty tale you've concocted to spare his backside."

Anne retreated, clutching her arms about her waist. She shook her head slowly and turned away toward the window. "Oh, Edouard."

"You called for me, Father? Oh, you are sitting up now!" Henri hurried forward and Edouard lashed out. The backhand blow sent his son reeling across the room. Clutching a fist to his mouth, the wide-eyed Henri turned and ran.

"Henri!" Edouard shouted. "Come back here!"

"You fool!" Anne cried. "You stupid fool! Could you not have listened?" Then she followed his son, calling out to him.

Edouard crawled back onto the bed and fell against the pillows, exhausted and sickened by what he had done. Other than infrequent swats to his nether cheeks for minor misbehavior, he had never struck his son. And even then, not in pure anger.

Never mind that Henri deserved the slap and more, it hurt Edouard sorely to chastise him. It hurt even more to know that he had failed to teach the boy that he must always protect women, no matter what you thought they had done. He felt like weeping as Anne had done earlier. A soul-deep cry to oust the sorrow from his gut.

She had returned. He knew before he saw her, before she spoke. Edouard closed his eyes and hoped his tears would not show, for he never wept. Never.

"You should be ashamed," she growled. "Were you not so ill, I would take a stick to you!"

He said nothing. What could he say? Anne cared for his son and he wanted that whether Henri merited it or not.

"Henri saved my life, Edouard," she said quietly. "He took control of the ordeal from the sheriff. Somehow he seemed to know what to do. He instructed me to force out all my air so that I would not float. With the ropes, he bound me in a position where I could not help but sink. He, with Rob's help, led us to a place on the loch where stones lay beneath the water, stones that they knew I could grasp and stay down. Had he not done so, I might well have been judged guilty and perished before you ever woke from your illness.''

''Oh, God,'' Edouard whispered, covering his eyes with his hand. ''What have I done?''

''Let that fever cook your brain, I think,'' she replied. ''Now when I bring him back here, you will make things right.''

''If ever I can,'' he promised.

But Henri did not return. Not that day or the next. He ignored all of Edouard's messages to him, be they requests or even pleas. He refused to see or speak to a father who would allow a son no hearing, a father who would strike him without just cause.

Edouard did not blame Henri in the least, for he had suffered the same himself for many years. He knew the feeling all too well. What little time they had spent together, his own father had been impossible to please, unwilling to grant the smallest hint of praise. Though the old comte had never been cruel to extreme, he had been quick to strike out. An unloving man obsessed by his quest for power and prestige.

As the day crawled by, the sad truth dawned. Edouard realized he had lost his son, that he had driven him away. Not away from Baincroft, for Henri had no other place to go and was bound by his oath as squire to remain. But the boy would never grant him the trust Edouard had enjoyed before. Regardless of their proximity, there would remain an unbreachable distance between them.

Anne had deserted him, as well. He would not demand that she come to him, partly because he thought she might refuse like Henri. He knew he had angered her with his treatment of his son, disillusioned her, probably made her afraid of him, as well.

This would not do. Edouard knew that he had to repair what he could within his family, even if it meant humbling himself. Humility had never been his strong suit, however. Point of fact, the quality was altogether foreign to his nature, and he wondered how to go about gaining it.

The next morning, Edouard quit his bed, arguing Meg's protest that he had not regained his strength.

"How am I to regain it if I lie here until I wither?" he asked. Though she dared to huff and shake her head over him, Edouard took heart from the fact that at least *she* seemed to care one way or the other.

He finished dressing himself and ventured down the stairs for the first time since he had fallen ill.

Someone had transformed Baincroft while he lay abed. His bright banners and exquisite tapestries enhanced the now painted walls of the hall. Polished boards on carved trestles had replaced the roughly hewn tables. He recognized two elegantly made chairs he had once commissioned for Morevin in Lorraine. The old lord's and lady's chairs, recently waxed to high shine, flanked the new. Gone were the primitive rushes, and the floor now gleamed damp from a recent scrubbing.

When he reached the bailey, he inspected more closely the renovations he had been able to see from his window and those he could not. After an exhausting hour-long tour of the place, Edouard felt satisfied that he had made a sizeable difference here. Once the bedchambers had been refurbished, no one would find fault with Baincroft.

Unless they noticed the attitude of its people. Some had offered a greeting when they could not avoid him, but he did not miss the sullen, underlying wariness. A few actually ran. He knew it was a direct result of what had happened between Henri and himself. They no longer regarded him as a just and reasonable lord.

Just then he spotted Sir Gui exiting the barracks. "Halt, Sir, I would speak with you," Edouard said as he strode toward the knight. Gui's overzealous bid for justice still infuriated Edouard, but he could not afford to hold this grudge. There was the long-standing oath between them, given and received in good faith.

"Yes, my lord?" Gui said carefully.

"Good God, I'm not about to ask you to fall on your sword. Straighten those shoulders. Have you seen my son?"

Gui braced himself. "He is in the bathhouse. We have just finished practice."

Edouard walked past him, unready just yet to mend the breach between them. He might never be, but he had already acted in haste once too often. Until his temper cooled, Edouard would not make this decision.

"Lord Trouville?" Gui asked as he passed. "Were your former words a final dismissal? Do you wish me quit of your service?"

"You have sworn to me," Edouard said evenly, not turning to speak directly. "You will stay."

He walked on, marking the sound of Sir Gui's heavy exhalation. Edouard wondered whether it signaled relief or disappointment.

The common bathing chamber was filled with several tubs and a fire hole to heat the water, a warm place conducive to camaraderie and relaxation. Edouard felt his muscles contract, in no way relaxed.

Robert, naked as a newborn, busily added a steaming bucketful to the large tub Henri occupied. When he had finished, the boy climbed in on the far side. Edouard felt a rush of pride in the promise of these coltish young bodies. They would grow into fine knights, fine lords, and he hoped, good men.

They both noticed him then. "Father," Henri said, his voice a clipped greeting, just short of surly.

Edouard decided he might as well have done with the business he had come for before tempers increased. "Henri,

I should have listened before administering punishment. The blow was unwarranted. Do you forgive me?''

"Yes," Henri said simply. It brought to mind Edouard's curt reply to Sir Gui.

"My thanks, then," Edouard replied, trying to bank his displeasure. He turned to Robert. "I hear you have begun your training at last. How do you fare with the sword?"

"He will be modest," Henri rushed to say, nodding with sudden enthusiasm. "But Rob excels!"

"In your opinion," Edouard commented dryly. "Is that so, Robert?"

"Aye!" Robert announced, and did so with a merry grin.

Edouard laughed. He could not restrain his delight, either in the boy's outrageous boast or in the first happy expression he had observed in far too many days.

He was still chuckling when he reentered the hall. So relieved was he that Henri had forgiven him, however reluctantly, that he almost stumbled into Anne. "Oho, have a care, my lady!" His hands reached out to steady her. "I was coming to find you, not to trample you!"

She stepped back, pulling out of his grasp. It was then he noticed her appearance. His wife looked as though she had been dragged through the swine pen. Though some of her gowns lacked the current style and rich trimmings, never once had he seen her attire or her person less than pristine. "You are dirty!" he commented.

"How perceptive you are, my lord," she said, throwing back her shoulders and raising her chin defensively.

"May I ask why?" he inquired, frowning. "A comtesse should not go about so." Surely he need not tell her that it was neither proper nor necessary under any circumstance.

Judging by the fire in her eyes and the way she pinched her lips together, she must have read his mind and taken offense. "I have been seeing to your *things*," she explained, her words terse.

"I see," he said, when he certainly did not. "My things."

"All of the so-called treasures with which you have *graced* my home!" She swept out an arm to encompass the refurbished hall.

"*Our* home," he replied none too kindly. "And I certainly never meant to inconvenience you. What is the problem with the *things?*"

She wilted visibly and allowed her arms to hang loosely by her side, her chin to rest upon her chest. "I tried to have all in readiness before you recovered and came down. The task proved larger than I imagined. We are not finished."

He placed one finger beneath her chin and raised it so that he could see her face. "Your eyes!" he exclaimed. There were deep purple circles beneath them. "And your hair!" It was covered with dust and looked rather lifeless. She had obviously been slaving like the veriest scullery drudge.

"Come with me!" he ordered, and all but dragged her toward the nearest chair. "Sit."

He shouted for a cup of wine. "Now tell me why you think it necessary to toil till you drop. We have all the time in the world to set Baincroft to rights. There is certainly no hurry, and I do have funds to hire additional help."

She brushed a wayward curl off her brow and sniffed. "You will not be content until everything is perfect around you. Above all, I would see you *content,* my good lord." Her sharp sarcasm stunned him to silence.

She pushed up from the chair. "Now if you will excuse me, I would go and make myself presentable so I do not offend your eye."

He watched her stride toward the stairs while he cursed his lack of tact. One of the first lessons he had ever learned in dealing with women was never to disparage one's looks.

Anne was likely right. That cursed fever must have

cooked his brain. Nothing he had done since awakening from it had been right. He seemed to have alienated every person within leagues of the place without so much as leaving his bed. Nor could he seem to make amends properly.

Edouard felt sorely tempted to return to that bed, sleep for several days, and hope that on awakening again, he would find this sorry state of affairs a horrid dream. How could matters have gone so blissfully at first and then degenerated into such disorder, near tragedy and confusion?

All that had gone wrong sprang from misunderstandings. Now that he had recovered and regained control of matters, he would set things aright. He was in charge here, after all.

Suddenly the convoluted workings of the French court seemed childishly simple by comparison.

Chapter Twelve

"He has ordered the barracks completely replaced, my lady!" Meg declared. "Says a larger one's in order. There's to be a new armory, as well. And he's bringing in a new smithy." She clicked her tongue. "Auld Tom's give out, I grant you, but what's he to do now? Herd sheep?"

"I will find Auld Tom some kind of employment. Tell him not to fret." She knew very well that Tom would never fret. Nor would he settle for another occupation. He would probably stalk off full of wounded pride and starve to death in the woods. She had never liked the smithy overmuch, but she would never have dismissed the man because of advancing age and surly ways.

Why could Edouard not accept people as they were? Could he not understand that everyone had foibles? Of course he could not. Therein lay all her problems bundled into one great mass.

Anne brushed a palm across her brow, wishing she could wipe away the ache in her head, an ache that seemed as permanent as Trouville's presence was proving to be. The man was wreaking havoc right and left, with Baincroft, with her peace of mind and especially with her heart.

He never made mention of leaving, even for a brief sojourn to tend his other properties. A part of her longed for the day when his king would recall him to France and give her a rest from this worry and necessary deceit.

Yet another, softer part of her yearned for a miracle to occur. She wished Edouard would suddenly acquire an acute and incurable case of tolerance. But it appeared that the longer he remained at Baincroft, the more determined he became to make everything matchless, impeccable, flawless.

His zeal frightened her. There were some things not even his wealth and steel determination could repair. Whenever he discovered those things, he discarded them without a second thought.

She leaned over the edge of the new holding pond and watched the trout swirling about in their temporary home. Meg fished another out with her net. Anne admitted some of Edouard's improvements, like this one, made life more convenient. But whenever he lessened work in one area, he demanded more in another.

The clang of steel across the bailey proved the point. Were it not for this over-full pond he had stocked in one day with huge nets manned by every available hand, the lads might be out fishing now. They could be enjoying this beautiful day on the bank of the burn, while providing food for the table. Instead, they slaved and sweated under his direction, absorbing the hard and hazardous lessons of warfare.

He drove Henri, Robert, and especially Sir Gui to absolute exhaustion every morning during their weapons training. They and the other men in his service never complained, but Anne saw no use in it. 'Twas not as though war was imminent and they needed such intense preparation.

The fact that Edouard also did not spare himself counted

for little. The man seemed driven, and heart-set on driving everyone else before him at like pace.

The sight of this husband of hers, naked to his waist, muscles rippling, his sun-browned skin glowing with a sheen of sweat, pricked her with an unwanted frisson of desire. Damn the man, did he have to display himself so?

She had held fast to her anger over his striking Henri that day. Edouard surprised her by permitting her to continue sleeping apart from him. He had asked only once if she would return to his bed. Her curt nay and his single nod had settled the matter.

That he had not troubled to argue about it only increased her ire. He might have insisted. That had been a fortnight ago and since that time, he had not offered a single longing look in her direction. So much for the charms she had hoped would soften his heart. If he even *had* a heart.

Mayhaps things had worked out for the best in that instance, however. She knew for certain now that there would be another child. Edouard might have noticed the changes in her body, however slight, for there was little that he missed.

Thank God one of the things he did miss was the fact that Robert could not hear him. Henri's diligence in preventing that surpassed even her own.

Anne could not help feeling that a huge sword hovered just above her head. Edouard would find out. Eventually he would discover her pregnancy, and Robert's secret as well. Unless he left here. She hoped that he planned to leave soon, and that his present fervor in perfecting Baincroft signaled his intention to do so. And yet, she would mourn his absence. She felt torn.

Sword practice ended as she watched. Sir Gui, two other of the men and Robert headed for the old barracks to clean and stow the weapons. Edouard had handed off his sword to Henri, pulled on his shirt and made directly for her.

Rarely had she seen her husband so disheveled, so hot, exhausted and ungroomed. The last time had been when he lay near death with that fever. Edouard prided himself on his appearance. His coming to her before making himself presentable told Anne that this would be no casual conversation. He looked upset.

"Good morn, my lord," she said as he approached.

His lips, pressed in a firm line, confirmed the fact that something had gone awry. He dismissed Meg with a pointed look, and only when she was out of earshot, did he return his formidable regard to Anne.

"Robert resents me," he declared without preamble.

"What? Oh, surely you are mistaken!" Lord, what had Rob done now?

Edouard blew out an angry breath, wiped his forehead on one sleeve, and looked at her accusingly. "If he would be forthright about it, I could understand and grant him that right, but he is not."

"What do you mean?" she asked. "Rob is never sneaking. What has happened?"

Edouard began to pace back and forth, obviously very troubled to abandon his usually calm and unaffected demeanor. "He ignores me completely at times. When he does deign to listen, he smiles sweetly as a saint. Then he acts completely contrary to my orders. When I correct him, he nods and says aye. Always *aye*! He mocks me, Anne, and I will not have it!"

Anne found she could not breathe, much less speak. How could she explain this?

Apparently, he required no explanation and only wished to rail at her. He pounded one fist into the other palm. "What have I done to warrant this, I ask you? Is it that he hates my taking MacBain's place here? Does he feel himself disloyal to his father? He called *me* his father once.

Freely he did so, do you recall? Why would he do that if he does not wish me to be?"

Anne could swear he sounded more hurt than angered. What could she say to him? Robert liked him very well, admired him greatly, and had never shown a jot of animosity. Not likely she would be able to convince Edouard of that now, given Rob's unintentional behavior. And if she explained the truth of the matter, all would surely be lost.

He continued, running his hands through his sweat-soaked hair. "Anne, I must ask you. Have you communicated your feelings toward me to Robert? Have you set him against me because of your own hatred? If so, I warn you that you do him no favor!"

Anne's mouth dropped open. "Edouard! I do not *hate* you! I never have. What foolish talk is this?"

He smirked. "You made clear that you do not want me. I know my actions toward Henri that day overset you, but it is more than that, is it not? Because of my sudden illness, you nearly died. You hold me accountable for that trial. Aye, I can understand that, and I do not fault you for thinking as you do. But I am doing all that I can to compensate." He threw out his arm, a sweeping gesture meant to point out all the improvements visible. "What more may I do to satisfy you, eh?"

"Edouard, listen—"

But he would not. "All I ask is that you allow Robert to form his own thoughts, Anne. Do not require him to echo your disaffection for me. Do not make him choose. It is not fair, not to him or to me!"

"I have not!" she declared. "If you will but heed me, Edouard, I would tell you that Robert does not hate you, nor do I! My ordeal was none of your doing. How could you help falling ill, or what happened after when you were insensate? True, your unfairness to Henri angered me, but

I know you struck before thinking it through. Every parent has done such at one time or another.''

''Ha!'' he replied, turning away and kicking a rock into the pond. ''I can just see you cuffing your Robert, all undeserved! I doubt me he has ever suffered so much as a thump of your pretty finger!''

Anne wished heartily that she could tell him all Robert had suffered, undeserved. Not at her hand, surely, but at MacBain's. Edouard would quail at hearing it.

She took a deep breath and said the only thing she could to bring an end to the matter for now. ''I will speak to Robert, Edouard. I do beg your patience.''

He nodded, refusing to look at her. ''Do you mean it when you say you have no hatred left?''

''I told you I never felt hatred. Only anger, which has since dissolved.''

''Then you will return to my bed. Tonight,'' he ordered, calmer now. Or mayhaps pretending to be. She thought she saw a flicker of uncertainty in his eyes, and a sudden gentleness in his voice softened the command.

''Very well,'' she said. Anne wondered why she did not feel any anger at this manipulation of his, for surely that is what it was. That might not have been his intent from the beginning of the conversation, for Anne felt certain his worry about Robert was real. But Edouard would never let an opportunity to have his way slip by him.

She admitted her anticipation in letting him have his way this time. Though it made no sense to court disaster by allowing him to reestablish their closeness, she could not summon any regret that it would happen. It was early yet for him to notice that she might be increasing with his child. He might even tire of her and leave before she began to show any outward signs.

''Tonight,'' she confirmed.

He strode away then without another word to her. Judging by his bearing as he did so, one would never guess the great comte de Trouville had ever experienced a troubling thought. She had to admire his aplomb, once he got it in place. The man thought he had fixed matters for all and good now.

If he would only realize that some things were beyond his control, beyond anyone's help. Anne shook her head sadly.

She would be a wife to him again, and for that, she could not deny her eagerness. If she applied herself, she might offer enough diversion that he would forget his problems with Robert.

If Edouard finally decided that all was well here, everything settled and repaired to his satisfaction, he might feel content to return to more important matters in France. As a devoted helpmate, one concerned for all her husband's far-reaching duties and responsibilities, could she not logically suggest such a move? She could, of course, and it would pain her greatly. Anne wanted him fiercely, and forever. But she could not have him that way. Why must life be so unfair?

That evening when they gathered to dine, Baincroft's new splendor did nothing to lift Edouard's mood. The new look of the place might stir awe in its simple folk and praise from his own retainers, but it only reminded Edouard of how other things had changed. And those things, not for the better.

Robert served at table with a care worthy of any well-trained page at court. As the younger squire, he had taken Henri's place at this duty until some future fosterling became junior to him. Edouard had noticed no fault in Robert's execution of this task, and so he applied courtesy and praise as he always did when merited. "Thank you, Robert. Well done of you."

The boy still wore that same bright and eager expression he had last Edouard saw him. No chagrin, no apologetic bowing of the head to indicate he had played his game too far.

"Wine, m'yowd?" Robert asked as he lifted the flagon.

Edouard glared at him. "How many times must I repeat it? It is my *lord*, Robert. Say it correctly." Anne tensed beside him and turned to interfere. He clamped a hand on her arm to warn her to silence. The boy would mock him no further. "Say my *lord!*"

Robert's eyes had widened as he fastened his gaze on Edouard's mouth. "My," he repeated obediently. Then he stuck his tongue to the top of his upper lip and blared, "Laud!" Then he laughed. The little bugger laughed as though he had uttered some proud jest. Edouard wanted to throttle him soundly.

"Get you to your chamber!" Edouard ordered, keeping his voice low when he wanted to shout. "Go. Now. I will deal with you later."

Anne made noises of concern, but he ignored her. Henri jumped up from his place to fill the void as well as Edouard's wine cup. Edouard placed his hand over the container and dismissed his son as well. "Go and tell Robert the penalty for mocking one's lord. He might heed you, for obviously he did not believe it when I warned him! God's teeth! What am I to do?"

"I've told you he has trouble with English, Edouard!" Anne declared. "He was not mocking you, I swear. That was pride in himself you heard. Rob only thought he had accomplished what you asked and he was glad!"

"Hmmph, a likely tale."

"'Tis true!"

Edouard released the angry breath he had drawn and with it, most of his anger. In its place fell disappointment and frustration. "Anne, I am at a loss here. You were to aid me in bringing Robert around."

She drew her palm along his arm, a gesture of comfort which should have done no good at all. Still, that touch, her sweet floral scent, and the timbre of her voice did erase some of his hopelessness.

If nothing else, he might count on putting the problem aside for a little while. She looked willing enough to cosset him a bit. But was she so amenable for his sake or for her son's? A foolish wondering, that, for if he were honest, Edouard knew very well why.

"Come to our chamber and put aside this worrying," she suggested. "Tomorrow all will seem better."

All the way up the stairs he had considered the events of the day as objectively as he could. Something was not right about it all. Something had not been right since he had fallen ill, possibly even before that time.

He could see it in the eyes of everyone who looked at him and then hastily looked away. Even Anne had done that at times. The only one who did not was Robert, who gave him guileless smiles, and then flouted his orders. Something was definitely amiss. But for the life of him, he could not divine what it might be.

Only when he had closed the door to their chamber did Edouard take up their conversation.

"Henri has not forgiven me, either," he said. "There is a look about my son that I have not seen before, guilt mixed with defiance. One or the other, he has offered up in plenty over the years, but never both at once. I confess it bothers me."

When she said nothing, he went on. "And Robert clearly taunts. You must know I shall have to remedy that."

"Forget the lads for now," she suggested softly as she sidled near and trailed a finger down his sleeve. "Surely you are too tired to trouble yourself tonight."

He pushed past her and took a seat before the cold fireplace, avoiding the bed so that he would not forget his need to discuss their sons' behavior.

"Hear me well, Anne. There may come another day when Robert thinks to amuse himself at the expense of a man thrice his size. For his own good, I need to disabuse him of the notion that he can do so and live to laugh about it."

She drifted around behind him and placed her small hands on his neck, her thumbs circling the muscles at his nape. In spite of his determination to remain stern, he allowed his head to tilt backward and lean against her. Her hands moved magically enough to melt his bones.

Edouard knew he must have his say here, however. She would hear it all and understand. The sensual movement of her palms and fingertips prevented his speaking sharply, but he would speak.

"Anne, You heard him tonight. Do not mark this up to a boyish prank. Such could well get him killed. For all intent and purpose, I am his father now. It is up to me to point out the error of his ways."

"Such a good father," she crooned, her voice flowing over him like warm honey. "And husband." He felt her reinforce the last whispered words with a particularly deep thumb stroke to his shoulders. The back of his scalp tingled where it rested in the valley between her breasts. She had such lovely breasts.

Her essence surrounded him, that subtle fragrance of wild jasmine, changed, sweetened by the unique scent of Anne herself. A heady mix that drew him under her spell as surely as a witch's charm.

Desire surged through his veins. He knew very well what she was about here. She meant to divert him, capture him within a web of longing that would dispel any thoughts save those of her and what they might do together. And her attempts were proving so wildly successful, Edouard could have laughed at his total lack of defense. Of a sudden, he cared for nothing except her hands upon him, the images they evoked, her body beneath him, her sweet voice in his ear.

Yet he did not move to take her and end the wondrous torment she aroused. Her hands slid upward, fingers threading through his hair, caressing, making his mind a near blank that immediately filled with further lust-filled imaginings.

Light as the brush of a moth's wing, her fingertips traced his brows, his eyelids, and feathered down his face to cup his chin. Then she leaned over him, her lips brushing his, her tongue offering a tentative invitation.

"You provoke me, lady," he murmured against her mouth as he tried to capture it for a deeper kiss.

"Sufficiently?" she asked, teasing unmercifully with small biting nips.

"Quite," he answered, capturing one of her hands and drawing her around in front of him. He took her lips with his as he fumbled with the laces at the sides of her gown. She broke the kiss and stepped away. Edouard opened his eyes, wondering if she meant to deny him now. He could not allow that. Not in the state he was in.

But no, she only meant to torture him more. His eyes grew heavy-lidded, hungry for her, as she drew off her cotta. The woven net that held her hair came loose as she removed the gown, allowing a dark spill of silken waves to surround her.

Edouard's hands ached to slide through the mass of it, to wrap it around his fists and draw her near again. But he waited, even more eager to see her disrobe and give him more to touch when they did come together.

She pulled the long chemise from her shoulders and allowed it to slide to a snowy pool about her ankles. The graceful movement of her legs as she stepped out of it nearly destroyed his will not to haul her against him and take her right there in the chair.

He groaned low in his throat when she knelt before him, the cape of her hair covering most of her as she tugged off his boots. Her palms slid up his leggings beneath his tunic and plucked at the points tied to his waist. Edouard's hands gripped the chair arms. "I'll never go the distance if you do not cease this play," he warned in a grating whisper.

She glanced up at him, those dark gray eyes full of promise. "Then we shall plan a second journey where you may finish with distinction."

Edouard gave himself up to her then, let her do as she would, and savored every instant as she undressed him.

He admired the bounce of her breasts as she went about the endeavor, their pert peaks already tightened without so much as a touch from him. She knew he watched her, for she tossed her hair back behind her to give him a greater view of her charms.

Edouard sighed loud and long, hoping against hope for endurance. She deserved her measure of satisfaction for these efforts. Still, he did not move to provide it now, unwilling to relinquish the dizzying pleasure she was wreaking on him.

He stood when she rose so that she could completely divest him. When she had, he opened his arms, waiting and beyond ready.

Anne smiled up at him, a bewitching display of dimples and daring, and moved slowly into his embrace. Edouard lifted her against him and closed his eyes, the better to feel her soft warmth. Holding her fast, he carried her to their bed and laid her down upon the rich coverlet.

For a long moment, he stood above her, treasuring the knowledge that Anne belonged to him and he to her. Neither spoke as he lowered himself so that they fit together.

Her groan of welcome proved enough to ignite the urgent fire within him. No longer could he deny the passion he'd kept banked for weeks. No longer could he direct his movements to ensure her surcease. And no longer could he hold back that which she demanded of either his body or his soul.

He gave everything he was and with all his will and energy, barely knowing or caring when she gave back full measure. They surged together again and again until her harsh cry against his ear spurred a release so intense, he lost both breath and mind in the maelstrom.

The power of it left him a deadweight pressing her into the softness of the bed. When reason returned, he wondered if he would ever move again.

But he must move. Anne lay gasping. He felt her weep, a hot wetness against his shoulder. Only with the greatest exertion did he shift to one side, first sliding one hand beneath her to keep them joined. He wanted them to stay so, though he had no real purchase within her now, spent as he was.

"Anne, love," he whispered, grazing her damp cheek with his lips, absorbing her tears with his lips.

"Shh. Sleep now," she said, her words little more than a sibilant sigh drawing him down into the beckoning darkness.

Chapter Thirteen

Edouard woke to midmorning sun shining through the window and the delicious sensation of soft limbs entwined with his own. Anne snuggled even closer and sighed contentedly as she began to stir. Nothing short of an attack on the keep could have dragged him from the bed at that point, no matter the lateness of the hour.

If he had thought himself too spent to love her further, his body assured him he was not. And hers seemed to agree. He smiled lazily as the lovely rose peaks of her breasts gave evidence of her arousal. Slowly she slid one silken leg down the length of his and sighed. Her delicate, womanly scent stirred him to an urgency he found amazing considering how fulfilled he should be feeling after last night's delicious encounters.

Several slow caresses later, he found her eagerness matched his own. Without any pretense of shyness, Anne urged him over and into her sweetness as naturally as wishing him good morning.

He loved her slowly, drawing out her pleasure and his own, until she arched beneath him and cried out softly. Even at the moment he poured himself into her, Edouard knew this time was different, more like a communion of souls. He felt at one with Anne, as near pure happiness as he had ever felt in his life.

Though tempted to relish their repletion and remain abed long into the day, Edouard forced himself to leave her there curling into the covers, eyes closed and smiling with contentedness. There would be tonight and every night hereafter.

He carried that image of her in his head throughout the morning as he went over Simm's accounts for Baincroft and the tally for Anne's adjoining lands. He could scarcely concentrate.

When he joined her for midday meal, her languorous look almost prompted him to ask her to go with him above stairs. But he did not. She must be exhausted, and in truth, so was he.

Instead, he bestowed a lingering kiss on her hand and promised them both that he would follow through the moment their door closed this evening. The marriage business was proving delightful this time around.

Edouard congratulated himself yet again on choosing Anne to wed. His heart nearly stopped each time he recalled how near he had come to losing her.

That evening Edouard allowed Anne's request to be excused. She promptly joined Meg at sewing after the meal had been cleared away. Her come-hither look told him that she meant to prolong his anticipation of the night's events. Two could play that game, he thought with a suggestive smile in her direction.

He had not forgotten the unfinished business that had preceded their lovemaking last night. They certainly needed to speak more on the matter of Robert's disrespect, but Anne seemed too distracted to pay much mind to anything he had to say about that now.

He hesitated to provoke an argument over it when everything else between them had resolved itself overnight.

Better if he left her for a while to the mundane things in which women found such interest. Embroidery, tedious as it appeared to him, must renew a woman's energies. He could not think why else they would choose to spend so blessed much time at it.

He watched the women settle comfortably beside the low-burning fire, frames upon their laps, heads inclined toward their busywork.

The hall did lend itself to such endeavors now that all the improvements had been made, Edouard thought with satisfaction. There was not the usual chill that, even in summer, sent everyone to smaller and more easily heated enclosures once the evening's meal was done.

How companionable it all seemed. None of the bustle of the court, no royal tempers to placate, no intrigues afoot. Just a home where he could feel free to be himself and enjoy life for a change.

There was the problem with Robert, of course, but even that did not dim Edouard's contentment at the moment. He would be patient and the boy would come to like him sooner or later.

Sir Gui approached, limping slightly, and slid into the chair Anne had vacated. "May I join you?" He set down his cup of ale and filled Edouard's empty one from the nearby flagon.

Many an evening they had spent just so before they had come to this place, Edouard thought. No more.

He looked pointedly at Gui's bandaged leg as the knight stretched it out before him.

Gui shrugged. "That wretched beast of mine threw me this morning. Your healer says the leg's not broken, though it pains me like a break."

As though he cared. Edouard still felt like breaking both Gui's legs. And his head as well.

"A game of gammon, what say?"

His mind occupied fully with Anne, Edouard had no desire to play at games, at least not with one of his knights. And especially not with this one.

Though Gui had served him faithfully for two years, Edouard could not oust from his mind what this man had almost done to Anne. He knew he needed to put the incident behind them, for he was sworn lord to this man. Before this happened, he had always liked Gui well enough. The man was sometimes pompous, and always ambitious. Most landless knights were, and Edouard did not fault him for that. However, Gui's accusation and Anne's near death stood as squarely between them as a thick stone wall.

"I am in no mood for gammon," Edouard answered honestly.

"Chess, then?" Gui tried again.

"No."

"You are still angry with me," Gui stated, his sandy brows drawing together in an irritated frown.

Edouard nodded. "The matter is too fresh, Gui. Leave it be if you are wise."

The knight bristled with resentment. He rose from the chair and shoved it back. "This is not fair of you, and I have always known you to be a just man. I did what anyone sworn to you would have done! I only thought to avenge you, as I hope you would do for me in like circumstance! You should be grateful!"

"*Grateful?* You nearly killed my wife," Edouard growled, his voice low and fraught with warning. "Leave me now and speak no more of it, lest words are said we cannot retract!"

"I repeat, I did no knowing wrong. You will not dismiss me like an errant page!"

When Gui moved into a defensive stance, Edouard stood to face him, one hand clutching the hilt of his sword.

For a few tense moments they glared at each other. Then

Gui spoke. "This cursed place has changed you. That woman has changed you more. You are becoming exactly like these people, using their crude and ugly speech, taking on their ways. It sickens me to see it. They make you question my loyalty at every turn!"

Edouard could hardly contain his fury, both at Gui for ignoring his warning, and with himself for his inability to absolve his man. Even so, he might have held his temper had Gui not persisted with the unforgivable.

"Will you break our bond, my lord? Over a puling *woman?*"

Edouard's next words, though deadly calm, carried throughout a hall that had fallen quiet to listen to the two. "Leave this keep, Sir Guillaume. Return to France or wherever you will. We are quit of one another as of this moment."

Anne rushed to the dais, her embroidery clutched in one hand, her other outstretched toward him. "Oh, Edouard, nay! I beg you do not! Sir Gui only—"

"Silence, Anne. This does not concern you."

She looked as though she might dispute that, but managed to keep her tongue still. Her eyes spoke volumes, however.

He marked disappointment, regret and not a little fear. Edouard tried to ignore her, training his eyes on Sir Gui's angry, slow-gaited exit from the hall.

Then he reached for the pouch of gold he wore at his belt and counted out twelve coins. "Henri? To me," he shouted.

Henri stepped forward from where he had been standing behind Edouard's chair. He had overheard everything, of course, judging by his frown.

"Yes, Father?"

"Take this coin to Sir Gui in the stables. Tell him that is his wage through Michaelmas."

Henri nodded. "Father, I would like to say—"

"Take it *now*," Edouard commanded, "and do not presume to argue with me!"

"No, sire," Henri said with a shrug. "I would not presume." Though he dared a last questioning glance, he hurried to obey.

Edouard wondered if he would ever again obtain obedience from anyone without an objection.

"That *did* concern me, did it not? Now that knight who was your friend is broken, cast out, and I am the reason." Anne's anguished whisper broke through his haze of anger.

"Do not speak foolishness, Anne. Sir Gui is gone because he lacks proper judgement. He is even more careless with his tongue than with that mount of his. I will not have about me a knight bereft of good sense. Sound riddance, and there is the end of it, do you hear?"

"I hear you well, my lord," she murmured and quickly retreated to the fireside to resume her sewing.

Now he had done it. She might be soundly frightened into submission or angry as hell now, and he had no way of knowing which.

It hardly mattered in the scheme of this night's plans. There would be no warmth in their bed when he reached it. None at all. He might understand little of a woman's mind, but he knew well enough that neither fury nor fear stimulated a female's desire to pleasure her mate. Edouard admitted that was not all he regretted. He did not like to see the guilt in Anne's eyes, especially when an act of his had put it there.

There were two choices here, as he saw it. He could apologize for his burst of choler, recall the knight and reinstate him. Or he could explain fully to Anne what had caused the uproar so that she could understand his reasoning. But apologies and explanations were so foreign to Edouard's nature and experience, he feared he would make hash of either one. And his rage had not calmed enough yet to try to change any ingrained habits.

Long after Anne and all the others had retired, Edouard sat at the high table, lost in his thoughts. How could everything turn so sour in but a few moments? In one instant, he had felt supremely confident that nothing could overset his newfound serenity. Now here he sat, despised. All he had ever wanted was the peace he had hoped this exile would bring.

The price of repairing matters would be humility, of course. He could send someone after Gui. The knight might return if he believed himself forgiven. But Edouard suspected that Gui's desire to quit Scotland lay behind his actions, both in accusing Anne of poisoning, and in tonight's inevitable encounter.

The man had always held this country and its people in low regard, especially Anne. He had been suspicious of her from the very beginning, willing to believe the worst of the foul rumors about MacBain's death.

Had he used the opportunity of Edouard's sudden sickness to try to get rid of their main reason for remaining here? A truly unconscionable act, and not worthy of a knight.

Even if Gui really believed Anne guilty of attempted murder, he certainly had left little to chance in the way of confirming it.

If only Edouard had explained to his men why he was leaving France in the first place, Gui might have made his preference clear then and remained there. He could well have served Edouard in some other capacity. But a knight followed his lord without question. And a lord should keep his own counsel, should he not?

All things considered, he knew he could not retract his banishment of Gui. Pride had little to do with it, Edouard decided. Even if he did bring himself to offer Gui reconciling words, they would be empty of meaning. An outright lie. He would always remember that Anne nearly met a horrid death on that man's orders. Nothing would change that, and nothing could make Edouard forgive it or forget it.

He could try to make Anne understand, but she would still feel guilt over this. Even if he explained exactly what was in his mind and heart that caused him to turn away the closest thing he had to a friend, she still would feel responsible.

He and Gui had not shouted the whole of their conversation, so Anne could not have heard but the last outburst, the dismissal. It might be best if he could make her believe that they had quarreled over another matter, one that had nothing at all to do with her.

When he had decided what that would be, Edouard made his way up the dark stairs to try to mend what Gui had thrown asunder.

The next morning, Anne's supposed confession to Father Michael held outrage rather than contrition. They sat side by side in a small alcove just inside the chapel, more like the friends they were than priest and penitent.

"I tell you, he broke faith with his man simply because Sir Gui may have permanent injury to his leg!"

The priest clicked his tongue, a sound of resignation. "Well, I suppose we shall miss that knight's saintly posturing, won't we!"

Anne rolled her eyes and huffed. "Sir Gui is no favorite of mine, as you well know, but casting him out is the act of a harsh lord, indeed! Do you not see the implications of this? First, he slew poor Rufus because of infirmities, then he threw out our smithy because of his age. Now, he cuts all ties with a knight who has served him faithfully, all due to a damaged limb! I shudder to think what might happen to the rest of us.''

Father Michael nodded and reached over to pat her hand. ''Robert, you mean.''

''Aye, Robert! But not only him. Now everyone seems at peril. Lord help us, Trouville will sweep Baincroft clean of all its people, do they not fit his notion of excellence! What must we do here?''

''Point out some fault of his, so that he might understand the failings of others?'' he suggested.

''Has he a fault?'' she asked, her words rife with sarcasm.

The priest grinned. ''So say you. He is intolerant. He is arrogant. He is ill-tempered. And unjust.''

She threw him a jaded look. ''He is a man. Those are not faults, but merely traits!''

''How your words wound!'' he returned, tongue-in-cheek. Anne could hear the amusement in his voice as he continued. ''Though my Meg would likely agree with you on all counts.''

''Be serious this once.''

He nodded and smiled. ''Aye, you are right. 'Tis no jesting matter. But, my lady, your husband and our lord has shown you nothing but kindness since he came here. Whenever he looks upon you, one cannot help but see he cares deeply. If you ask me, I believe he sent Sir Gui on his way because of that man's hasty judgement of you and the ordeal you had to endure as a result.''

''He says not. I assumed that was the reason at first, but he denied it. And if that were so, why did he not do this immediately after it happened? Why should he lie to me about it now?''

''I cannot say.''

''What can I do?'' she asked, pleading for answers she knew Father Michael did not have. He would tell her to pray, of course. She did so much of that, her knees were bruised and God must be heartily sick of her voice by now. She grasped his slender hand. "Other than prayer," she clarified.

"Strive for perfection?" he suggested with a grin.

She flung his hand away from her. "Wretch. Trouville will likely get rid of you for lack of piety! He already questioned your right to a wife. Did so the first day he was here."

Michael sighed. "And he was right to do so. My marriage is against all the Church teaches. But you know the reason behind it, and that I could have done no differently. I love Meg and our children. If my soul is in peril, then that is my concern and God's. We have made our peace with it. Should his lordship not accept that, then we shall leave when he says we must. Thus far, he has not berated me or Meg about it."

"Probably because he does not know you are wed to *her*. Oh, he knows you have a wife, but since he has not seen you paired together with a woman, he has probably forgotten. He sounded surprised when I mentioned you had a wife, but then he said no more about it. You need not worry, really. I only said that to tease you. He does not care one way or the other."

Father Michael remained in quiet thought for a moment. "Could it be that his lordship is not so intolerant as you believe, Anne?"

She shook her head sadly. "Aside from ignoring—or more likely forgetting—your marital status, I am afraid his actions do speak for themselves."

He shifted, folded his hands together, and assumed a more dignified position on the bench they shared. "Well, I doubt we shall solve this tangle today, and you are here to confess. It is near time for Mass and we should get on with it."

Anne stood up. "Go ahead and make ready, then. I've nothing else to bother you with this morn."

"Not even an impure thought?" he asked innocently.

Anne felt her face heat with a blush, and quickly turned away from him.

"Go in peace, my child," he intoned solemnly. She did not need to see the twinkle in his eyes to know it was there.

Anne wandered back through the hall, mingling with the others who were gathering for Mass. She had left Trouville asleep earlier. He had come late to bed, and his explanation about Gui's dismissal had kept them both awake even later. Neither had made any overtures toward intimacy after that. She had been too worried, and he had seemed somehow weary.

Now she saw that he had arrived downstairs and was engaged in earnest conversation with Meg.

As she drew near enough to hear their voices, he turned to greet her with a smile. "Ah, here she is now! Good morn, my lady."

"My lord," she answered. "I thought you might sleep through the morning's service."

He inclined his head toward Meg. "I was just thanking our esteemed healer for her good care of us, and telling her how fortunate we are to have her. Why did you not tell me that Margaret is Simon of Oldfield's daughter? I know him well and have for years! A good knight and worthy opponent on the field, though I believe he has retired his sword by now."

Anne prevaricated. "I did not believe it would be of interest to you." She shot a questioning look at Meg. Whyever had Meg told him about her father? And why had she given him her full name? No one ever called her Margaret anymore. Edouard had charmed her, that was it. He had entirely too much charm for his own good. Rather, for theirs.

Edouard smiled at them in turn. "Oh, but it is of great interest! I shall have to write to Simon and extend an invitation to visit us."

Meg's hand flew to her mouth, probably to stifle a cry of protest.

"Nay, do not do that!" Anne advised him, realizing belatedly that she must give the reason. He would know soon enough, and it would be best if she did not seem to make any great secret of it. Lord knew she had enough to conceal already.

He probably would not cause trouble about it. Especially if she gave him the very excellent reason it had happened in the first place. "Sir Simon did not sanction her marriage. He and Meg are estranged."

Edouard frowned with disbelief. "Did not sanction it? But how can that be?" He turned to Meg. "What is the circumstance that caused defiance of so worthy a father? Or were you wed by force? Where is this husband of yours?"

"Later," Anne promised. "'Tis time for Mass."

"Nay!" Edouard demanded. "I would hear it now."

Meg opened her mouth to speak, but Anne silenced her. "I shall tell him myself."

She glared up at Trouville, daring him not to understand. "This will be brief, so do not interrupt me. Margaret was fostered here with my husband's first wife not long before the poor woman died. When MacBain decided the young lady would make a winsome addition to his bed, Father Michael did the only thing he could do to protect her. He married her, and threatened my husband with eternal damnation if he so much as touched a hair of her head. There you have it." She turned away and started for the chapel door.

"Wait a moment!" Edouard said, stepping in front of

her. He motioned for Meg to continue on her way before he asked, "Married her to whom?"

"To himself. Rather, he had an itinerant priest do it."

"But why?"

"I told you, to protect her!" Anne explained again. "None of us knew where to find Sir Simon."

"There were convents, surely!"

"Aye, but all of Scotland was in turmoil then, and travel unsafe, no one to offer her escort. Michael was the only one left here of suitable rank to wed her. He also knew that my husband feared for his soul, and threatened MacBain with damnation for adultery if he touched her. Michael saved her. It is that simple."

Trouville still wore a look of incredulity. "But he is a *priest,* a man of God!"

Anne nodded sagely. "And closely related to King Robert. So do not mistake him for one you can deny his living without dire consequences!" With that, she stepped around him and went inside to take her customary place for the service.

She knew she tread a thin line here. True, Michael was related to the king. But not beloved of either Bruce or the man who had fathered him. Michael's family had thrust him into a monastery before he was old enough to protest. In fact, before he was old enough to know any other kind of life. He was given to the church in penance for Neil Bruce's sins, and had little choice but to take vows the moment he reached the age to do so.

The fact that he was still a priest had nothing to do with any call to God or inclination in that direction. But he'd been trained to it, knew nothing else, and was reluctant to break any more of his vows than necessary. Anne respected that.

All through the mass, as Edouard stood beside her, she could feel his consternation. She should never have told him. There would be repercussions from this and they would likely happen as soon as Michael had issued the benediction.

Anne had a horrible feeling that everything would come to a head on an issue she had thought inconsequential. To think, she had centered all her fears on Robert's fate and hers. How remarkably selfish she had been these past weeks.

Lord, she wished Edouard would find some tolerance. Most of Baincroft's inhabitants might soon find themselves eking out a living in the nearby forest, while her righteous husband sat wondering where he could find other folk without any flaws to people his new keep.

Edouard paid little attention to the Mass. He stood or knelt when everyone else did, but his mind leapt from problem to problem. This whole new life he had made for himself seemed to be unraveling like a poorly done weaving. His closeness to Anne, Robert's regard of him, his son's affection, were precious threads that had come apart at the touch.

He probably had not convinced Anne that she had nothing to do with Gui's leaving. Now, in addition to that guilt, she worried that he would dismiss her priest and her friend because she had told him of their marriage.

God only knew what Robert thought to accomplish by that merry insolence of his. Even Henri was becoming a stranger to him instead of the dutiful son and squire.

Though these issues presented enough worry, he felt some other thing eluded him, some greater problem. There were secrets here at Baincroft. Secrets everyone seemed privy to but himself.

Could they not see he had their good in mind as well as his? Did each suspect him of some foul purpose? Did they all fear him?

If so, he supposed he had himself to blame. Though he had tried both by word and act to dispel the belief that he was that cynical and dangerous man he had portrayed in his former life, they must still think that he was.

Edouard examined his behavior these past few weeks and could not see exactly where things had gone awry. Had it been the death of that hound? Nay, Robert had understood that, though Henri obviously had not. Anne had not mentioned it again since Edouard had recovered from his sickness. There seemed to be more to this than that one incident, however.

At least he could establish *some* goodwill between Anne and himself if he accepted the matter of the priest's marriage. Though the fact that Father Michael had wed the woman surprised Edouard, he certainly did not intend to do anything about it. What could he do, save deny the couple their living and send them on their way? That would not resolve a thing. They would still be married. God could solve that one whenever He saw fit.

But what could he do to ferret out the true cause of dissension within his family?

It might be that he had no talent for honest discourse, a tactic so long unused he had nearly forgotten how to employ it. Had he dealt so long with conspiracies and hidden meanings, he naturally thought first of tricking out the truth? But surely his wife and children would be forthright with him if he was so with them. Simple questions that required straightforward answers. As soon as Mass was over, he would begin with Anne.

Anne filed out just behind him as everyone left the chapel. He turned immediately and took her arm as they entered the hall proper. "Come to the solar. I have things I wish to ask you."

She shot him a belligerent look, but did not pull away. So she still thought he intended to dismiss her friends.

Edouard smiled. Anne would be relieved about his reaction to that.

As soon as they were seated, he came right to the point. "Father Michael and Meg may stay. I care not if they are wed."

Anne pursed her lips and gave a wary nod. "Fine."

"Is that all you have to say?" He had thought she would show some gratitude, and that it might lead to openness on the other issues he wished to address.

"What else would you hear?"

"Why are you angry with me? I would know," he said.

Her perfect eyebrows flew up. "Angry? Who says I am angry?"

Edouard rolled his eyes. "No one has to say it! You show it with every expression on that lovely face of yours this morning. Or do I mistake it? Is it fear, then? Do I make you afraid?"

"Have I reason to be?" she asked.

He took one of her hands and laced his fingers through hers. "No. I promise you on my life, Anne. Nothing could make me do injury to either your person or your happiness. But I must know what makes you unhappy. I cannot read your mind."

She relaxed a bit, her fingers closing naturally around his. "Ah, but I wish I could believe you, Edouard. I do wish it."

"How, then, have I failed you thus far?" he demanded. "Something is wrong. Tell me."

For a long moment, he thought she would.

He encouraged her with a smile of reassurance. "I promise you, I am very good at banishing problems."

Her fingers stiffened and her guard came up. "I have none."

Edouard studied her eyes, which had silvered over with

a sheen of tears. Something troubled Anne very deeply, but nothing she was willing to share with him.

Her lack of trust hurt, but he supposed she thought it justified. Why, he could not fathom, but he would. If straight talking would not provide answers, then he must rely on the old and devious measures he had hoped to discard.

"Very well," he said. "Then let us go and break our fast. Such blissful content as yours surely must be shared with everyone else, since they do seem to take their moods from yours."

Chapter Fourteen

"**Y**our priest's wife appears to have lost her appetite," Edouard observed with a nod toward the lower table. He speared a sliver of cold pork and offered it to Anne. "Would you not care to ease her mind? I suspect she is wondering how quickly she must pack and be off."

Anne shrugged as she accepted the bite of meat and began to chew thoughtfully. When she had swallowed, she finally met his gaze. "I would have done so, but to give her false hope would be cruel indeed. I thought I might wait to see whether you would change your mind."

Change his mind? Edouard sat back in his chair, his hands braced on the table's edge. He regarded the eating knife he held as though it contained an answer to the question she raised. How was it this woman could goad his fury with so few words?

It was not as though he did not know the scheme she played. He had played it himself, many a time. Remind a man that his honor was at stake if he reneged on his word, and everyone would know. It was not this ploy, but her lack of trust that infuriated him.

"I have said they may stay, Anne," he said smoothly, unwilling to allow her to see his anger. "Have you ever

known me to play false with anyone? You have no reason
to insult me with these doubts of yours. I always keep my
word.''

She swiveled to face him fully. ''As you did with Sir
Gui? He did you no disservice. His leg will heal, Meg says,
and he will serve you well again. Go after him. Make
amends.''

''No,'' he said, sliding the knife firmly into the chunk
of cheese on his trencher and crossing his arms over his
chest. ''That would not be wise.''

''Then you have played him false, have you not? He
swore to you, and you to him some years ago. As his lord,
you are bound to offer him protection, even when he is
disabled. 'Twas no great injury. Had he sustained it in battle, you would not cut him from your service, surely.'' Her
eyes, as well as the whole set of her body, challenged him
to deny it. She probably knew very well that he had in-
vented the reason for sending Gui away.

If Edouard admitted the truth, that Gui's injured leg had
nothing whatsoever to do with the matter, then she would
regret her role in the dismissal. As much as he did not want
her to suffer that regret, neither did he like her to think him
so shallow that he would break his bond as lord to Gui for
such small cause. He would give her a half-truth, then.

''Sir Gui never wished to come here. Everything he said
and did bespoke the fact that he wished to return to France
and to the court. He is an ambitious man who must know
by now that he could never further his fortune significantly
if he remains with me. Attached to some other lord, he may
gain lands. I will not offer him any. Now let the matter
rest.''

Her dark brows lowered as she considered his words.
''Did he ask to be released?''

''In a way, he did. When I warned him to hold his

tongue, he did question whether I wanted to break our bond.''

''And in your anger at that, you ordered him away,'' she guessed.

When Edouard said nothing, she placed a hand on his arm in supplication. ''Please send after him, Edouard. Do not let things end this way between the two of you. The day will come when you will regret what passed between you. He was your friend.''

''*Was* is the word to mind. Why do you care so much what happens to him?'' Edouard demanded, unable to mask his ire completely. ''The man nearly made an end to you! How can you think that is nothing? I swear you confound me!''

She leaned her head back and closed her eyes. ''So I was right. This is about me. About the ordeal.''

''Not entirely!'' Edouard argued. So much for the practiced deviousness on which he prided himself. He blew out a breath of defeat. He could not lie and make her believe it.

Neither could he deny her anything she asked. ''Very well, I shall send for him since you insist on it. I will not have you hold yourself accountable for this. You certainly did nothing wrong.''

''I know,'' she said, assuming that excruciatingly formal tone he hated so. ''I do not blame myself at all. But when your choler with Sir Gui fades, you might blame me. Now if you will excuse me, my lord, I shall go and tell Meg and Michael they may stay.''

He looked up at her as she stood. ''Is there anything else you wish of me today, my lady? My will seems to work at your pleasure. Shall I leap off the wall-walk?''

Edouard experienced a short moment of discomfort as she paused to consider that. Then she looked down at the lower table where their sons were laughing together with the steward's boy and a lovely little girl. Anne's eyes narrowed as she pressed a finger against her lips, tapping gently while she thought. Edouard could see calculation warring with her trepidation. She wanted to ask something of him, and he knew precisely when she decided to press her advantage.

"Aye, there is another thing you can do," she said decisively. "Have Thomas trained with Henri and Robert. Make a knight of this lad, too."

Her request surprised him. "The steward's son, a knight? Why?"

Wearing a look of confusion, her gaze flew to his. "Thomas is not Simm's lad. What made you think so?"

Edouard shrugged. "He is ever with the man, poking about in Baincroft's business. I just assumed..." Then he knew. "Aha, let me guess. Young Thomas is a product of our infamous cleric, am I correct?"

She smiled down at him, another challenge. "He is. And also your good Sir Simon's grandson, if you will remember. We are preparing him for the stewardship under Robert. I gave my word on this. Would you break it?"

"You push your authority, madame. Quite sure of yourself, are you?"

"Is my word worth nothing, then?" she questioned with a hauture he would not have guessed she possessed. "If you pride yourself on yours, husband, should I do less? Would you destroy my honor and make me a breaker of promises?"

Edouard pondered that for a moment. She had no right under law or custom to choose the one to administer her son's estate, either now or in later years. But she had given her word, and he felt disinclined to rescind it. At least not entirely.

He decided on a compromise. "Very well. I will grant Thomas a trial period," he conceded. "If he possesses the proper ability, I will consider making him a squire. But knighthood, he must earn. No promise there from either of us. He must be tutored, of course. Reading, writing, and a proficiency with numbers will be required of him."

She smiled. "He has that already, thanks to his father."

Edouard sighed. He should have known she would leave nothing to chance. "Future stewardship must remain in question until he proves himself," he warned. "Fair enough?"

"Fair," she said, hope shining in her eyes. "Thank you, Edouard."

He rose then to stand beside her. "Dare I hope Thomas is an only child? Or do they have others earmarked for our largesse?"

"Only Jehan," she murmured while she fiddled with the keys jingling against her skirts.

"Mmm-hmm. The future herbwoman, I trust?"

"Not exactly," Anne offered warily. As she swept around him and descended from the dais, she spoke over her shoulder. "Chatelaine. Lady of Baincroft."

"What!" he thundered. "Chatelaine?"

"Robert's wife," she clarified, from a distance now. "They are betrothed."

Edouard dropped back into his chair, apalled. *Betrothed?* That contract would not have been MacBain's doing. No lord with any sanity about him would betroth his heir to his own priest's daughter.

The child would bring no land, no dowry and no important alliance to her husband. Father Michael might well be related to the Scots king. But Edouard knew this cleric was no favorite or he would not remain immured here on this obscure little estate. Vocation notwithstanding, The Bruce would have elevated him to some position of power. No, this betrothal was Anne's idea, an unfortunate and surely a very recent arrangement.

Edouard stared at the woman hurrying away from him,
and wondered what other information she had decided to
withhold.

God's truth, he must assert his authority immediately if
he was to have charge of this place! He had had more say
in the administration of France itself, than he would have
in that of Baincroft Keep, if Anne had her way.

She would keep him ever in the dark with regard to the
goings on unless he pressed her, piece by piece, for the
truth. And he had the distinct feeling that he had merely
scratched the surface of her little cask of secrets.

Some other thing bothered her, some greater worry than
his learning her plans for the priest's children or the business about Gui. And she did not mean for him to know of
it, whatever it was.

Quite right that she should be concerned, he thought.
Unearthing plots and conspiracies was a talent he had de-
veloped to a science in his lifetime. The time had come to
employ that talent with all seriousness.

Sir Gui arrived that night, brought back by a message
Edouard had sent after him by one of Anne's men-at-arms.
She saw almost immediately that she might have made a
mistake in instigating this. Edouard's knight appeared none
too pleased when he hobbled into the hall just after the
evening meal.

"You proclaimed it urgent that I return," he stated, glaring at Edouard. "So, here am I. What is it you wish of me
now? Were the wages you sent a mistake?"

Her husband wore an expression of studied calm, all feeling suppressed. Anne wondered if she had prompted some
horrible confrontation by insisting on this reunion. But
Edouard responded without ire to the knight's belligerence.

"I wish to speak with you privately, Sir Gui, concerning
our last words. Now that tempers have cooled, I would

discuss how we might go on. Would you join me in the solar?''

Gui marched toward the door, neither answering nor waiting for Edouard to rise and accompany him. Anne jumped with surprise when Edouard took her arm, indicating that she should join the parley.

Sir Gui frowned as she and Edouard entered together. ''I understood that we were to speak privately,'' he snapped, raking Anne with a disdainful glance.

She could feel the tensing of Edouard's arm beneath her hand. This forced patience of his would not last long, she feared.

When he did speak, he sounded calmer than she expected. ''My lady believes that I acted in haste by dismissing you. I would that she witness this.''

''This what?'' Sir Gui pressed. ''Do you recant?''

Edouard's nostrils flared and a muscle ticked in his jaw. Anne thought his knight must be truly mad to test him so. They might come to blows if she did not intercede.

Anne took a small step forward, her hand still resting on Edouard's arm. ''Sir Gui, I did wish my lord husband to offer reinstatement of your bond. We both understand now that your loyalty and concern for him prompted your accusal of me. You have been his knight for years. Will you not consider reconciling?''

The knight looked from one to the other, his truculence diminishing even as she watched. He shifted one foot to the other for a moment, then sidled forward and dropped awkwardly to one knee. ''If you wish it, my lord. I shall remain your man.''

Both gazed down on Gui's fair head as he knelt. Edouard still appeared reluctant to accept Sir Gui, even after this evidence of humility. If he did not, sooner or later he would forgive Sir Gui. Then he would blame her that he had lost this trusty knight. Edouard looked up at her then. Anne nodded her encouragement.

He frowned as he placed his hand lightly on Gui's head. "So be it. You may rise."

Sir Gui looked up with a slight narrowing of his eyes. "Shall I not pledge again?"

"I do not ask it," Edouard said evenly. "We shall forget all that has happened and go on as before."

"As you will, my lord," Sir Gui answered as he got to his feet. He bowed briefly before Edouard and then Anne. "If that is all, then I bid you both good-night."

"Good night," Edouard replied in a tone without expression. Anne marked that he had shown no sign of forgiveness or any relief that he had regained Gui's services. She wondered again if she had made a mistake.

"You might well have been right," Anne admitted. Weary and unsure of herself, she took a seat in one of the solar chairs, folding her hands in her lap. "He does not seem altogether thrilled to be back, does he?"

Edouard looked at her as though she had just grown horns. "Nor am I enraptured with his presence, but you would have it thus, so for good or evil, here he is!"

"He misses France, you said. Do you not miss it, Edouard? It must have been exciting at court. I cannot see how you manage to endure here for this long a time, when you could be enjoying the revels and all that august company there. If you wish to return, I will certainly understand. Sir Gui would be happy, and you would be—"

"Miserable," he said. He lowered himself to the chair just opposite her and issued a rough sigh. "I shall not go back."

"Ever?" Anne gasped. He sounded so definite. She had resigned herself to the fact that he would not leave immediately, but how could he ignore indefinitely those responsibilities Uncle Dairmid had spoken of? She sat forward, imploring. "But you will have to do so! You are needed there!"

He shrugged. "Not so long as Philip is king."

Anne quickly lowered her eyes so that he would not see her shock. It seemed more like surprise, however, and not all that unwelcome. Why didn't she feel hopeless? She *should* feel so. All her plans had rested on his leaving Baincroft eventually and staying away for long periods of time. But he would stay.

Even when he had invested so much of his wealth in improving Baincroft, she had assumed his motives were pride and his own temporary comfort. He would not want his name associated with a poor keep, she had thought. When he had commenced these renovations, Anne had truly believed him a man with more coin than he knew how to spend.

But if that were so, why had she never questioned his taking *her* to wife? She wondered now, of course. Why would he wed a woman with so modest a dowry, a widow of twenty-seven years with a half-grown son? He could have had anyone. It seemed she was not the only one with concealed motives for this marriage.

"The French king is not to your liking?" she asked, probing none too subtly his reasons for staying in Scotland.

"No, he is not," he said simply.

Anne knew she must unearth his reason for abandoning king and country, for taking a Scottish wife and changing his life-style so drastically. If she did not understand these decisions of his, how on earth could she begin to change them? How would she convince him to leave? She must do that, of course, even though his going would leave an emptiness within her.

She had only another month at most before he would guess she carried his child. That knowledge would ensure his remaining here until after the birth.

"Will you tell me why you do not like your king?"

He took a deep breath and sat back in his chair, elbows on the armrests, his long fingers steepled under his chin. He studied her for a long moment before speaking.

"I am unused to explaining my decisions, Anne. But since you are my wife, I shall tell you. King Philip and I had a difference of opinion and he ordered me out of his sight. My sovereign is not a reasonable man, but one given to deadly fits of temper. It would not be wise for me to return to France until I discover what punishment he intends. Most likely it will involve relieving me of my title and my estates. Although, it could prove worse."

Anne said nothing, but she was certain she looked properly horrified. Because she was. This certainly explained everything, but was in no way a relief to her.

Edouard had come to Scotland looking, not for additional properties to add to his income, but for primary estates to replace those in France which he would no longer own. Estates for himself and for his son. Thanks to her uncle, he had found two, those belonging to her and her son. Her adjoining lands, he owned now by virtue of their marriage. And Baincroft, he would have by right of possession. As soon as he discovered that he could legally wrest it from Robert.

"Did my uncle know you are out of favor with your king?" she asked.

Edouard laughed. "What do you think? Of course he did not know it. If so, would he have offered you to me? Not likely. Ironic, is it not? He was after gaining a bit of influence at court through our alliance."

Anne knew that very well, since Uncle Dairmid had made it quite clear. She just hadn't known that Edouard understood his motives. "What will you do now?"

"Now?" he asked smoothly, as he crossed his arms over his chest and smiled. "Why, I have already done it, my sweet. I have established a home for myself and Henri right here with you and Robert. Even were I free to return to France, I would not exchange what I have found here for any other place in the world."

There was little left to say, she decided. He could not make matters much plainer than that. Though she wanted a future with him desperately, it could never be. He was a dire threat to her children. "Forgive me, Edouard. I am afraid I feel rather ill."

He stood and leaned forward, all concern, and quickly felt her forehead with the back of his hand. "You are perspiring!" He strode to the solar door and called, "Meg, to my lady! She sickens!"

Anne protested, but he paid her no mind as Meg came running from the hall.

Before Anne could object, he swung her up into his arms and headed for the stairs, talking to Meg over his shoulder. "She's likely caught the ague I suffered. We must get her abed!"

Anne groaned. She wanted to be abed right enough, but not with him hovering and barking orders. All she wanted was to curl into a ball beneath the covers and weep. With Edouard in constant residence, he would soon know everything. All would be lost.

Mayhaps it had been from the first day he came here. What had she been thinking to believe she could outwit a man like him? The comte de Trouville would never allow a small lad to stand in the way of owning Baincroft outright, be that lad hearing or not. Hadn't Edouard already made this keep his own?

Once he had put her to bed, Anne did not weep as she thought she might. Succumbing to that particular weakness would solve nothing at all. It might even make her as ill as Edouard seemed convinced she was. Even so, she could

not decide what must be done. For hours she thought on
it, considered every alternative, as she pretended sleep.

He lay beside her, turning at least every hour to feel her
brow, while trying not to wake her. She wished he would
take her in his arms and make love to her, though her mind
was likely too troubled to involve herself completely. She
did want him. She feared she would always want him.

And she loved him. That truth was not exactly new to
her. A part of her rejoiced that he would be staying. Her
selfish wish to have him with her angered Anne, but it
would not be denied. She must be a mother first, she told
herself repeatedly. And while she now admitted that she
loved Edouard, she still did not trust that he would be fair
in the matter of Rob's inheritance.

She no longer believed that he would cast out Robert
and herself with no means of support. Edouard was no
beast, and he did care for her. But surely he would feel
constrained to prevent Robert's taking charge when he
reached the age for it. Now that she was to have another
child, however, there was so much more at stake than Rob's
losing Baincroft.

Dawn came at last. "Are you awake?" Edouard whispered. Again, he pressed a hand on her brow and exhaled
with what sounded like relief. "Still no fever, thank
heaven. How do you feel this morn?"

"Well enough," she answered. "I merely felt a bit faint.
I told you last night that I would be fine."

He got up and began to dress himself. His voice sounded
muffled as he drew his tunic over his head. "I'll go and
tell Robert and Henri. They will be very concerned about
you. Why don't you remain abed today and rest, just to be
safe?"

Just to be safe. Anne squeezed her eyes shut and wished
to God she could feel safe. Just once, she would love to
embrace that feeling. "For a while," she agreed softly. In

all truth, she simply did not want to face the day as yet. Surely, a momentary weakness would be allowed her.

He kissed her gently and left, greeting Meg as she met him at the door. "Keep her abed if you can," Anne heard him whisper. "She is better, but not yet well." Then he was gone.

"You look as though you need more sleep, but I'll warrant you're not down with ague," Meg declared. "I brought you something to settle your stomach." She set a cup and chunk of bread down on the bedside table.

"Thank you, my friend. I do not know what I would do without you." Anne sat up and reached for the posset. When she had finished most of it, she set it down again and looked at her friend. "He is not planning to leave as we had hoped. *Ever.*"

"His lordship? Did he give a reason?"

Anne explained all Edouard had told her about the inadvisability of his returning to France.

Meg pursed her lips as she sank down on the edge of the bed. "Do you think when he finds out about Robert, he might want to abandon the babe when it arrives? Would he expose it to the elements?"

"Oh, God forbid! I had not thought of that! Surely, he would not wish it to die!"

"Nay, nay, of course he won't!" Meg patted Anne's hand with sympathy. "You are right, he could not. Forget that I even thought it. MacBain might have been one to do that had he known from the first days. It was the old way of disposing of babes who were…lacking in some way. But even he could not be so cruel once he found out about Robert. Not after having him around for nigh on two years."

Anne scoffed and punched the pillow with her fist. "He thought of it, even then. He decided to end our marriage instead, and disown Rob. But I managed to convince him that Rob's deafness was not from birth, rather due to a fever in the ears when he was just a weanling. I promised there would be more sons. MacBain was a brute, as you know, but no murderer. He wanted to believe me, I think.''

Meg brightened. "Do you think that could be the true cause of Robert's deafness? If so—"

"How would I know? 'Tis true Rob was ill at one time, but not seriously so. I made up the story so MacBain would not think all our issue would be so affected.''

"And you were careful not to disprove it with another babe,'' Meg said softly.

"Aye. But I fear the proof may come all too soon that I have lied.'' She brushed a palm over her stomach.

"Lord Edouard is not the man your first husband was. He treats everyone with respect, Anne. He is not like MacBain in any way. Nay, I cannot believe he would allow a child of his to die for any reason. I'm dreadfully sorry to have mentioned it at all. And now I've given you more to worry on.''

Anne sighed and lay back, closing her eyes. "I want so to believe in Edouard, Meg, but I am afraid. Who knows what they do in his country in a like circumstance? If there is but the slightest chance that he would—"

They sat for a while, each mulling over the possibility. Then Meg announced. "Well, we both know you must tell him about the child, or very soon he will see for himself. But I think we should all continue to keep Robert's secret until the new babe has his lordship's heart involved. Then it will be too late for him to do anything but love it and do what is right.''

Anne nodded. "'Tis the only solution. And if he should find out about Robert somehow, I shall give him the same story that I gave to MacBain about Rob's illness.''

Meg agreed. "We should inform Michael, all the children, and Simm of the plan to continue the deception,'' she said. "They must take great care if we are to succeed in this."

"How long can we keep it up, I wonder?" Anne asked dispiritedly. "I only wish I could confess it all to him, Meg. I love him and do not like to deceive him. But I dare not take the risk of trusting too soon."

Or trusting at all, she thought.

Chapter Fifteen

Rob answered the summons to the solar, grateful to have his lessons with Father Michael delayed. Doing sums was not his favorite thing. Henri, Thomas, and Jehan were coming as well. He wondered if Mama meant to take them all to task for some unwitting transgression. Had he been asked to come alone, he would have figured that she had somehow found out about his old father's sword.

He worried that she would. No one had seen him take it out of the chamber after his father died, however. And he had been careful to hide it away for fear she would not allow him to have it. If she knew he played with it in the tower chamber whenever he could sneak up there, she would take it away and put it with all the others in the armory. The smaller one his new father had given him for practice was much easier to handle, but it bore a very dull blade. Safer, he supposed, but not much use to a man if he needed protection.

"Ah, here you are," Mama said as they entered. "Father Michael, I apologize for interrupting your lessons, but I needed to speak with you and the children." She looked out into the hall, nodded once as though satisfied no one else would come, and then closed the door.

Mistress Meg was here, too, as was Simm. Rob did not miss the fact that Father had obviously not been summoned.

Mama took a deep breath and began to speak. Her hands trembled a little as she included a few of the signs they had made up to help him understand her. Her face looked sad. He always marked the expression first to see whether she was happy about what she said or otherwise. Definitely otherwise. Now he must mind the words to discover why.

"So we cannot let him find out," she was saying, looking directly at Rob.

"Fathah?" Rob asked, to make certain he understood who she was speaking about.

"Aye," she said, nodding. "We must not let him know. Do you understand, Rob?"

"Know what?" he asked. There were not that many secrets she had asked him to keep, but when Mama wore a worried look, it always paid to get everything absolutely straight.

Her face looked pained, as though she did not wish to voice the words. "That you cannot hear," she said, shaking her head and touching one of her ears.

Rob glanced at the others, and to a one, they watched him expectantly, as though the decision rested with him. They served her well, and would never go against his mother's wishes. Neither would he, willingly. At least not without good reason.

Mama had asked him to pretend that he could hear, and he had done so as well as he could in order to please her. Henri and his new father might not like it if they knew how special he was, she had said.

Special, she called him. Mama always tried to make it seem as though he were somehow blessed, but Rob knew better. He did not mind so much that he could not hear everything. After all, he'd never known what it was like to do so, and he did possess skills others did not.

His old father had hated him because he could not hear well, but no one else seemed to care. Mama had been wrong about Henri. His brother said it mattered not at all to him. Rob could not imagine that his new father would think ill of him over such a small thing. If Father knew, it would help explain why Rob could not always make out the words he and Sir Gui spoke to him as they practiced with the weapons. There would be no need to make believe he did, and then have them frown at him when he did not.

Robert decided to question Mama's decision on this. "Fathah is good. We teh him."

"We cannot tell him!" she argued.

"Why?" he asked.

She made a grasping motion and then spread her arm wide as if to encompass everything about them. "He will take Baincroft and your lands from you."

Rob knew she was mistaken about that. Father did not have to take the place. He already lived here. "Nay, Mama. Teh him."

He spared a glance at the others. All watched him as though they feared this. But Rob knew he was right. A person's goodness was so easy for him to see, right there in the depth of the eyes, the carriage of the body, almost like a light around them which came from within. Rob understood that somehow listening to that person must interfere with the seeing of all this, so Mama was not to be blamed for her lack. Father might be demanding sometimes, but he was surely no thief. He was good.

Rob admitted to himself that he could be mistaken. But if he had no skill in judging a person's worth, then he had nothing at all with which to govern his people. He would soon know the truth, about his own judgement and about Father. "I teh him."

"I said *nay!*" Mama declared. "And I am your mother!"

Rob paused to form the words in his mind, to determine

exactly how they should fit on his tongue so that no one would misunderstand. Then he did a thing he had never dared before in his life. "I am lord," he stated with all the authority he could muster. "And I say *aye!*"

He strode to the door, head high and using big steps, just as Father always did. Even though his back was to the others, Rob knew they would be putting up a fuss. Mama especially. He did not look back. His mind was made up and that was that. It was *his* secret, after all.

Back in the solar, everyone stood staring at the door, unwilling to believe they had heard Robert's declaration. Anne recovered first. She shook her head as though to clear it. Rob had never asserted his dominion over anyone or anything before. What had come over her son? He must believe very strongly about this. "Mayhaps he is right," she murmured, more to herself than the others.

She wished she could afford this blind trust that Robert had just exhibited. He obviously idolized Edouard, simply because the man had been kind to him for the most part. The training, the attention, and lack of beating must seem like love compared to MacBain's treatment.

"Do not fret," Henri said, interrupting her thoughts. "I doubt Father will understand Rob even if he does tell."

"Aye!" Thomas added. "Even if his lordship does ken what Rob's saying, we could all pretend it is a temporary thing. Rob's ears have been hurting, swelled up inside, and—"

"Hist, Tom," Father Michael admonished. "Would you lie outright? Have I not taught you better?"

"Oh, but he lies right well, don't he, Da!" Jehan announced with a honeyed smile.

Anne threw up her hands. "Each of us has lied, if only by omitting the truth! And it is no more right that we do it than if Thomas does. What sort of example am I setting for our bairns to require this of them? I might as well tell Edouard everything. Why delay the inevitable?''

"Because of…'' Meg began, looking at Anne's midsection, "You know.''

"You think I have forgotten that?'' Anne almost shouted. "Heaven help me, I think on nothing else! What am I to do?'' She covered her face with one hand and sniffed, containing the tears that threatened to undo her. Now was no time to fall apart.

Father Michael patted her back. "I believe it will go better for everyone if you are the one to impart the truth to Lord Edouard. You would surely make a better explanation of it than Robert could, and more easily temper his lordship's reaction to the news.''

"Aye, you are right. You said he rode out earlier, Henri. Did he mention how long he would be away?''

The boy shrugged. "He left for the stables immediately after weapons training this morn instead of joining us in the bathhouse. He was nowhere about when we went to Father Michael for our lessons.''

Anne nodded. "I shall keep a watch for his return and speak with him directly when he comes. If any of you see Robert, tell him he must wait and allow me to have my say first.''

"Mayhaps we should ask him nicely, Lady Anne,'' Jehan suggested with an impish grin. "Lest our *wee lord* chops off our heads for impertinence!'' She streaked a finger across her throat.

Meg swatted her backside. "'Tis my wrath you dare with that jest, my girl! Robert *is* your lord, and mind you do not forget it!''

Jehan dashed from the room giggling. Robert would never intimidate that one, Anne thought with a wry smile. She should take a lesson from the child with regard to arrogant lords.

Then Anne reminded herself that she had stood firm and won out on the matter of Michael and Meg's marriage and Gui's dismissal. God grant she would prevail in this, as well. She could play on Edouard's honor, his charity, and the vow he had given to protect those weaker than he when he won his spurs.

She would not share news of her pregnancy yet, however. He would not relish that, coming directly on the heels of the facts about Rob. Later, when he had grown used to the idea of Robert's deafness, once he saw that it could be conquered in a way, she would tell him of the babe.

Robert left her no choice but to trust Edouard, but she would do so only insofar as it affected Robert. If her son lost Baincroft because of this decision of his, then she would do what she could to provide for him. She knew in her heart that Edouard would never expose an afflicted babe to the elements, else she could not love him as she did. But if she birthed another with Robert's infirmity, he would no longer have her as wife. No man would.

A convent might accept her and the babe if Edouard set aside the marriage and offered enough coin to support them. But the nuns would never take a half-grown lad. A monastery might, depending upon the order. However, some priests would consider Robert possessed by the devil and she had no way of knowing which those were.

This left no alternative for her except to rely on Edouard's sympathy and generosity. Unfortunately, she had no idea how far he would extend either one when he found she had deceived him.

Anne could only count on one thing for certain. Whether he set her aside or not, she would no longer have a loving husband.

Edouard looked forward to a long, hot soak as he sighted Baincroft's gates. After a particularly spirited sword practice and then his ride over to Anne's property, he reeked of sweat, his and Bayard's.

The ride proved a productive outing, however, for he had determined the exact site for building. Anne would love the place he'd selected, he felt certain. The master mason and workers he had hired should arrive any day now.

He would have a bath and then go to tell Anne about the plans for their new home. That should make her feel better if she had not already recovered. Thoughts of how delighted she would be curried an inner smile. His mysterious Anne.

So preoccupied, Edouard had to rein in sharply when a small figure leapt into his path. The instant he had Bayard calmed, he dismounted, spewing curses.

"Damn you, Robert! Have you no sense at all? This bastard could have trampled you flat with one hoof! What do you here? I distinctly told you not to leave the keep alone."

"Come," Robert ordered, ignoring the remonstrance. He marched toward a large stone at the side of the road and leapt up on it. They were eye to eye when Edouard approached him.

"Well, what have you to say for yourself? Or are you planning to knock out my lights from up there?" he asked, resting his hands on his hips. "I suppose it is time we settled matters between us. You do not care much for me and I know it. Are you now ready to tell me why?"

Robert copied his stance and demanded, "You take my keep?"

Edouard glared at the boy, dumbfounded. "Baincroft? I will maintain control of it until you are older, make no mistake about that. But if you ask if I mean to steal it—"

"Aye o' nay, Fathah. You take my keep?"

"No! Certainly not. Is this why you have acted the way you have? You think I intend to take advantage—"

"You like me?" Robert said, cutting him off. The words were blunt, each very deliberately formed and clipped to the point of rudeness.

"Well, when you are not exhibiting such atrocious manners and hurling these accusa—"

"Aye o' nay. You like me?"

Edouard almost laughed. He could not believe this stripling had jumped up on a rock and faced him down this way. Even Henri would not dare do such a thing. Knights with weapons in hand would not dare it. Courage was commendable, but such foolhardiness was ridiculous. But the boy looked so deadly serious, Edouard knew that his answer mattered very much to them both.

"Aye, Robert. I like you. Now if you'll jump down, we can converse like gentlemen and decide how we might get on together."

"I canna heah you," Robert declared rather loudly.

"Do not be impudent! If you want me to shout it to the world at large, you will be sadly disappointed. I have said I like you, and you shall have to be satisfied with that."

"I canna heah," the boy repeated insistently, though more softly now. His tawny eyebrows rose over widened eyes. He leaned forward a bit as though awaiting a reaction to his announcement.

Something clicked inside Edouard's brain. Robert meant the words literally, he realized. The boy's poor speech! A wonder that he could utter a sound. His seeming inattention when he faced away from someone. Not rudeness, then. "You...you truly cannot hear?"

Robert shook his head. "No' wuds." The blue-gray gaze bore into Edouard's, and the voice dropped to a whisper. "You like me?"

Not a plea for pity, that question, however softly spoken. Edouard understood that Robert really needed to know. The courage required and the trust offered in Robert's admission staggered Edouard.

After a moment's silence, he nodded, and replied so there could be no mistake, "Aye."

"Good!" Robert shouted. He laughed aloud and hopped nimbly off the boulder. "Home. Wide?"

Ride. Edouard nodded. He slowly mounted Bayard and reached down to give Robert a lift to the back of the saddle. He remained stunned as they finished the short trip and waited for the gates to open.

Only as they rode through did Edouard begin to understand the far-reaching implications of Robert's announcement. *This* must be Baincroft's secret. The truth everyone here had known but himself.

Robert let go of Edouard's waist the moment Bayard came to a halt. "Wait!" he cautioned, but the boy nimbly slid to the ground using the edge of the saddle and Edouard's leg and stirrup like vines of a tree.

With his feet finally planted on the ground, Robert looked up, grinned and offered a jaunty salute. "Big wide. My tanks, Fathah." Then he rattled off a few other incomprehensible sentences and laughed merrily.

Edouard nodded, amazed that the boy felt comfortable enough to converse with him this way. Not a shred of animosity remained. Edouard wondered whether it ever existed at all, or if he had imagined it because of the boy's lack of understanding. Every time they had spoken before today, Robert had only granted him one or two words at most.

Edouard dismounted, intending to continue the strange little discourse so that he could find out exactly how extensive was Robert's vocabulary. But when he turned, the boy had disappeared.

"See Bayard has his special oats after you groom him, Tiernan," Edouard ordered, and handed off the reins to the stable lad. He certainly had more to do at this moment than pamper the horse himself.

His head was full of questions about Robert's confession. Foremost among them was why he had not been told of the boy's condition. Anger and disappointment over that gnawed at his insides, but he would not give way to it just yet. Surely there must be some good reason why no one had trusted him with this knowledge.

Why had Anne not trusted him? There lay the crux of the matter. His own wife had not seen fit to tell him, and try as he might, Edouard could think of no logical cause for her to keep it from him.

Now that he considered more carefully, he realized that not only had she kept it from him, she had lied outrageously to prevent his finding out.

Gaelic, indeed. He would bet his last coin that Robert knew none of that language. Try as he might, Edouard could not envision how the boy had learned words of any kind since he could not hear them spoken.

The deafness certainly explained everything about Robert's attitude toward him. Now he must find something to account for Anne's.

She met him at the hall door. "Edouard! You are home!" With one hand to her chest, she sounded rather breathless and looked a bit flushed.

"Come with me." He took her elbow and practically dragged her to the solar. "You have some explaining to do."

She said nothing, but he could see fear in her eyes. A dreadful fear he wanted to erase. But first he must find out what had put it there.

"I know about Robert," he said without delay. "Why did you not tell me of this?"

Her shoulders drooped as though the weight of the world

had just descended upon them. Long lashes swept down to hide the desolation in her eyes. "Is it not obvious?"

Edouard turned from her, unable to chastise or comfort at this point. He only needed the truth. "No. I cannot fathom why you would keep such a thing from me."

She sighed, a dispirited sound he hated to hear from her. "Who told you?"

He rounded on her. "Robert, himself! He appears to be the only one at Baincroft with a dram of honesty about him! And even that was late in evidence. Everyone knew, did they not? Everyone but me, Gui and Henri."

She shot him a look of guilt, then glanced away, worrying her bottom lip with her teeth.

Edouard threw up his hands and huffed. "Do not tell me. They know as well?"

"Henri knows," she whispered. "He guessed soon after you came here."

"And I did not," Edouard said. "One has to guess, then. One is not told, even when that one is to be the father?"

She declined to answer, but he had not expected her to.

He grasped her shoulders, feeling the tension flare within her, the fear grow to trembling proportion. "Anne, how could you trust me with your body, with complete dominion over your life, and yet not with this truth about your son?"

Even as the question came out of his mouth, he knew. She had not trusted him at all. She had used her person, her seeming content with the marriage, to distract him.

"I believed at first you would go away and leave us alone," she said. "Uncle Dairmid said that you would."

Shock held him silent for a while. He released her shoulders and stood away from her, unwilling to touch her more. Finally he asked the question he dreaded for her to answer. "Then why did you agree to wed me?"

"Because of that," she admitted reluctantly. "Because I

believed you only wanted income from my lands, and that you would leave.''

''Why marry at all, if you did not want a husband here?''

Her head came up and she faced him directly, her spirit returning even as he watched her eyes. ''I had no choice, my lord. No choice.''

The breath left him in a rush. Another unwilling wife. ''Hume?'' he asked, knowing the truth of it. ''What did he threaten?''

''To take Robert away. I could not allow that. You see why I could not.''

Edouard pounded a palm with one fist. ''I should have slain that bastard four years ago.'' But then he would never have met Anne. It might have been best if he had not, he decided then. All of this, as unfortunate as it was, still did not explain her fear about Robert. A fear that must be over-whelming to have attempted deception for so long a time.

He strolled across the room and stared out the window for a time, replaying all that had happened between them, seeing each event, each conversation in new light. When he finally reached the last, his confrontation with Robert on the road, understanding dawned. ''You believed I would dispossess him, did you not?''

''Aye,'' she admitted in a dreadful whisper. After a small silence, she asked, ''Will you?''

He turned and regarded her with a sadness that he could not hide. ''I do not know. If I do, it will be for his own good and for the benefit of Baincroft. You must believe that, Anne.''

With a sharp little cry of dismay, she grasped a fist full of her skirts and ran to the door. Before he could reach her, she had thrown it open and dashed through.

Edouard let her go. She would weep, plead and wring promises from him he might not be able to keep if he followed. He needed time to ponder this and decide what he must do without his concern for Anne's feelings muddling his mind. Edouard knew from recent experience that she would use any ploy, any advantage, be it tears or intimacy, to hold this place for her son.

Despite the soul-deep ache it caused him to know that Anne had no care for him at all, Edouard could not fault her for pretending as she had. Would he not have done worse if he thought it would save Henri his birthright? He might even have agreed to that bit of spying Philip had suggested, if he had known beforehand the cost of his refusal. No, he could not blame Anne, but neither could he dismiss the pain she had caused him.

"A word, my lord?" Father Michael said as he entered.

Edouard shook his head and turned away. "Not now. Go away."

The priest ignored that. "I must insist. Lady Anne looked extremely overset just now. She needs to know what you will do about her son."

Edouard whirled around and began to pace. "She needs to know, does she? To put her mind at peace? Where is *my* peace, then?"

He stalked right up to the priest and glared at him. "Press this issue at the moment and I'm like to set you all on the road with naught but the clothes on your backs! Hume cheated me of my hope for a willing bride. Anne sold herself on the chance that I might be one to leave her alone. Everyone in this blasted keep has lied to me, even the son I love more than my own life! Everyone save for that poor, sad boy who knows no better! So, what then do you expect me to do? Say all is right and meet and let it go at that?"

The priest closed his eyes and pressed his lips tightly together. In fervent prayer or exasperation, Edouard could not say. Nor did he care at the moment.

"Leave me to my thoughts, Father. Do pray they take a kind turn, for at the moment, I wish you all to perdition!"

"Lord Robert is not sad," the priest persisted. "Neither is he poor, unless you choose to make him so." He held up a hand when Edouard started to speak. "Nay, I'll not ask for your answer on that, given your current mood. But I do believe you need more information than you have been given in order to make your decision."

"Oh?" Edouard countered, struggling to find some source of calm objectivity within himself. "I understand the boy is deaf. Anne conspired to hide the fact instead of trusting me to do something about it!"

Father Michael raised a questioning brow. "What, my lord? What would you have done if you had known?"

Edouard resumed his restless pacing. "There are physicians who might—"

"Alter the deafness?" the priest asked. "How so? Do you not think the MacBain considered that? He sent to Paris for the best when the lad was three. Naught can be done, other than what Lady Anne has done herself."

Edouard stopped and looked at the man. "What could she do that a learned physician could not?"

"Taught him to speak, a thing that all said could not be done. He's becoming canny with his numbers, too. And has always been an astute judge of character. I suspect he thought long and hard before placing his faith in you, my lord. Aye, our Robert may lack hearing, but he does possess a sharp wit and the keenest of eyes. You'd do well not to underestimate our lad."

"*Our* lad?" Edouard taunted. "But you forget yourself, Father. Robert is now *my* lad, to do with as I will. Lady Anne must hold herself accountable if my decision is not to her liking. She gave up her will to mine when she wed. Whatever I decide, she must by law uphold that decision."

Father Michael raised both brows then and pursed his lips as though to quell a smile. "If I were you, I think I would not count overmuch on that supposition, my lord."

Edouard could swear he heard amusement in the man's words, though he could see no reason on earth for its being there. "I assure you, my wife will never wheedle me into giving way on this matter, regardless of what you might believe."

The priest did smile then, shaking his head as he turned to go. "Nay, my lord. I grant you she is never one to *wheedle.*"

Chapter Sixteen

Anne's appearance at the evening meal surprised Edouard. He had expected she would hide away in her old chamber, wringing her hands and despairing that her deception had fallen apart. Instead, she entered the hall with head held high. Her eyes looked clear of tears and her bearing as calm and unaffected as though nothing untoward had happened.

As always, her beauty captured all his senses the moment he first observed her. She invited touching, tasting. He longed to loosen her braid, bury his face in the floral scent of her hair, and drink in that small sigh she always made when they came together.

He usually welcomed the overpowering ache all this engendered, because he looked forward to easing it once he and Anne sought their bed. The anticipation only added to the pleasure. Tonight, however, Edouard now resented the sensation. How could he allow a woman to affect him so?

Only after marshaling his errant thoughts for a few moments, could he bring his mind back to the problem at hand, a problem of Anne's making. He could not afford to get so caught up in his desire for her that he forgot she could be devious.

She had not begun to love him, as he had hoped. He

must accept that. His love for her, he would need to keep well concealed or she would use it. Not against him, of course, but for her own purpose and that of her son. Just as the painful fullness of his loins would do, the hurt in his chest would diminish with time, he promised himself.

But how could she remain so unaffected? Women did not experience lust the way a man did, of course. He did understand how she would not be troubled by that as he was. But how could she wear that smile and come so easily to his company showing no remorse over her trickery? Had Anne no feelings whatsoever?

He could not believe she had taken him in so with her pretense at caring. Edouard felt used, undone, and greatly embarrassed that everyone knew about Anne's chicanery. And how he had tumbled for it like the greenest of the green. The more he thought on it, the more his anger increased.

"Good even, my lord," she said demurely as she approached her chair.

"Is it?" he asked, as he rose for her to be seated. "I had not noticed."

"You are angry," she stated.

"You are observant," he replied.

That rattled her. He did not miss the way her pale, small hands trembled before she clasped them out of sight in her lap. Could the lady's serenity be as false as her response to his loving had been? He dearly hoped so.

Edouard determined to put the best face on the evening. He refused to let loose his ire and make himself a further laughingstock. He and Anne sat alone on the dais. Henri wisely had elected to sit at the lower table. Though Edouard had not taken him to task yet for his part in this, Henri sensed he had fallen out of favor and made himself scarce.

Robert stood just behind them, eager as always to do his service. At least *he* would not overhear, Edouard thought wryly. Impatiently, he thumped the empty wine cup. Robert stepped forward quickly and filled it, gaining not so much as a nod for his effort.

Edouard could not help recalling the instance, with great humility, when he had roundly chastised the boy for his manner of speaking. To hear another attempt at this moment, so identical to that other, would only make matters worse. Later, he would deal with his regret over the mistake. Now, he simply ignored Robert.

Anne noticed, of course, reading it as a deliberate insult. She looked directly into his eyes, without a hint of trepidation. "Edouard, I beg you, do not visit my sins upon my son."

He returned her look with one of feigned amusement. "What say I *visit* them upon you, then? How would that be?"

She did not quail as he expected, but looked quite sure of herself. Unquestionably at odds with her words. "I cast myself upon your mercy, my lord, and pray you take your vows of knighthood seriously."

He could not suppress a spurt of genuine mirth. "My God, but you are a veritable mistress of strategy! You've played upon my passion, and now you tweak my honor. If this fails, what try you next? My charity?"

She cocked her head coyly and shrugged one lovely shoulder. "I suppose that would be the logical progression. Do you feel at all charitable?"

"Not in the least," he assured her, downing half the contents of the wine with one long pull.

"Ah, well, then, mayhaps I should give it up. Simple rustic that I am, you are too worldly a man, too wise for *me* to cozen."

He set down the cup and clapped his hands slowly, three times, regarding her all the while from beneath his hooded lids. "My pride. You finally recalled that I have some. Tell

me, my sweet," he probed suggestively, "is there anything
of mine you would not use to get your way?"

She lowered her eyes to simulate humility, or so he
thought. But when she finally raised her gaze to his again,
he saw only fierce determination, a will of iron. "There is
nothing I would not do to ensure my child's welfare,
Edouard. Nothing."

"Even bed a total stranger," he remarked.

She nodded. "I have done so."

He waited as one of the servants delivered the soup, then
continued as though uninterrupted.

"And you fawned over him as would a loving wife,
feigning your pleasure."

"Nay, the pleasure was real, Edouard. I assure you," she
looked away as though she could hardly bear to admit that,
to relinquish that one small vestige of her own pride. "You
will not believe me, but I have come to love you."

"Love!" He scoffed. "You are quite correct. Belief in
that certainly eludes me."

Edouard raised the wine Robert had just replenished and
downed it. He thunked down the cup and raised one hand,
ticking off the fingers with his thumb. "Honor, passion,
charity, pride and now love. You seem to have run down
your list now. Is there aught else you would have me consider?"

"Understanding. That would serve very well, I believe,"
she said, still not cowed by his sarcasm or his acrimony.

"Understand *what?*" he demanded. The temper he tried
to hold in check burst forth as his fist banged the table.
"How you could deliberately set out to lead me around by
my southern appendage like some callow youth? How you
flaunted your beauty so I would notice nothing else about
me? The way you dripped honeyed words in my ears to
block out the truth everyone else already *knew?* How dare
you ask understanding of such things?"

The deadly quiet around them finally penetrated his fury. He had shouted. The woman stole his very reason. Fear permeated the hall, suffusing every face. Except Anne's. She appeared as serene as ever she had, though the color was missing from her cheeks.

"I humbly beg your pardon, my lord," she whispered, but her voice carried in the silence. Not a happenstance, either, he would wager. Everyone hung on her words, expecting him to backhand her out of her chair, no doubt.

He nodded once, not to grant her request, but so that everyone would go back to their supper and stop staring at them. When the chatter and usual noise finally resumed, he said in a low voice, "I know very well what you are about, Anne. Do not think to turn this around so that I appear the villain in this."

She shook her head and toyed with the edge of the table linen. "Once your wrath with me abates, you will see that you are mistaken, Edouard. I have hope that you will be fair-minded then. My son was born a baron and will forever be that unless King Robert himself revokes the title. Baincroft is entailed. You cannot change that yourself. The law is on Robert's side."

He raked her with his gaze. "I suppose you do not recall the very precedent you related to me which involves your neighbors?"

At her swift intake of breath, he almost relented enough to offer her sympathy, but her glare stopped him cold. So be it, he thought.

"Anne, I do understand that you wish Robert to assume the lord's duties here at Baincroft when he comes of age. My wrath aside, I can assure you that this will not happen. No matter what you have done or what you will do, it cannot be."

A visible and violent shiver shook her body. For a long moment afterward, she simply sat there unmoving. Then she rose, her meal untouched. She did not look at him again and said nothing more. Neither did Edouard.

He watched her glide across the floor toward the stairs and ascend with all the grace of a queen. Why did the crack in his heart grow wider with her every step? Why could he not gloat at her failure to twist him round her finger? Why did he ache so for her, when she obviously felt nothing at all for him?

She must know that Robert could never rule here. Love for the child had skewed her mind. He had not denied her that because of her deception. The boy simply would never be capable. Did he allow it to happen, the first opportunist to arrive here would wrest the place from Robert before anyone could come to his aid.

He turned slightly to see Robert staring after Anne, a worried look on his face. Edouard touched his arm and waited for the boy to face him. "Go. Take some food to your mother," he ordered softly as he removed the flagon from Robert's hands.

With a nod of understanding and a soft pat to Edouard's sleeve, Robert hurried to obey.

That sunny, trusting nature of his would play against him, Edouard thought. The deafness would disallow understanding, both with Baincroft's people and with neighbors who might be needed as allies. For all that Robert was a winsome and pleasant boy, Edouard knew that he would remain just that even into manhood. Such a one could never hope to hold his own in these savage times.

The necessity of denying Robert his place saddened Edouard, and he knew it must devastate Anne. If he ignored the way she had slashed his pride to ribbons, he had to admit that he admired her for her diligence. She had left no path untried in her attempt to secure her son's birthright for him. A woman could only do so much, but she had done all within her power.

Once she accepted that she had failed, Edouard meant to put forth the rest of his decision. They would have another son as soon as God willed it. When that happened, Edouard would petition King Robert to grant that one the estate in Robert's stead. Perhaps that would ease Anne's disappointment somewhat.

By that time, Edouard would have forgiven her. Accepting that she would never love him would be difficult, but he would manage. That had been a fool's wish he should never have entertained.

He slept beside her that night, but respected Anne's need to keep to herself. She needed time to come to terms with her defeat. How much time was the question that troubled Edouard. A day? A month? Half a century?

The next morning, he worked out his frustration on Sir Gui. Together they presented a demonstration of trickery one might encounter in a desperate sword fight with no rules.

Gui proved more proficient than usual, but still lost his sword, narrowly escaping impalement. Edouard welcomed the release of energies, and even managed a smile as he explained the moves to the young ones.

"Now, go to!" he ordered. Thomas and Henri paired off, as did Robert and Hamel, the armorer's boy, whom Edouard had selected to train as well.

"That Thomas moves like a cowherd," Gui observed. "Breeding will tell."

The comment irritated Edouard. "Thomas is nobly born."

Gui clicked his tongue against his teeth. "To a *Scot*." Before Edouard could speak, Gui leapt forward. "Robert! Lift that shield! *Dieu*, you will never learn!"

"Robert does very well," Edouard stated. "And save your breath. You know he cannot hear you."

"True enough. Why on earth do you bother with him

now that you know? I confess I was not that surprised. I had already noted how thick-witted he is. Cursed of God, those like him. The Church says as much.''

Edouard itched to kill the man where he stood. Just run him through and hope the scavengers would not gag when they feasted. But he would not. No, he had brought Gui back here, knowing full well he would always hate the man for what he'd done to Anne. Living with that decision would continue to pose a trial, but there was no sound reason for enduring these insults of his.

''Ah well, Gui, you are so religious, I wonder that he doesn't send you running in fear of contagion.'' Edouard paused, pursed his lips for a second, and then issued fair warning. ''You should listen well to my next words, for your life depends upon them. Mind what you say of my sons. And of any other in my care. You treat these boys with the respect they deserve for their efforts. If they step wrongly, correct them. But if I hear one more slur out of your mouth, it will be your last. Am I understood?''

Gui shrugged, his eyes still on the mock battles before them. ''Very well.''

He watched a moment longer and then turned to Edouard. ''I did overhear what you told Lady Anne last eve. I agree with you that Robert has no place as master of this keep. You are wise to make other arrangements. Who will take it over?''

Edouard did not mistake Gui's reason for asking. He felt like throwing up his hands in utter frustration at the man's gall. Gui's description of *thick-witted* stuck in Edouard's mind, but not in conjunction with Robert.

''You truly believe that *you* would be a good candidate, do you not? That I would consider you?''

The knight shrugged again, a mannerism Edouard found highly annoying due to its frequent repetition. ''I would like lands of my own.''

"Here? In Scotland?" Edouard asked, truly curious as to whether Sir Gui would place his greed above his prejudice against Scots and this country.

"I do prefer France, if you're offering a choice," Gui said succinctly, "But here will suffice. I am landless, after all."

And would remain landless so long as he served a Trouville, Edouard thought. If the man ever gained a plot of land from this quarter, it would be well under the surface and covered over with stones.

"So you see the wisdom of rewarding me now?" Gui asked with a sniff. "That *would* be wise."

Edouard stared, shaking his head in disbelief, as well as denial. "That would be *mad!*" Then he turned and walked away.

He wished he could get rid of Gui. It was all he could do to tolerate him after what he had done. But both Anne and Gui assured him that the act stemmed from Gui's loyalty. Now everything he did and every word out of his mouth grated.

Gui's attitude toward Scots, that they were a backward race lacking civility, was one shared by most Frenchmen. Gui only mouthed what he had been taught. His concept of deafness was almost universally held. Cursed by God, indeed! Robert was only an unfortunate coping as well as he could with what life had dealt him, no different than one who had lost a limb in battle.

The very fact that Sir Gui approved his decision to supplant Robert as lord of Baincroft made Edouard rethink his decision. No matter how he turned the facts around, however, he knew it had to stand. That was not to say he believed Robert useless, by any means.

The boy proved quite proficient with his sword, given the short time he had been in training. He was strong for his age, agile and tireless. Loyal, of course. Courteous and kind. He might make a competent household knight. But he could not begin to acquire the skills necessary to manage an estate, even one so small as this.

Thanks be to God that Robert's care had fallen to him and not some other. At least he could place this new son of his in a worthwhile position.

Edouard only hoped that Anne would come to appreciate that he did have Robert's best interest at heart.

Three long nights passed as Anne continued to sleep beside Edouard, determined not to leave his bed until he requested her to do so. She decided that she would give him no further cause to set her aside.

But her reasons went deeper than that. In her heart of hearts, she longed for him to turn to her, forgive her all the secrets, and say again that he loved her.

She dreamed that he granted her wish for Robert and welcomed the news of a new child. Then she would wake and find him turned away from her, ignoring their marriage as surely as he disregarded her wishes.

When he did notice her pregnancy, she would admit it. She would brazen this out, allow him to hope for a bairn who was perfect. That could happen, after all. Who was she to say this babe would share Robert's deafness? No one seemed to know what had caused him to be so.

Edouard still trained Robert each day and he never mentioned turning him out of Baincroft. He never mentioned much at all. They rarely spoke now, and when they did, it was of mundane matters. A question here about glazing the barracks windows, a comment there about the use of spices in a certain dish. Nothing of import at all.

He came to bed after she slept and did not touch her. Together they lay like two strangers, which she supposed they still were in essence. She had no clue to his thoughts and doubted he cared at all what hers might be.

But life went on, and Anne thanked heaven Edouard had not yet seen fit to set her and her son outside the gate to make their way as best they could. Difficult as it was to endure, his cold courtesy was definitely a lesser evil than that would have been.

The lord's court convened four days after their confrontation at supper. Edouard sat to judge it, as was his right as acting lord and Robert's guardian. Though the sheriff saw to cases involving serious crimes, the day-to-day conflicts arising among the inhabitants of Baincroft lands, and her adjoining property, were always settled here.

Anne, accompanied by Rob, had presided over the court since MacBain had become ill and before Edouard came. Though she resented her husband's usurping of this duty, she held her peace on the matter.

Nevertheless, she did take a seat beside him when he offered it. Father Michael sat to Edouard's other side. Robert wandered the hall, his displacement quite obvious to everyone.

The first complaint involved two brothers who lived upon Anne's property. The elder stated that Baincroft's steward, Master Simm, had paid a sum for their cutting extra firewood to be used within the keep. He declared that he had labored to cut it all, and his brother had done nothing but deliver the wood and accept payment for it. Now the younger refused to hand over the money. The younger, of course, argued that he had both cut and delivered it, thereby earning all of the coins himself.

While Edouard considered the matter, Robert marched directly up to both men and grabbed their hands by their wrists. He turned them palms up and inspected them carefully.

Curious to see what he was doing, Edouard leaned over the dais. Robert turned and pulled both men closer, pointing out the raw blisters on the younger man's hands. The elder's hands were hardly even callused. Robert gave the man a short shove. "You lie."

Edouard sat back, both surprised and pleased. "Judgement to young Matthew," he declared. "Keep the coins. And you," he said pointing to the older man, "will furnish a like amount of wood for half the pay. Lie in this court again and I shall have your tongue."

He then nodded his appreciation to Robert and summoned the next complainants.

Agar, the chief herdsman, dragged his daughter before the dais. "She be carryin' a bairn, my lord, big as life, and wilna say what scutling done th' deed!"

Edouard leaned toward Anne, his voice almost inaudible as though he spoke to himself. "Judging by the girl's truculence, she probably has no idea who it was. I suppose we should select a husband for her."

She heard a sudden commotion of whispers and chuckles. Edouard straightened immediately. His attention settled on Robert, who was tugging forth to the dais a bashful, red-faced young man. Anne saw that it was David, one of the older stable boys.

The girl's frightened cries almost drowned out her father's curses.

"Silence!" Edouard demanded.

Robert grabbed the reluctant girl's hand and slapped it on top of David's. "Banns?" he suggested to Father Michael with a knowing quirk of one sandy brow.

The priest ducked his head in a quick nod, barely suppressing his grin.

"Do you fear this man?" Edouard asked the girl, for she still looked stricken. "Has he hurt you? No matter the pregnancy, I will not tie a woman to her rapist."

"Nay, my lord. I but feared Da would kill him if I told! I love my Davy!"

"Then have him," Edouard said with a roll of his eyes.

He turned to the priest. "Need we banns, Father, given the circumstance?"

"Nay, but I am curious. Robert, how did you know 'twas David?"

Robert answered promptly. "Look!" He pointed to the assembly with a sweep of his hand and mimicked their curious and somewhat salacious expressions. Then he gestured negligently toward the guilty party and assumed such a woebegone, love-stricken face that Edouard laughed aloud.

Anne barely caught a giggle behind her hand as their eyes met. She forced herself to look away, lest she forget where she was. But out of the corner of her eye, she saw the quick, surreptitious motion of Robert's hands.

No question that he thought to hide the motions from her and impart them only to Edouard and possibly Father Michael. He rapidly touched a finger to his chest, to his eye and then made an obscene gesture with both his hands that no one could mistake. Definitely not one of the signs she had concocted for him. He had seen the couple in the act, and he wanted no doubt left as to David's culpability.

"Does he miss nothing?" Edouard asked wryly, over the noisy congratulations to the pair just betrothed.

Anne cleared her throat and clasped her hands before her on the table. "Robert is quite thorough."

"And knowledgeable for one of such tender years," he commented. "How does he know that the act could result in pregnancy, I wonder?"

"Because I told him. He needs to know these things."

Edouard grunted a small laugh of disbelief. "Shall I just ride out hunting or some such? It seems my talents are quite useless here. Is he always right?"

Anne shook her head. "Not every time. We all make mistakes. But he reads a man well. Or a woman, for that matter. Robert can tell if one is trustworthy or not."

Edouard smiled with what seemed a direct taunt, questioning her own ability to judge such a thing. "He did see fit to trust *me*."

"Well, my lord, as I said, we all make mistakes."

She regretted saying the words when she saw his sudden frown.

If he would only be fair. Why could Edouard not see that Robert was perfectly capable of doing what he was born to do? Had he not proved himself just now?

A bud of hope opened slightly, wanting desperately to blossom in full. What if Rob continued to show Edouard all that he had learned? Not only in how to settle disputes, but in other things. He understood the accounts of expenditures necessary to keep Baincroft running smoothly. Sums were not his favorite thing to do, but he did them well. Aye, this could work, she thought.

Suddenly the possibilities seemed endless. True, keeping the secret had roused Edouard's wrath, but he *had* allowed them to stay here. His grudge seemed to be wearing away, even though his thinking was still wrong. Considering that things had not gone as badly as she once feared, Anne made up her mind. They would win Edouard over.

He did look kindly on Rob and he had offered admiration—however reluctantly—for the antics here in court. And not once had he really snapped at her today. In fact, he had even deigned to include her when considering the girl's plight.

Anne smiled to herself. She might save everything yet if she kept her wits about her. Edouard might pretend to be immune to the feelings that had grown between the two of them, but Anne knew better. The light of desire had shone like a golden gleam within those dark brown eyes only moments before.

What if she gave free rein to the love she felt for him? Suppose she gave it unconditionally? There was a chance he would love her back. A small chance, true. But if he did, Edouard might willingly and of his own accord, give her what he knew she most needed.

"Aye, everyone makes an error now and again," she added, to counteract her sharp retort to him only moments before. "Though I will admit that I could be the one mistaken about the trust in this instance."

When he looked down at her in surprise, Anne smiled, aiming for the same expression Rob always used when he sought to charm her out of too much marzipan.

It unsettled her just a little when Edouard returned it in kind.

Chapter Seventeen

"Would you ride out with me today?" Edouard asked her after he declared the court's business at an end. "I trust it has been a while since you have visited your property."

The reason for his impulsive invitation intrigued her. "I have never seen it," she admitted.

"Not ever? Imagine that." He took her arm to assist her down from the dais. "Why?"

Anne knew she had shocked him, though he phrased the question politely enough. "Not for lack of interest, I assure you. Before I came here to wed MacBain, I lived in my father's castle, which lies to the west. The dower lands, which came to me through my mother, lie northeast, as you know. So, we did not pass through them to arrive here."

He had tucked her arm through his so that she had no choice but to accompany him as he left the hall. They descended the steps and leisurely crossed the bailey toward the stables.

"That was eleven years past," he said. "Surely there have been opportunities for you to see it since. The ride takes less than an hour."

"I do not ride."

He laughed. "You jest. Everyone rides! There are several

suitable mounts in your stables. What of hunting? Simple exercise?''

''Neither my father nor my husband would allow it.'' Anne answered, looking anywhere but up at him. ''They were probably afraid if they permitted me with the means, I would not return.''

He sobered, those ebony brows drawing together in a frown. ''Then how do you get about?''

Anne shook her head. ''I do not *get about,* if you mean leaving Baincroft lands. They brought me here in a covered cart, and here I have remained.'' When his frown deepened, she tried to make light of her virtual imprisonment. ''I do walk in the wood now, gather herbs, trek over to the loch to enjoy the view.''

''When you're not sinking to the bottom of it,'' he muttered under his breath. He wore an expression of anger Anne knew was not directed toward her. ''I'll wager you were not granted even those outings you mention until six months past, am I right?''

''You are,'' she admitted with a small laugh, hoping to coax him into lighter banter. ''But I explore farther each time. Soon you may call me an adventurer! I hope you do not fault me for neglecting my lands. I was but minding my place here. Simm has seen to everything and, of course, Robert and Thomas help.''

''Would you learn to ride?'' Edouard asked, his voice brisk and devoid of the sympathy she saw clearly in his eyes.

Anne could not bring herself to reveal her fear of trying this new thing. Edouard offered out of kindness. And after that smile he had just given her in the hall, she felt he also might be trying to reestablish some goodwill between them. This seemed a perfect chance to begin accomplishing that. Surely, if Rob had mastered a mount by the age of six, she could do so at her age.

"Aye, Edouard. I believe I should like that very much."

Their ride provided exactly what Anne hoped for. Mounted on a small gray mare of gentle disposition, she kept Edouard hovering near with his larger gelding. No riding master could have been more attentive, offering more warnings and instructions than she could digest.

"Surely we have ridden more than an hour!" she said, feeling a numbness in her nether parts she had never experienced.

"Longer by far," he agreed, pretending high impatience. "I usually do not travel at a slow walk! I swear these nags have grazed most of the way. When we dismount, I fully expect their girths to be dragging the dirt." She watched the corners of his eyes crinkle when he suppressed a smile. "I believe we should return at full gallop."

"Nay!" she cried, laughing aloud. "She will bounce me off!"

He reined in and slid from his saddle, then reached up to lift her down from hers. "Come, I've something to show you."

They walked hand in hand to the top of the hill. He presented the lovely view with a sweep of his arm. "Our castle will lie here."

"*Our* castle?"

"Yes, of course!" he said proudly, and pointed down the slope. "See those few dwellings there in the distance? When the mason and the workmen come, they will settle there near the quarry. Then my man, Sir Armand, will be organizing the major effort here once he arrives with proper building tools."

All of the information after his first sentence barely registered in her mind. "You are constructing a castle."

"I plan to make it roughly twice the size of Baincroft. Still small, but large enough to support a number of my knights and those workers from my estates in France who might wish to come here to live.''

Anne's legs felt nigh to giving way under her, so she lowered herself to the plush grasses and sat. ''When did you decide to do this?''

He joined her on the ground, resting his forearms on his upraised knees. ''When I first came through here. That depended upon whether we suited, of course.'' He smiled. ''And we did. I considered every location. This site seems perfect, does it not?''

''Aye, perfect.''

''I'm happy that you like it.''

Anne looked around her and noticed several stakes that someone had pounded into the ground to mark one thing or another. ''I like it well,'' she murmured.

For some time, Edouard continued relating the details of the structure he intended. His enthusiasm grew such that he rose and began pacing after a while, gesturing with his arms, and smiling down at her where she still sat. For the love of her, Anne could not bring herself to stand. He was building a castle. For them.

Simm had told her there was a keep somewhere on her lands, the skeleton of a place unfit to inhabit. Anne had supposed Edouard might make it habitable someday. But, if he had bothered, she'd envisioned his giving care of that to one of his men while she either remained with Rob at Baincroft or took refuge in a cottage hereabout. But Edouard would not be returning to his wealthy estates in France. He would build a castle. For them.

Since she had found he was not returning, Anne had thought he would simply take Baincroft for his own. Now she wondered what he would do with it once he completed this grander castle. Give it to Henri, she supposed. She plucked a long blade of grass and nibbled on it as she thought.

There was no point in asking what he intended to do
with Robert. If he meant to send him away, surely he would
have said so by this time. If Rob was to stay, she was not
certain she wanted to hear in what capacity just yet. Best
to avoid the subject for now. She still had high hope of
Edouard realizing that her son was worthy to govern his
own lands. Once Edouard voiced what he had in mind for
Rob, he would not likely go back on his decision.

When she glanced up at him, he wore a questioning look,
as though he had just asked her something. "I wonder,"
she said, "how deep you must dig to find water hereabout." The distraction worked. While he launched into a
detailed explanation, Anne was free to examine further her
feelings about Edouard's plans for their future.

For the first time, she allowed herself to admit she was
glad he would not leave her. Despite his intention to take
all that belonged to her son, Anne felt that Edouard would
surely see to Robert's welfare. And he had not indicated in
any way, even when he raged at her, that he meant to set
her aside as his wife. Her worst fears, that she and Robert
would be rendered homeless and without any means to live
other than begging, would not be realized.

Edouard had not yet said that he feared their future children would be afflicted as Rob was. Either he assumed
Robert's deafness had resulted from sickness or accident,
or he simply had not thought about the why of it one way
or another. He would eventually. Anne had the fever tale
ready. But the birth of this new child seemed far into the
future now, as she sat half attending Edouard's grandiose
plans for their new home.

At the moment, all she wanted to do was sit here in this
peaceful place and pretend they were two people, newly
wed, and looking forward to life together.

When he fell quiet, she spoke her true feelings to him.

"I had no notion how wonderful it would be to feel so...so liberated."

"How far would you ride, then?" he asked, again dropping down to the grass, only much nearer this time. "To the coast, to see the ocean? To the west to visit the Isles?"

She laughed. "Someday I might!"

"May I come with you, Lady Free?" he asked softly, taking her hand and bringing it to his lips. "Such wondrous things I could show you."

Anne turned and regarded him quizzically. For a brief moment, Edouard's countenance wore neither jaded amusement nor the arrogance he usually assumed to mask his feelings. In the darkness of his eyes, she clearly saw a need. Not a desire to accompany her on any fantastical journey she might make, not even for the satisfaction of the body. This was a plea for her to assuage his loneliness, a state she thought a man like Edouard would never have experienced.

How could he even know what lonely meant, this privileged noble, cosseted and waited upon his entire life? Anne doubted he had ever heard the word *no* from the lips of anyone, save mayhaps his king. Edouard could have anything. Anyone. Still, he sat here, holding her hand so tightly, and beseeching her with those eyes of his to...what? Be his friend? Love him?

She did love him. If he only knew how much. The one time she had tried to tell him so, he had not believed her. He would not believe it now, and why should he? She was not his friend yet, if that was what he wished. She might never be. For love could, and did, coexist with dislike at times. Or even hatred.

"Do you hate me?" he asked, not intensely as she might have expected, but impersonally, as though he were asking if he thought it might rain. How quickly he managed to conceal his feelings. The fact that he seemed to have read her very thoughts disconcerted her, but he had done that before.

"Do you have the Sight?" she asked.

He laughed, releasing her hand to lie back on the grass and abandon himself to his mirth. It rang with a bitterness he did not even attempt to hide.

"I did not mean that to sound so," she said sincerely. "Nay, I do not hate you."

With a long exhalation—she hoped, of relief—he got up and offered her his hand. "Come, we must head homeward now or we shall miss our supper."

They did not gallop, but rode sedately side by side, discussing all the amenities he proposed for the new castle.

By the time they reached Baincroft, Anne's heart had grown so light, she hardly noticed the aches she had gained as a result of her questionable riding skills.

Edouard also wanted peace between them. Possibly more than that. She would try to be his friend, after all, Anne thought. He was making an effort toward that end. How could she do less?

If they were in sympathy with each other, there would be opportunity for her to point out to him all of Robert's talents, just as she had hoped. She would change his mind about Baincroft.

Once she had that settled, there would be months in which to plan for this next child. Edouard would be happy about it at first, she knew. He would come to adore it once it was born.

Why not dwell on his goodness, instead of those traits she would wish away? He was nothing like MacBain. Never once had he raised a hand to either her or her son. Though he meant to deny Robert his due, it was only because he needed enlightening.

She knew well that this husband, for all his wry barbs and loud growls, was quite capable of love. He might not love her, but he loved Henri dearly. There was no reason to think he would not love this babe, as well.

Later, if a problem surfaced, as it had when Robert outgrew his infancy, she would manage it. By that time Edouard would have observed how well Robert got on, and would understand that dealing with deafness was quite possible. This time she would be free to enlist the father's help in training.

A husband such as Edouard should be properly rewarded for his goodness of heart, she thought, smiling to herself. And a wife like herself ought to provide such desserts. She quite looked forward to the bestowing.

Edouard lingered in the hall after their supper and allowed Anne time aplenty to finish her bath. He had no wish to destroy the fragile bond they had begun to form.

Sleeping with him was one thing, but allowing him to intrude on her bathing, seeing her unclothed and performing such intimate rituals, would constitute quite another. Later, perhaps, when and if they established a true closeness, he might suggest they bathe together.

Tonight, however, he would content himself with finding her already abed and hope for more of the pleasant conversation they had enjoyed during the afternoon and throughout the evening meal. That could lead to lovemaking if she were willing, but Edouard doubted if she was ready for that at this point.

He understood her feelings of helplessness with regard to Robert's plight. Anne's loyalty to her son came first with her. Though, by law, she should support her husband in all things, he knew she did not agree with him at all on this issue. Edouard's anger over that had dissipated and the blow to his pride did not sting quite so much anymore. At least she had wisely realized that enmity between them served nothing. One had to admire her pragmatism.

Just as he had done, Anne had carefully avoided any reference to his relieving Robert of future responsibilities at Baincroft. Edouard hoped she might have begun to accept that he knew best, but he seriously doubted that she had.

For some reason, she had initiated a sort of truce between them. The relief and eagerness with which he welcomed that gesture disturbed Edouard. Because of that, he determined that he would not rush headlong at this olive branch only to have it slap him in the face. Women were notorious for their changes of mind. Judging by her quick turnabout at Lord's court this morn, Anne was the rule rather than the exception.

He also suspected there was more behind this sudden amiability of hers than she made evident. The very abruptness of it made it questionable. And yet, he could not bring himself to spurn her efforts. A small possibility existed that she might have accepted his edict concerning Robert, and be quite sincere in her wish to reconcile.

He approached their chamber quietly so as not to wake her. But the moment he entered, she spoke.

"Would you care to bathe?" she asked softly, her voice warming him with a pleasant tingle of desire. He could enjoy that without giving it free rein, he thought.

She sat on the edge of the bed, brushing out her hair. Though the pale blue bedgown covered her body entirely, its folds draped close about her in an enticing way. Edouard drew in a deep breath and with it, the sweet scent of the herbs she had used in the water.

Flickering candlelight lent visual warmth to the radiant heat of the low-burning fire, both casting golden light and soft shadows about the chamber.

Edouard recognized a seduction scene quite readily, having arranged a number of them himself. He should have expected this, he thought. Anne's little campaign was not yet finished.

He could save her the trouble and tell her that the scheme would not work, but it seemed a shame to waste all this. And, truth be told, he felt just angry enough about it to take full advantage of her just now. Why should he be noble about the matter when she was not?

"A bath sounds inviting," he said, employing his most suggestive tone. He had already washed in the bathhouse after their ride when Henri removed his chain mail. Slowly, and with all the grace he could manage, he began to remove his belt.

Her eyes widened slightly as he dropped it on the floor and lifted his tunic. Holding her gaze, sending lascivious promises mind to mind, he threaded his finger through the ties of his shirt and slowly pulled them apart. He lingered over the removal of that, flexing the muscles of his arms and chest as he pulled the soft linen over his head.

A small sigh escaped her, sending waves of heat through his loins. She admired his body, so she once said. He decided she might have spoken truly in that instance, gauging by her present reaction. The knowledge appealed to him. He did not consider himself particularly vain, but neither was he modest.

Bare chested, he strode languidly toward the stool beside the tub and sat down to remove his soft leather boots. She watched him rather avidly. He could feel her gaze like a caress against his skin.

Edouard slipped off his boots and stood again to untie the points of his hose. Again, he made slow work of it. Daring her to look away, he lowered the heavy, clinging knit past his thighs and calves and stepped out.

She glanced quickly away and then back again, fastening her eyes directly on the only garment he had left to remove. That barely contained what it protected now and would leave precious little to her imagination. With a slow smile, he turned his back to her and unfastened his loincloth.

Her swift intake of breath did nothing to hurry him into the tub full of water. He looked over his shoulder to find her staring wide-eyed, lips parted, and appearing rather ravenous. His own hunger tested his control. Hers nearly snapped it completely.

"You have dropped your brush," he remarked with a lift of his brow. He turned toward her. "Shall I retrieve it for you?"

"Aye," she breathed, staring avidly now that she could witness his readiness.

He did not rush as he crossed the room, but reveled in her avid perusal of him. The brush lay on the bed beside her. Edouard picked it up and smoothed the bristles with one long finger. Her fascination with the gesture prompted him to ask, "Would you like me to help you, Anne?"

"Wh-what?" Her eyes flew to his.

"Brush your hair. Shall I?"

"Nay," she said, swallowing hard. "Never mind."

"Nonsense," he crooned. "Allow me."

He raised the brush to her crown and drew it down in a long, lingering stroke, following the flowing length of dark satin that draped over one shoulder and breast.

When the firm bristles raked over the peak beneath her tresses and the clinging fabric of her gown, she moaned. Her eyes closed. Edouard smiled.

"Now the back," he whispered near her ear. With his arms surrounding her, he applied the brush to the top of her head, just behind the center part of her hair and smoothed it downward. As he did so, the front of his body brushed her knees. He shifted closer, wedging her legs apart so he could rest between them.

With each stroke of the brush, he pulled her forward until

only the softness of her gown lay between her heat and his own.

"Is—is it warm in here?" she murmured unsteadily.

"Too warm for the gown," he whispered, abandoning the brush. Fighting his urge to rush, Edouard reached down and slowly lifted the fabric to her waist. "Cooler now?" he asked suggestively, his gaze traveling from her dazed expression, downward to where their bodies almost joined.

"Nay!" she exclaimed as though nearly devoid of breath.

He slid his hands beneath her and lifted her slightly so that they fit together. When he pushed into her, she uttered that same sweet cry he dreamed of, the one he craved above all to hear.

For a long moment, he remained still, battling the need to thrust madly and without thought until he gained surcease. He leaned into her while pulling the gown up her body and over her head. Then he gently pushed her back so that she lay prone.

"How beautiful you are," he whispered, smoothing his palms over the silkiness of her skin, shaping her neck, her shoulders, her breasts, pausing to circle carefully over their taut peaks.

"Do not," she cried. "Do not wait!"

He felt the sweat of his brow run in rivulets. His muscles bunched and he trembled with the need to move. Control almost slipped. Edouard withdrew, relishing her cry of protest.

Quickly now, he lay down and drew her above him. "Take it as you will," he invited as casually as his urgency would allow.

She took it as she would. Edouard clenched his teeth together. He squeezed his eyes shut and fought to think of other things than the grasping heat within her. But nothing quelled the fierce compulsion to hurry. He clutched her waist with his hands and guided their mating to a paradisiacal and hasty conclusion that left him gasping for air.

They lay there for some while, Edouard wondering what to say next, while she drew slow circles in his chest hair with one finger.

She finally broke the silence. "I thought we might never do this again."

"You must have planned to emasculate me then?" he said, unable to imagine a lifetime of celibacy in this bed.

"Nay," she answered with a lazy laugh. "But do not think the thought did not cross my mind. You provoke me to such anger betimes, it frightens me of myself."

"Remind me to keep a civil tongue around you!"

Anne rose on one elbow to look down at him. "Edouard?"

He met her gaze directly. "Yes?"

"I am happy that we can talk sensibly now. Before today, we seemed at cross-purposes most of the time. That is behind us, is it not?"

Ah, here it comes. He wished he had gone straight to sleep. He heard a hint of proposed negotiation in her question and, as much as he disliked the necessity, the time had come for him to stand firm.

"It would be, if we could both remain sensible, as you say. But I fear we are still at cross-purposes, Anne. I have told you quite clearly that I will not bend on the matter of Baincroft's disposition."

She sighed dispiritedly and lay back on her pillow. "Will you at least give Rob the chance to prove what he can do?"

"I know what he can do, Anne. He does have good instincts when it comes to judging in Lord's court. He rides well for one his age. And he is amazingly good with weapons. You need not tell me these things, for I have witnessed his abilities. But you must admit he lacks the ability to make himself understood and to understand."

She sat up and glared down at him. "He lacks neither!"

"Aside from that, Robert trusts too easily, which can be fatal to a man. He is too accepting, Anne. Too naive."

"He is but ten years old, Edouard! *Ten!*"

Edouard took her hand in his, and it required some strength to hold it. "Listen to me. Your Robert has had more reason to mistrust than anyone of his age ought to have, and yet he does not. See how easily he took to me as a father? He blithely ignores Gui's disdain of him. He never questions a man's motives. I think it never even occurs to him to do so. Robert is like a gamboling hound pup that assumes everyone finds it pleasing until it gets kicked! This attitude is dangerous, whatever the age."

Tears streamed down her face. Edouard desperately wished he could hold her and comfort her. No chance at all that she would allow that at the moment. But he would not lie to her just to give her a temporary measure of peace. This thing must be settled here and now, for all time.

"Anne, I care for you more than you know. Believe me or not, I truly care for Robert, as well. Did I not, I would agree with what you want for him. But your son can never defend Baincroft. The people here deserve a strong lord who will see to their interests and protect them with his wisdom and his sword. Please try to understand that."

She raised her chin, sniffed once, and blinked away her tears. "I understand well enough. You want this keep and know that you can take it with guile and without wasting any of your men. You would steal it from its rightful lord!"

He released her hand and met her glare with a look of regret. "I need not steal it, Anne. I have it already. Should we have another son together, Baincroft will be his. I will petition Robert Bruce, and you know he will grant me this."

She wept no more, nor did she rail at him as he expected.

Instead, she lay down quietly and deliberately turned her back to him.

Edouard knew that all his hopes for a peaceful future and a loving wife, hopes almost fully rekindled in spite of the caution he intended, were now dead. Anne would hate him to her last breath.

There would be no sleep this night. The air, so heated during their lovemaking, began to chill.

He got up, donned a pair of hunting braies, and went to stoke the fire. He should go downstairs for ale, he thought, just to get out of the chamber. But he decided that drinking in this particular mood might be unwise.

God help him, he really wanted to recant. He wanted to give Robert this insignificant place in eight or ten years, and wish him well of it. But he knew if it were Henri facing the challenge with such a limited ability, the decision would remain the same.

Thank God it was not Henri. Guilt over that relief troubled Edouard and made him feel small-minded. What would he have done if it had been so? Exactly what he planned to do now. He would have another son to take charge and look after him.

He wondered if the loss of Anne's regard was worth standing on this principle of his. A lord's responsibility to his people was an awesome charge that could not be taken lightly or left to a steward to handle. He considered how much care he had put into selecting the strongest and most intelligent castellans for his own estates in France.

A castellan! Why on earth had it not occurred to him before? Because Robert would never be an absentee lord, that was why he had not thought of it. Though there was no law that said the lord could not remain in residence and still have a castellan, but it was not done that he knew of. Those with only one estate, especially one the size of this, did not need such a man. Robert would.

Acquiring the right person would be critical, however, when the time came. A man trained well enough to serve as castellan would also be able to usurp Robert's property permanently, perhaps even make a bid for the title himself.

The bed seemed much more inviting now, but Edouard did not want to wake Anne and suggest this alternative just yet. He must give it more thought.

Relief relaxed him enough that he thought he might rest for a while. Then he might go down for ale or wine and have himself a private celebration, while planning how to tell her about his inspiration. He leaned back in the chair and closed his eyes, entertaining thoughts of her gratitude if this did prove a worthy idea.

He drifted into a pleasant chimera of Anne showing her delight. She would love him then, surely. The family would become whole as it had not yet been. He could almost hear the happy murmurings of a crowd gathering for celebration.

By the time he realized the voices were neither happy, nor within his dream, the door flew open and men burst into the chamber.

Edouard leapt out of the chair to find a weapon, but they fell upon him too quickly. Anne screamed.

For a second, he broke free, but a sound blow to his head from behind staggered him. He dropped to his knees and then knew nothing more.

Chapter Eighteen

Anne recoiled, scrambling back against the headboard and clutching fistfulls of the covers to her neck. A huge man wearing a *breacan* turned toward her, grinning. *A dreaded highlander!*

"Dress yersel', Lady Anne. We'll be awaitin' ye in th' hall. Dinna be afeared. We've come to save ye." He quirked one eyebrow as he held his torch aloft and examined her face. "God's own truth, he was right! Ye *do* have th' look of Honor!"

Before she could summon enough wits to speak, he and his men had dragged the unconscious Edouard through the door and firmly shut it behind them.

Free her? Of what? Edouard? Worry for his fate tore the fear right out of her. She had to get to him before they did something worse than knock him senseless. Anne's own father had been a highlander. She knew how fierce and unreasonable they could be.

Anne threw back the covers and ran for her clothing chest. She grabbed the gown on top and yanked it over her head, not even bothering with *surcote* or belt. Her soft house shoes sat nearby and she almost fell stepping into them. Poor Edouard. And what of Robert and Henri? Had they taken them, as well? She flew to the door and flung it open, rushing after them.

By the time she reached the hall, Anne saw that someone had hastily set up the table on the dais. The leader of the brigands sat in Edouard's chair. Two of his men stood on either side of Edouard who lay facedown with his hands bound behind him. Another one held Anne back.

"Stand away, Lady Anne," said the one who had spoken to her in the bed chamber. "You'll not need to trouble yersel' more about this one."

"What do you mean, *trouble myself?*" she demanded. "Who are you and what do you do here?"

He smiled again, a proud expression as if he had just done something wonderful instead of attacking them in their home. Then he turned the smile on one of his men. "Jamie, wake him up."

The man he addressed bent down, rolled Edouard over and began slapping and shaking him none too gently.

"Leave him be!" Anne screamed, struggling with the brute who held her arms.

"Calmly now," the leader ordered. "There's no call to get upset. He canna harm ye."

"Harm me?" Anne cried. "He's my husband! What are you doing to him? What do you want of us?"

"Ach! Pardon my manners. I should have introduced myself. I am Sir Alan of Strode, husband to Lady Honor, your cousin. My lads and I have come to relieve you of this troublesome lackwit." He inclined his head and clicked his tongue. "I coulda sworn he had better sense than t' show his face again this side o' th' water, after I warned him."

Anne had spent the last moments looking to see whether they had rousted anyone else out of their beds. Obviously they had not, for none were present save those who usually slept in the hall, the spitboys, several of the kitchen maids and Simm. Another of the strangers had herded the fright-

ened servants and her steward together in one corner and
stood by with his sword at the ready.

"Trouville's men are contained within the barracks,"
said Alan of Strode. "We plan to make short work of this."

Edouard groaned and opened his eyes. Anne watched as
he focused upon the man who was speaking to her. She
marveled that Edouard seemed not at all distraught. "Ah,
Strode, the illustrious hero. I wonder why I didn't expect
this."

He rolled to his side, managed to get to his knees and
then stood.

Strode laughed. "Turnabout *is* fair play, Trouville." He
turned to Anne. "Did he boast to you about the time he
dragged me from my slumber just so, intent on making *my*
wife a widow? If I'd no' shamed him inta giving me a
fightin' chance, I'd be dead, and he'd be wed to her now."

He leaned forward toward Anne, wriggled his dark red
brows and whispered conspiratorially across the table, "But
God tickled his nose, y'see, and that sneeze was his un-
doing. And if he's thinkin' I'll give him a sword and depend on yet another boon from th' Almighty, he's dead
wrong!"

Anne looked from one to the other, confused. She did
not know Edouard had ever come to Scotland before.

Edouard stepped toward her, "Anne, I should have—"

"Silence!" Strode thundered. One of the men rammed
his sword hilt into Edouard's midsection. "There's a good
lad."

Strode continued as though uninterrupted, his voice perfectly friendly. "I see you are completely in the dark, my
lady. Your uncle, Hume, is father to my wife. He arranged
a betrothal between her and this offal here some four years
past. But courageous lass that she is, Honor escaped to
Scotland. Trouville came to claim her back. Now we find
our situations reversed! Ha, he pales now."

Strode offered Edouard a nasty grin. "Didna want her to
know she was second choice, eh? Well, I'll be givin' ye

this, she's nigh as bonny as her cousin. Hume came t' see our new bairn and confessed this last wee trick of his. Said puir Annie here did her duty as she was told. Did he beat her inta it, then, or starve her as he did my lass? Did ye watch, all proud of gettin' a docile wife?''

"No one beat me!" Anne declared. "Or starved me, either. I wed him willingly! Ask anyone! Now you release my husband at once and cease this nonsense!"

"I think not," Strode said thoughtfully. "I know Hume threatened ye somehow. No woman would wed this bugger wi'out some force applied. But I intend ta fix matters once and for all. He'll no' be keeping one of my Honor's kin agin her will. I warned him not ta come here."

Edouard cleared his throat and straightened to his full height. He looked directly at her, narrowed his eyes slightly and glanced toward the kitchens. She averted her own gaze to see what he was trying to tell her.

She saw two forms slide silently through the shadows at the back of the hall and disappear. Judging by the size, she thought it must be Rob and Henri. Pray God, they would hide themselves. Anne shoved at the man holding her to create a distraction and keep all eyes upon her. "You will not give him a hearing?"

They both looked at Edouard. "Have yer say, then," Strode said evenly to Edouard. "If ye think ye can explain yer way out of this one, I'd dearly like ta hear it."

"I would not have my lady believe that I took her in another's stead, Strode," Edouard said. "I love my wife."

"Oh, aye, and ye said once ye loved mine, as well. Would ye have me show our Annie th' truth of th' matter, then? That ye took a look-alike when ye couldna have my Honor?"

He motioned one of his minions toward the door of the hall. "Go and fetch our lady from outside the gates. Leave her guards there ta mind th' mounts, since we've all under control inside."

He shot Anne a smug look. "There's none ta give us

trouble here save yer fine lord, anyways. I'll have ye free of him in a sword thrust. Or d'ye think we should hang the bletherskite?''

"Neither!" Anne answered, frustrated beyond bearing. "You cannot kill him!" She looked at Edouard, who stood facing his nemesis without any fear. He wore an expression of bored amusement. If she wanted rid of this husband of hers, now was certainly the time.

She might convince Strode not to kill him, but to escort him and his men to the coast and set them on a ship away from Scotland instead.

No matter what Edouard had done or planned to do here at Baincroft, whatever the consequences of his remaining, Anne did not wish him dead, or away from her, permanently or otherwise. He was her husband and she did love him.

As much as she loved Robert and wanted him to have what was his by right, and as much as Edouard's expected reaction to the new child troubled her, she did not want to give him up. She must save him if she could, and trust him to do what was right for all concerned. He said he loved her. Were those words for show here, or did he fear she would side with this heathen highlandman against him?

They waited. And waited. Though plenty of time had passed for his man to go outside Baincroft's gates and back again, he still did not return with Lady Honor as instructed.

Strode grew restless, and Anne could understand why. He had only one man guarding Simm and the small crowd of servants, one holding her, and only one now minding Edouard's movements. There must be others set to watch the barracks where Baincroft's other men were being held. God only knew how many waited outside the gates with her cousin, Lady Honor.

"How did you get in?" Anne asked, trying to distract Strode from his obvious impatience.

He preened as he kicked back in the chair and propped one foot against the table and addressed Edouard instead of her. "Happened on one of yer men out takin' th' air yestere'en. Bribed him ta unbar th' postern gate in the wee hours. Said ye'd done him an ill turn, keepin' him landless after all he'd done for ye. He'd see ye pay for that."

Edouard exhaled loudly and shook his head. "Gui de Perrer, I presume."

"Aye," Strode answered. "If ye was bent on coming here, ye'd ha' done well ta leave that laddie in France, Trouville."

"For once we agree on something," Edouard said thoughtfully. He looked at Anne. "I shall have to kill him for this."

Strode laughed merrily as he stood up and ambled around the table. Hands clasped behind him, he paced back and forth, taunting. "Even did ye find the chance, he's gone. Took out soon as he opened the back port for us."

"He would," Edouard said with a snort. "The coward."

Anne could not abide this, their talking together as though Edouard were standing free and not under threat of death. "I demand you release my husband and get you gone from my home! You have no right to come here and—"

Suddenly Anne heard a loud *thwack*. The highlander whirled to see who'd struck him. A like sound broke the sudden silence and Strode dropped to his knees, clutching his forehead.

The man guarding Edouard ran to his fallen master. Rob dashed from the entrance to the kitchens. He brandished a dagger and dragged a broadsword Anne recognized as MacBain's. Rob dropped the sword at Edouard's feet and quickly slashed the wrist bindings with an economy of movement that held Anne spellbound.

Edouard grasped the fallen sword with both hands.

The skinny guard holding Anne pushed her aside to engage Edouard. Anne's rage erupted. She leapt at the man's back, dug her fingers into his neck and kicked at the backs of his legs. He tried to turn, but went down, thrashing, with

Anne on top. Robert jumped on the man's outstretched sword arm with both feet and Anne heard the crack of bone. She scrambled off as Rob grabbed up the abandoned sword and shoved his dagger at her.

Simm had followed her example and attacked the distracted man guarding the hall folk. The spitboys and the others added their weight, overwhelming their guard.

The one who had rushed to aid Strode turned, his sword ready. Now Edouard faced two, one guard and Strode himself, who had barely gained his feet. Edouard engaged the guard.

Rob dashed past the combatants toward Strode. For a moment they stared at each other. Then Rob raised the heavy sword aloft. Strode answered the challenge. Their blades met, steel ringing like a death knell.

"Do not kill him!" Anne screamed. She threw the dagger, which bounced harmlessly off Strode's shoulder.

Edouard quickly disarmed his opponent, knocked the man cold with the flat of his blade, and wheeled around to rescue Robert.

With blood streaming from the stone cut on his forehead, Strode laughed drunkenly as he caught Rob's blade on his own. "God's truth, yer whelp's a wonder, Trouville!"

Clang. He easily checked Rob's next swing.

"Stop!" Anne cried, throwing herself toward them. "Do not hurt him!"

Edouard blocked her way. "Strode!" He approached the man from one side. "He is Anne's! Leave the boy be!"

Again Strode chuckled, leaping back to avoid Rob's labored thrust. "Leave *him* be? Ha! He wants blood, this lad! Let him fight."

Edouard moved closer, but Strode circled, keeping Robert between them. The huge man still smiled and risked throwing Edouard a wink. Rob's sword dipped, accidentally catching Strode's knee with the tip. "Ach! Canny move, lad!" He danced backward yet again, almost tripping.

Even Anne saw that this was no real battle. Strode

merely met Rob's thrusts and swings with defensive measures, though he put on a good show of it.

She darted a look at Edouard and saw him mask a grin. He was also marking the position of Strode's fallen comrades to see that they did not rise and gain the upper hand again. No worry there. The one he'd struck lay still as death. Simm had the other disarmed and buried beneath a pile of clinging servants. Her own guard had rolled into a useless ball, weaponless now, and clutching his broken arm.

Anne jerked her attention back to her son. Robert grunted loudly, obviously using up the last of his strength to raise the weapon once more. He made a mighty swing, which Strode allowed to knock the weapon from his hand.

With a huge, theatrical groan for mercy, Strode fell prostrate on the floor.

Sweat-soaked, red-faced and heaving, Robert scurried forward and positioned the broadsword, fully intent on impaling his adversary.

"Hold!" Edouard shouted, barely reaching Robert in time to snatch the sword away. Robert looked up, questioning the move. "Mercy, Robert," Edouard advised. "He begs mercy."

Anne ran toward them and grasped Rob in her arms. "Oh, Rob!"

"Back away, Anne," Edouard said in a low voice. "He's no child."

"But he *is*," she whispered, even as Rob struggled in her embrace.

"Let go," Edouard demanded, his hand gripping her shoulder hard enough to leave bruises.

Anne complied. Robert offered his hands to help her rise from her knees. How hard it was to look past the child and see the man he would become.

Edouard laid an arm across Robert's shoulders for an instant and returned the heavy sword to him.

"Get up, Strode," he ordered, nudging the man with his foot.

Henri's voice reached them from the hall door. "We have secured the others, Father."

"And took your time about the matter," Edouard growled in response. "Any in need of care?"

"Robert's wicked with that sling. One could lose an eye. He is being tended. There are more without, but we cannot determine how many. I count eleven mounts and a cart of some kind, but it is too dark to be certain."

A few of her men trooped in with Henri. She supposed the rest were standing guard over Strode's.

The highlander stood now, grinning and brushing off his plaid. Then he bowed to Robert. "I'm no match for ye, lad. I never seen th' like."

Rob raised his chin and threw back his shoulders. "You le' my Fathah be. Go a-way. You die."

Anne watched a look of serious consideration suffuse the man's face. "Yer *father,* ye say? He's guid to ye, lad? And yer mam?"

"Aye!" Rob declared as he stepped nearer Edouard, so that they stood side by side, blades ready. "Good!"

Strode's eyes met hers, and then Edouard's. He obviously remarked the true parentage by Rob's resemblance to her. She could read the understanding even as it dawned on their intruder. Edouard was more than welcome here, as husband to her and father to her son. "Well, then. I beg yer pardon," he said with a firm nod.

"As well you should!" Anne said, crossing her arms over her chest.

Edouard spoke up. "I suppose now you believe I will spare your life?"

Strode shrugged. "Weel, I did spare yers four years past, Trouville. And we are kin now."

"We were *kin* a quarter hour ago when you would have killed me," Edouard reminded him. Suddenly, he expelled a weary breath and lowered his sword. "Look, Strode, all this is Hume's fault, you know. We should go after him together."

"Aye," Strode agreed. "Tell me, did ye give him reason to want ye dead? Why else would he ha' made certain I'd come?"

Anne knew why, and they might as well know, too. "My uncle found out about Robert's deafness, and feared you would learn of it and blame him," she explained.

"Blame him?" Edouard asked. "He caused it? How?"

"Nay!" Anne said with a roll of her eyes. Men could be so thick-witted. Then suddenly Anne realized that women could, too. Her, in particular.

How could she explain that Hume feared Edouard would not want her bearing his children if he knew? That he would find her flawed as a wife and blame her uncle for arranging the marriage? Damn her for her hasty tongue!

Well, if she could not avoid this truth altogether, she could at least postpone it until they had settled the matter of what to do with Alan of Strode. "Never mind. I shall explain it all later," she said firmly. "At the moment, it appears we have guests. This foolish man has dragged my cousin half across Scotland and left her out there in the dark."

Chapter Nineteen

Jealousy struck Anne with all the force of a swift summer storm. It caught her out in the open with no warning at all and she felt drenched with it.

Oh, she had heard Alan of Strode nattering on about Edouard's former betrothal to her cousin Honor, but under the circumstances, she had not dwelt on it then. Anne's main concern had been Strode's intention to kill her husband, and then the ensuing fights.

Once Sir Alan had accepted the fact that her marriage was to her liking, he and Edouard behaved like allies. Edouard had called for ale and they drank to a truce, amusing themselves highly by concocting in turn the most outlandish punishments for her cowardly uncle. All very well and good until the men Strode sent outside the gates to retrieve his wife returned with her.

Anne had seen Honor only once. She remembered her as a thin, shy, dark-haired maid of about twelve years who had accompanied Uncle Dairmid and Aunt Therese to Anne's wedding to MacBain. When her cousin arrived this time, Anne saw that she was no longer thin, shy or twelve. Small wonder Edouard had fought for the woman.

Anne felt rumpled and unkempt and at a strong disadvantage when facing the Lady Honor. Dragged from sleep, hair hanging in tangles, hastily garbed, and undone by her scuffle with the guard, Anne dearly wished to hide. Instead, she forced a smile and a welcome. "Cousin, how good it is to see you after this long time."

The other woman laughed. "Here we come to save you and give you comfort, and you have all in hand without us. Alan's man explained the mistake to me. I do apologize for this intrusion, Anne. Do say you'll forgive us, for we did mean well."

Anne noticed then that the lady's maid stood behind her holding an infant about six months of age, and the hand of a small, fair-haired girl child. "You have brought your bairns?"

"Yes. I am still nursing Adam, and Kit would not be left behind. Alan feared you might need me here once he had rid you of the comte." She smiled apologetically. "It seems we sorely misjudged the circumstances."

"No matter," Anne said, though it certainly *did* matter. Her voice sounded stilted and insincere, even to her own ears. She regretted that, but this was a woman Edouard had claimed to love. One he might still have feelings for, since he had married the cousin Honor greatly resembled. "I shall have rooms readied for you at once."

"Oh, there is no need for that," her cousin said, laying a hand on Anne's arm. "It is almost dawn now. I believe my husband and I should say our farewells and begin our journey home."

Not likely, Anne thought to herself. She would not stand here next to this woman who was dressed like a princess garbed for court, and leave the comparison between them in Edouard's eye forever. *Never.* She would at least make herself presentable.

"Nonsense!" she said, more sincerely this time. "You

shall stay with us a while. We should become acquainted since you have no other kinswoman in this country.''

''Befriend each other?'' Honor said with a doubtful expression. She glanced toward Edouard and Sir Alan, who now approached them, drinking together like old companions. ''I suppose we had better. Would you look at those two?''

Love shone in her cousin's eyes. Anne only hoped Honor directed all of that toward the man in plaid.

Their husbands were as unlike as any two she had ever seen. Edouard appeared the courtier, even though he wore only a pair of wrinkled braies. His hair looked nigh as tumbled about as her own. She supposed it was his sophistication and unruffled demeanor that lent him the appearance of a noble gentleman, no matter what he wore. As for the other one, Strode looked a rough sort, though right handsome in his own way. Jolly, a bit wicked, fierce, and yet compassionate, judging by his treatment of Robert. Both were fine specimens of manhood, but as different as the night was from the day.

Both men came toward them now, and Anne tensed. Did Edouard still love Honor? Did he wish with all his heart he had not been forced to settle for a pale imitation of this woman?

''Lady Honor,'' Edouard greeted the cousin and took her hand within his, raising it to his lips. ''We bid you welcome. I trust your journey proved none too discommoding?''

''Not at all, my lord,'' Honor said with a touch of mischief. ''I trust our unexpected arrival did not...put you out in any way?''

Edouard smiled down at her as he rose from his bow. ''Why no, my lady. All is being prepared for your visit, even as we speak. My documents all hidden, the jewels concealed, the weapons locked away. No reason at all for us not to embrace your company with all joy.''

When Strode's face reddened, Anne feared another fight. She quickly offered her hand to distract him from the thought. ''Sir Alan?''

He cleared his throat, still glaring at Edouard over the thinly veiled insults. ''Aye.'' Then he raised her hand rather perfunctorily and planted his lips upon it.

Anne did not view these next few days with any expectations for a congenial family gathering.

Edouard only half listened to Strode's rambling on about Hume. That one would get what was due him when he reached France. King Philip would not take kindly to anyone seeking favor through a kinship to the comte de Trouville.

Edouard's attention remained focused on Anne as she ordered the tables fully set and food prepared for their guests.

As soon as she had done, she excused herself and started up the stairs. Edouard quickly did the same. Their state of dress—rather undress—provided excellent reason for them to go above and speak alone.

He desperately needed to explain about his former betrothal. After the apprehensive looks she had offered both him and her cousin, Edouard had no doubt how Anne felt. She believed herself but a poor consolation offered him by her uncle when his marriage to Honor came to nothing.

Of course, the fact that she really *was,* would not be an easy matter to deny. If ever there was a time for a judicious bit of lying, this surely qualified. No woman of his acquaintance would ever accept the role of second choice. Anne might be exactly that on the face of things, but not in reality.

The two had more in common than he had first thought. That would make this foray into diplomacy even more difficult. Anne looked much like Honor, that he had always granted. Their ages were but four years different, Anne the elder and certainly the wiser of the two. Now, how many women would want to hear how much he admired her wisdom? Not one.

Very well, Anne's greatest attribute was her serenity. Yet earlier in the hall, Honor had appeared the soul of calm while Anne had been the one to fidget. He could hardly blame her for that after being held in terror, overcoming that surly knave who had restrained her, and then watching her only child challenge a full grown man. Lord above, most women would have fainted dead away before they ever left the bedchamber. No, he could not fault Anne for her uneasiness. Or for anything else. She was his one and only love, and he must somehow convince her of that.

He loathed explaining. In the weeks he had spent here, he had made more damned explanations than in all his former years combined. Even if this one proved successful, however, Edouard had no hope that Anne would forgive him for all his past errors. His one desire at the moment was to prevent Anne's loss of inner pride. God, but she had such a wealth of that. He would not see her sense of self-worth diminished in the slightest way, and certainly not because of something he had done.

"She is very beautiful. I can see why you loved her," Anne said the moment he entered the room.

Edouard thanked heaven her back was toward him so she hadn't seen his wince. There would be no wading into this. He had to dive and pray the water would be deep enough. "I suppose Honor is lovely enough. But her hair is too straight."

Anne whipped around with a disbelieving laugh. "Her hair?" She flipped her own mass of tangled waves off one shoulder.

Edouard smiled as winningly as he knew how. "I saw it down about her once. Strings, I swear."

She shifted her hands to her hips and glared. "And just when did you see all these *strings* down about her?"

Edouard ventured farther into the room and into the fray he feared he'd created. "Uh, the night I attempted to reclaim her hand."

"To kill her husband, you mean!" She threw up her hands and paced angrily in a tight little pattern, well away from him. "Aye, he did say you played out this same bit of foolery upon them. You loved her so much you would have slain him there in his own hall! Did you not?"

"Loved her?" Edouard repeated. Where was his diplomacy now that he needed it? "No, Anne. But she had tweaked my pride in running from me, so I went after her to appease it. I only saw her a few times about the court with her father. How could I love a woman I hardly knew?"

"You said you did!" Anne accused.

Edouard shook his head. "Will you listen? Honor was different from the jades at court. I needed a wife, a mother for Henri. She seemed a likely choice, so Hume and I made an agreement. I admired her, I do admit that. When she defied us all, it angered me. That is the reason I came after her. The only reason. Pride! And Strode dispatched that quickly enough. She loves him and he loves her. Surely you can see that."

She remained quiet, tapping one foot and staring out the window. He continued, "Hume did suggest you as a wife for me, else I'd never have known you existed. I still needed to wed, as much for Henri's sake as for mine, so I agreed to come here and see whether we would suit."

He struggled to find words that would reassure her. The truth would have to do. "The moment you appeared before me, I knew you were the one. The *only* one who would ever do. Whatever I once felt for your cousin four years ago had nothing to do with that decision.''

''Except that I look somewhat like her,'' Anne reminded him. ''At least when I am got up decently. Even then, you see me as a poor substitute. You still love her. That is obvious.''

He ran a hand through his hair and blew out a sharp breath, holding on to his calm by a slender thread. ''You sorely mistake me, Anne, and see only what you fear.''

''Fear!'' Anne shouted, throwing up her hands. ''You believe I *fear* you love her? Why should I? What care I whom you love?''

But she did care, Edouard thought with an inner smile. She cared very much. He approached her carefully. ''Anne, I love *you*. Have you any idea how beautiful you are to me right now?''

''Ha!'' she cried. ''Do I know it! A wrinkled, dirty gown, hair flying like an unkempt horse's tail! I can well imagine how you see me next to that girl.''

''Yes, a girl, Anne. But you are a woman. Four years wiser and grown into your full beauty. As for your state of dress, you have Strode to blame for that. He is the one who rousted you from sleep with threats of mayhem, not I.'' He paused and grew thoughtful. ''And I thank him for it.''

''Thank him?'' Anne stilled, her brows lowered, her carriage tense. ''Are you mad?''

Edouard shrugged, but he did not mask his feelings. He let her see all of the admiration he felt for her. ''Had Sir Alan not done what he did, I might never have seen you this way. I might never have witnessed what courage you have! What fiery spirit!''

He had seen Anne's courage and her spirit many times these past few weeks, of course, but truthfully not put forth with such vigor. Edouard needed to touch her, hold her, and embrace that fire, but knew it was not yet time.

"Anne, you are a wonder to me always, but I have never loved you more than I do at this moment. And for all your disarray, I have never found you more beautiful."

That stopped her cold. Edouard watched expressions flit across her face, one after another. Surprise. Disbelief. Hope. Denial.

Then her eyes narrowed and she crossed her arms over her heaving breasts. "Then you are a blind fool! I am a mess." She looked away from him, hugging herself. When she spoke, she sounded resigned. "Would you leave me now? I would wash and dress suitably for our…company."

"To hell with the company, Anne. I'll not leave you in such a state, doubting yourself this way."

He moved closer, arms out to enfold her, but she shrank away from him. "It's not myself I doubt, husband! It is *you!*"

She doubted both of them and Edouard knew it. His patience slipped. "Fine! But if you are so eager to be rid of me, why did you beg Strode to spare my life? My death would have solved all your problems, would it not? If he made you a widow as he came here to do, you would be free of all this doubt! Free of me!"

She sniffed, but he could not tell why since she had quickly turned away from him again. A curt dismissal. A rejection, if he had ever seen one.

Frustrated that he had failed, Edouard marched to his clothes chest, grabbed up clean garb, and quit the chamber without another word. He stalked down the stairs, heading for the bathhouse.

Let her stew. What did he care? She would never love him now. Not that he had held much hope of that after their last argument about Robert.

He might have set her mind at rest on that score, as well, had she not thrown his love back in his face, all unwanted. Devil take her, then. He had survived two loveless marriages already, and he could damn well weather another if he had to.

He rubbed his chest, wishing to God he could rid himself of the hollow ache. But Anne had made certain of its permanence and Edouard knew he must live with it.

He had hoped he would not find a crowd within the bathhouse, but the boisterous noise as he approached told him he would have to deal with just that.

His sons dashed water at each other from separate tubs as Alan of Strode joined in their laughter. Things were altogether too merry to suit Edouard's mood.

"Henri!" he shouted over the melee. "Cease this play at once!"

Silence fell and all three faces regarded him expectantly. He saw that none held any fear. Had he completely lost his ability to intimidate people? Instead of testing the matter now, Edouard managed a pleasant enough expression. "You two get dressed and be off to help your mother. We have guests to entertain." He looked pointedly at Strode. "I shall tend to this one."

The boys obeyed instantly, hopping out of the water and grabbing up drying cloths, which they had wet with their splashing. Henri popped Robert with one end of his, gaining a yelp and a garbled threat.

Edouard ignored them as he undressed and sank up to his shoulders in the tub Henri had vacated. Blessed quiet ensued after the young ones dashed out, slamming the door behind them. He leaned back carefully, resting his head on the tub's padded rim. The blow that knocked him senseless and all that followed, had left him with an aching head.

"I like yer lads," Strode said lazily. He lay back as well, arms outstretched, tapping his fingers lightly against the edge of the tub.

"Fine. You may have them," Edouard replied easily as

his eyelids fell shut. "Do tell me you all plan to leave immediately."

Strode chuckled. "If yer the least bit serious, I would be honored to foster either one or both."

"Over my dead body," Edouard said evenly, not even opening his eyes. "And you've had your last chance at that."

Strode sat up with a sloshing sound. Edouard looked over at him in the event Strode might be considering it again, but the man was only soaping himself vigorously. After he had done, and dunked beneath the water to rinse his head, he spoke again. "Yer Robbie took down three o' my men in th' bailey wi' his wee rocks and sling. Henri bound 'em fast and then released yer men. They work together well."

Edouard uttered only a grunt, though he felt pride surge through him like a storm's wave. His fine sons.

"Robbie saved yer life, y'know?"

"Mmm-hmm," Edouard acknowledged. "But he knew very well you had no intention of killing him even before he challenged."

"Ye think so?" Strode asked, obviously worried. "I shoulda given him a better show of it then."

Edouard laughed and said with certainty, "He knew before he raised that blade or he would never have done it. Robert's a good judge of character. He counted on your inability to kill a child. That was his real weapon."

"And how would he know such?"

"Your eyes," Edouard said. "I would wager he looked into your eyes just beforehand, did he not?"

"Aye," Strode admitted readily. "But th' wee bugger woulda killed me right enough, had ye not stopped him!"

"I do believe so," Edouard agreed, unable to contain his huge smile. "So then, you must have counted on *my* tender mercy."

"Not exactly," Strode confided. "But I didna believe

ye'd let Annie's lad bear th' burden of my death. Or do the killing for him and hurt his pride.''

''Then that was your weapon against me. Am I right?''

''Weel, at least no one died.'' Strode sighed loud and long. ''All this reasonin' makes me hungry.''

He got out of his tub, found a cloth, and scrubbed his hair. ''Since ye kept me alive, th' least ye can do is feed me.''

''Already, you make me see the error of my ways,'' Edouard grumbled as he reluctantly abandoned his bath and began to dry off.

''Will ye be goin' after that knave who helped us?'' Alan asked.

''Perrer?'' Edouard asked as he donned his shirt. ''No need. After the way he betrayed me, no one will hire him on.''

Strode grinned. ''Then we'll have ta see word gets about, eh?''

Edouard could not help a liking for this great, hairy lout. Even four years ago, enraged by unaccustomed defeat and the loss of his betrothed, Edouard had understood that Alan of Strode was a good and honorable man. He lacked civility. He could do better, but he still spoke like an uncouth highlander.

He sometimes dressed like one, too. Edouard glanced at the Scot belting on that devilish *breacan* of his. But Strode might be a powerful force to call on in times of trouble. If the man were willing, that is. He seemed almost too affable, and quite incapable of holding a grudge. Concern for his wife's cousin had brought him here, not revenge. He might even become a friend.

Edouard did not believe he'd ever had a true friend, one who owed him nothing and wanted nothing from him. The idea seemed a little foreign, but interesting to contemplate.

"Tell me, Strode. If we could put all our differences behind us, could I count you as an ally?"

"Nay, not that," the knight said quite seriously.

"Ah, I see. Because of Honor," Edouard guessed, accepting the denial. He looked away and adjusted his belt over his tunic, hoping Strode would not notice his disappointment.

"In part, because of her," Strode admitted. "And there's yer Annie, too. They are first cousins, after all, so we'd be family, not simple allies. 'Tis a bit more binding."

He grinned and slapped Edouard on the back as they headed out the bathhouse door. "One good thing about it. See, ye have ta be nice to yer allies. But family? Ye can beat 'em about th' ears when they irk ye. Right, Ned?"

Ned? Yes, beating Strode about the ears did sound appealing. Edouard laughed instead, and it felt good. His mood had lightened considerably, in spite of his ongoing troubles with Anne. Now that he thought more on it with a clearer head, that jealousy of hers could not signify hatred. She did care for him, whether she admitted it or not.

Chapter Twenty

Anne held the babe. Since Honor had thrust it at her, there had been little choice in the matter. She cuddled it close and the soft fuzz of its hair tickled her nose. The sweet milky scent of the child made her own womb swell with anticipation.

She pressed her lips to the innocent little head and was suddenly glad her cousin had given the maidservant leave to go after they had supped. Until now, her worries about how Edouard would react to the new life within her had almost obliterated her joy at becoming a mother again.

After winter melted into spring, she would hold her own bairn this close and love it with her whole heart, just as she did Robert. Anne decided then and there that she would no longer allow her worries for her babe to cloud her happiness. She would cling to her hope for its well-being, but if that hope was crushed, then she would deal with this child just as she had with Rob. And she knew that she must trust Edouard to help her do so.

He did not despise Robert now that he knew everything about him. He simply did not credit all her son's abilities. She could hardly blame him for that. No one, save those who loved Rob well and had witnessed his accomplishments these last ten years, would believe him worthy to draw another breath. *Cursed by God,* they would say. Just as MacBain had believed. But Edouard did not think so. Nothing he had done since he'd found out gave any indication that he held such a notion. And if he did not believe Robert cursed, then he surely would not believe it of his own child.

Honor's babe yawned and nestled closer. Anne felt his soft breath against her neck. She longed for the day when she would hold her own just so. Edouard's child. A dark-haired, dark-eyed treasure that would remind Anne that her husband had at least *liked* her well for a small space of time.

She regretted her sharp words to him earlier in the day. With all there was to do in preparing rooms and seeing to the meals, Anne had found no time to try to make things right. Nay, not true, she admitted. She had avoided Edouard except at table where that was impossible. He treated her with all respect as though nothing had happened to prevent it. That only stoked her guilt.

He had treated Honor with the same courtesy, which increased Anne's jealousy. Guilt and jealousy. Such base feelings, she thought with a sweep of self-loathing. How could she foster any liking on Edouard's part if she clung to these dark emotions? If her husband still possessed tender feelings for Honor, Anne knew she'd never dispel them with angry accusations. How she wished she could cast away her devils, run to him now and throw her arms around him. Trust him fully.

Honor had just made the suggestion that she, Anne and the little ones leave the solar and join the men who sat gaming beside the hall fire. Small wonder she had done so. Their visit in the solar had not been at all comfortable, considering they were two cousins reunited after so long a time. Anne accepted the blame for that with a flicker of shame.

Honor had come all this way with two bairns in tow, just to comfort her in a time of trouble. Even Edouard, who had been the victim of their good intentions, had offered their guests a welcome once the truth came clear. How could she do less?

Edouard looked up and offered her a gentle smile from across the hall where he played at chess with Sir Alan. Rob and Henri sat nearby with a gammon board, playing at being men themselves.

Honor had retreated back into the solar to extract her daughter from beneath a chair where she had cornered one of the tabby mousers. Anne stood at the doorway, waiting for them.

She glanced within, amused by Honor's ungainly position. Her cousin crouched on all fours, backside higher than head, pleading with her four-year-old. Anne sympathized, as any mother would, and her heart suddenly felt much lighter.

Honor looked up, exasperated. "She seems to be stuck!" she declared.

Anne pursed her lips to keep from laughing. "Cat or bairn?" she asked finally.

Her cousin rose to her knees and then plopped backward, impatiently tucking loosened hair beneath her lopsided coif. "I give up."

Anne rejoined Honor in the solar.

"You wish us gone," her cousin said, "and I promise we shall be as soon as we've had a good night's rest in a bed."

"I have not been at all gracious, Honor, and I am the one who is sorry for it. We shall begin again, you and I!" Anne declared. "But first, take the babe and let me help you with—"

Just then the tabby erupted from its sanctuary with an earsplitting yowl. Honor's daughter, her small fingers locked around the cat's tail emerged halfway.

"Let go, Kit!" Honor cried. "Release the beast this instant!"

The cat struck out, clawing two streaks along the child's arm. Once loose, the animal made a dash for the solar door, tripping Sir Alan. The huge knight fell forward, his plaid flying up to reveal a rather interesting sight.

Anne had backed against the wall, cradling the wakened babe, who set up a howl fit to shake the dead from their vaults.

Her eyes met Edouard's as he rushed in. Lips drawn tight and shoulders shaking with mirth, he offered Sir Alan a hand. Then he lifted the heavy chair off the screaming child, while her father bent to lift her up.

"Excuse us, please!" Honor shouted above the horrendous din. She relieved Anne of the screaming, squirming bundle that was her son. "We are off to bed!"

"Good sleep!" Edouard roared back. Anne would have scurried ahead to escort them, but he took her arm. "Send Rob! He's the only one with any defense against the din!"

Anne collapsed against him, helpless with laughter. When she had recovered, their guests had found their own way. Distant wails indicated a long night in store for the cousins.

"Anne," Edouard said softly, smiling down on her with such tenderness. He cradled her face in his hands and leaned to lay a soft kiss on her parted lips. "If only you would believe how much I love you."

"What of Honor?" she whispered against his mouth.

"Honor who?" he asked, drawing her close, renewing the kiss, deepening it until her knees grew too weak to support her.

When he finally released her mouth, he kissed her ear.

"You must mean that lady who shouts like a battle commander and crawls about on the floor. Most unbecoming. Strode should take her in hand, though I cannot say much for his own dignity."

Anne smiled up at him. "You're not being fair."

He leaned down and nibbled her earlobe. "Ah, but you are fair enough for the both of us. Fair Anne, who is all a woman should be." His hands slipped upward to cradle her breasts. "Shall we make ours an early night, as well, O fair one?"

"Aye," she agreed, breathless with need.

Together, arms about each other, they left the solar for their bed. When Edouard stopped in the hall for a night candle to light the way, Henri and Robert glanced up from their game and bade them good-night.

"They are truly brothers now," Anne remarked, as she and Edouard climbed the stairs together.

"Comrades and friends forever," he agreed. "A shared battle can accomplish that." He looked down at her, his large hand caressing her waist. "Would that you could be the same to me after what we've been through this past night and day."

She returned his look. "I would be more."

"At last," he said in that wry tone of his. "I must have said something right for a change."

"Aye, you did. And I have much to say to you, Edouard," she confessed as they entered their chamber.

He set the candle down and took her in his arms. "If it consists of more than three words, it will have to wait for morning."

Anne knew the three words he wanted, but there were others that must come first. "Please, Edouard. Do listen."

"Now you have had your say, with one word more than I allowed. So like a woman."

He shook his head in mock despair, then lifted her up and set her down on the fur coverlet. "Time for bed."

"So like a man," she admonished, even as she reached for the ties of her overgown.

Edouard unbuckled his belt, whisked off his tunic, and was free of the remainder of his clothing before Anne could get out of hers.

Anne was well aware of his urgency as he helped her finish and joined her on the bed. But he did not move to take her immediately as she thought he would. Instead, he lay down, propping on one arm so that he looked down at her. "Now then, what is of such import to you, love? I will hear it."

Anne wondered how to begin. Hesitantly, she placed her hand over his heart, feeling its quick rhythm. Heat emanated from his body like a well-stoked brazier. "I know you want me, Edouard. I want you as well. Desperately."

He moved to kiss her, but she held him away. "This first, or I shall lose my courage." She met his eyes. "I must trust you, Edouard, and you have no notion how difficult it is for me to do so."

He smiled and stroked her cheek, lifted an unruly wave that nearly covered her eye and tucked it behind her ear. "I would never betray your trust, my sweet. Never."

She swallowed hard, determined to give him what she had once decided to grant no man. She loved him beyond reason. He had said he loved her, and she must believe it. Anne reminded herself that Edouard had never done anything to harm her or her son.

In the incident with Alan of Strode, Rob had exhibited a recklessness that made even Anne wonder at the wisdom of his ruling Baincroft. He had attacked a man thrice his size, just as Edouard had once warned he might. At the moment, Robert's inheritance was the lesser of her problems.

She had to share the secret she carried within her. Edouard must know everything, even the worst of her fears.

"We are to have a child," she whispered, almost choking on the words.

Edouard's hand stilled upon her cheek. A look of wonder crossed his face. "Oh, Anne! I have hoped for this!"

She stared into his eyes, ready to search for a lie. "Will you love it? No matter what happens, will you promise me that? I would have your word."

He laughed, a short sound charged with disbelief that she could ask such a question. "What foolishness! Of course, I shall love it."

"Even if it can never hear you say as much?" she asked softly, cringing inside as she watched his understanding dawn.

He closed his eyes and released a harsh breath through clenched teeth. When he looked at her again, she saw his tears. They did not fall, but glazed the grief there.

"It may not come to pass," she said, unable not to share the small measure of hope in her own heart. "What caused Rob to be as he is remains a mystery. Though I have been told that deafness often visits members of the same family. My mother once told me that her father could not hear well."

She felt Edouard's quick tremor as he deliberately dispelled his shock. "That would be Hume's father."

"Aye," Anne agreed.

He smiled, but it appeared forced. "Your uncle certainly hears well enough. Mayhaps old age caused your grandsire's affliction. Lady Honor's children appear well enough."

Anne nodded, grasping at any reassurance he would conjure. "True, though I have to say that daughter of hers does seem *unwilling* to listen. It is probably too soon to judge her babe's condition."

Edouard's mouth quirked in what seemed a more genuine mirth. "Well, we do know neither is mute!"

Anne appreciated his ability to find any humor in the matter, however dark. She had always felt guilty for doing so, though Rob himself oft times jested about his inability to hear. He also used it to his advantage more times than she would like.

Edouard lay back and settled her head on his shoulder, stroking her hair. "Robert's is not a true deafness, is it? He heard you whistle him down from the castle wall that day."

"A whistle, his hawk's cry, the beat of a bodhrun when there's music. High sounds and low." Anne sighed. "I used to ask myself why *my* son should suffer this when he is such a fine lad otherwise." She turned her head so that she could see Edouard's face. "He has a true heart, Edouard."

His expression looked thoughtful. "You need not tell me this, for well I know it!"

"I have accepted that you will not allow him Baincroft. After his reckless antics last night, I freely admit you could be right."

Edouard raised up again, dislodging her abruptly from her comfortable position on his shoulder. "What? Reckless antics? Is that what you call defending his keep? Saving my life?" He appeared almost angry with her. "Anne, I have never in my life witnessed such courage in one so young! He took down four full-grown men with that sling of his, then challenged Strode without a second thought!"

Edouard made a sound of self-derision. "And to think I considered making him a layabout, household knight! More fool, I. That one will make a finer lord at ten years than most I know at thrice the age." He scoffed at himself again. "Oh, our Robert shall manage this place, right enough, the moment he gains his spurs!"

Anne laughed through her tears as she threw herself

against his chest and held him tight. "I love you, Edouard. I love you more than I could ever say!"

He hugged her back, a none too gentle embrace that felt a little desperate. "Well, of course you do." His voice held the cynical tone Anne now recognized as his defense against his own tender feelings.

She felt his lips brush her neck and settle a passionate kiss where it curved into her shoulder. Chills of anticipation rippled through her as the warmth of his mouth began its exploration. His spicy scent surrounded her, permeated her senses with visions of the exotic pleasures he had offered in their past loving. His hands slid down her back, tracing her spine, setting her body afire as he drew her closer still. The firm, velvety ridge of his arousal pressed against her, an insistent pulsing that echoed through the empty space awaiting his sweet invasion.

He made a wordless, urgent sound that stirred her own body more profoundly than any coherent entreaty might have done. Then he rolled to his back, still holding her fast so that she lay atop his body. Firelight danced across features drawn tight with a rare, unguarded expression of need as he lifted her forward and joined them immediately.

Her sigh of welcome was lost in his harsh exhalation of relief. The hands which grasped her hips now traveled up her body, followed the curve of her waist, and shaped her breasts. Dark eyes held hers with a naked demand.

Gone was the sardonic, teasing courtier who once taunted her so sweetly with his expertise. Edouard needed her. Not only for this, she realized. She sensed a hunger far deeper than that, an ache within his soul that must be eased.

All the loneliness, the lovelessness he had ever endured lay open for her to see. His words were not necessary. Pride would not allow them, but he spoke to her heart with his own in that moment.

Anne leaned forward and plundered his mouth with hers,

touching and claiming him everywhere, moving with him. She reveled in the swift, sleek, slide of their bodies and his groans of deepest pleasure as he filled her again and again.

Her own explosion took her unaware, the intensity of it almost eclipsing the recognition of his release.

With one final surge, both fell still, savoring the ebb of their passion, struggling for breath and clutching each other in the wake of the storm.

"I do love you," she said again to reassure him. And in hopes he would say it as well.

"Yes, I know," he gasped with a breathless laugh and a confident hug.

"Certain of yourself, are you not?" she murmured, twirling strands of his chest hair around her finger.

"Very," he agreed.

She had one more question, one she felt driven to ask. No other doubts stood between them now. She wanted to hear the whole of the tale and how the rumors came about. "Edouard, tell me, did you kill your wives?"

He pushed her away and looked down at her, one eyebrow raised. "Not really. Did you kill your husband?"

She raised her own brow and met his stare. "Not exactly."

His laughter broke their standoff. "You never thought I was guilty of that, any more than I believed it of you."

She smiled a lazy smile. "Think what you will."

"I think it's a very good thing I decided ours would be a love match." He kissed her softly and then settled her back in his comfortable embrace. "And so it is."

Anne snuggled against the broad warmth of his chest, amused at his pretended conceit. "I had nothing to say to it, then. 'Twas all your doing."

He laughed again, the faint rumble of it sweet against her ear. "A simple matter to arrange. No trouble at all. I recognized at once what a gentle, biddable woman I had found.''

She gave his chest hair a sharp tug. "In all your wisdom, you are never wrong, I suppose."

His strong fingers clasped her chin, raising it so that she looked directly into his glowing eyes. "Often wrong, my love. I can admit that now with all humility. But about this, about how we love one another, I *know* I am right." A brief, almost unrecognizable, doubt flickered within his eyes. "Am I not?"

Anne grinned, her heart full of love. And trust, at last. Sweet trust.

"What's a gentle, biddable woman to do but agree with you? A love match, indeed, if you would will it so."

"I command it," he said, his smiling confidence fully restored. He trailed his fingers down her neck, their destination aching for his touch. "Now let us see just how truly biddable you are."

Anne reached for him, her touch demanding. "Biddable, you say? Must I also be gentle, my lord?"

In the hours that brought them to dawn, she proved neither. And both. Just as she always would.

Epilogue

Edouard idly paced the roof of their new keep, glancing impatiently toward the road leading up from the south. Today they would celebrate the arrival of the first guests in the castle that had taken five long and happy years to complete. Anne leaned against one of the merlons, enjoying the summer breeze that cooled her cheeks and toyed with her veil.

"They should have arrived by now," he grumbled, hooking his thumbs in his belt.

She laughed. "So eager to show off our new home? Or is it that daughter of ours you'd preen about to Alan?"

He clicked his tongue at that. "Our Alys has manners, unlike that hellion of theirs. Kit terrorizes every animal about the place, humans included!"

"She's nine now, surely past such prankishness."

Edouard huffed. "Well, even at eight, she should have known better than to plait the ponies' tails together. No reason about her, that child!"

"You know you love her, Edouard," Anne teased.

"Kit can be winning when she wants. Only she so rarely *wants*. The first time I saw her as a babe in arms, I offered Alan a match between her and Henri. Can you believe it?

I said it in a jest, but the very thought of it now gives me chills of horror!''

"Careful how you criticize Kit, Edouard. Our Alys is no saint, you know."

"Ah, but she is! Did she say her new rhyme for you this morn? The one Robert taught her?"

"The one in Scots?" Anne asked, pulling a wry face.

"Aye, that she did. Would you like to learn the meaning of the words?"

He worried his lip with his teeth. "Do I want to?"

"Nay, trust me. You do not," Anne advised. "But you might want to prevent her reciting it for our guests. Unless, of course, you wish Alan to injure himself when he falls down laughing."

Edouard's brows drew together in a frown. "I shall have a word with that son of ours, make no mistake! His progress with lauguages is remarkable, considering, but teaching his sister—"

"There. They come," Anne said, pointing toward the road. "All is ready on your end for the knighting ceremony tomorrow?"

"Oh, yes. Henri will do us proud, Anne."

"How we shall miss him, though," she said sadly. "Paris is so far away. But I suppose he must complete his education before he assumes care of your estates." Fortunately, he would *have* care of them, since the new king honored no grudge held by King Philip. Edouard had worried about Henri's birthright almost as much as Anne once had about Robert's. Now both their sons would prosper.

"At least we will have Robert by us for some years to come," Edouard said by way of reassurance. "Even when he's knighted and takes charge of Baincroft, he'll not be far away." He grinned as he took her hand in his. "And our Alys will remain here forever, of course, since no man will be worthy of her."

Anne looked at him askance as they began descending the pristine, whitewashed stairway of their new keep. Halfway down, he turned and took her in his arms. "Even when they are all gone, Anne, I will be here for you."

"Oh, thank you, my good lord!" she said dryly. "You are so terribly benevolent."

"So I am," he announced. "Do not forget it!" He kissed her soundly and then drew back his head, his arms laced around her waist, his hips pressing hers against the curved stair wall. "What a vision of contentment you are! My fault, of course."

"No doubt in your mind, eh?" she said, pursing her lips invitingly.

"None." He kissed her, a quick, friendly, childish token, and then cocked his head to one side and grinned. "Life rarely goes as planned, no matter how carefully I try to arrange it. Things go awry with such constant regularity, I almost expect it. Yet, by chance or divine plan, all the dreams are coming true. Did you ever notice that?"

"Oh, every day," she said, laughing softly, knowing that his droll grin and the teasing light in his eyes only masked a deeper, heartfelt happiness. A happiness that was her fault, of course. No doubt in her mind.

* * * * *

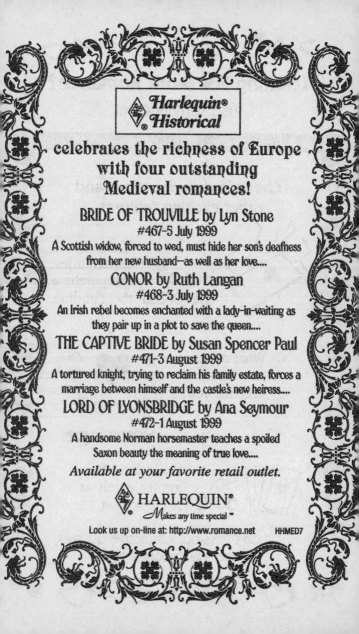